WELCOME TO DAMNATION . . .
where every living soul is as dead as a doornail. Except one.

Buddy Baker is a dead man. Literally. After gunning down more men than Billy the Kid—and being hung by a rope necktie for his crimes—the jolly, fast-drawing fugitive reckoned he'd earned himself a nonstop ticket to hell. Instead, he finds himself in Damnation: a gun-slinging ghost town located somewhere between heaven and hell.

There are no laws in Damnation. Only two simple rules: If you get shot, you go directly to hell. If you stay alive without shooting anyone for one year, you just might get into heaven.

Hardened outlaws pass the time in the saloon playing poker and wagering on who will get sent to hell next, while trying not to anger the town's reclusive vampire or the quarrelsome werewolves. Buddy winds up in everyone's crosshairs after swearing to protect a pretty gal who arrives in Damnation pregnant. Her child might end up a warm-blooded meal for the supernatural residents, or it could be a demon spawn on a mission to destroy them all.

Visit us at www.kensingtonbooks.com

D1487085

Books by Clark Casey

Dawn In Damnation
Jesus Fish and Slaughter Bird
Pale Male and the Infertile Girl
The Perfect Defective

Published by Kensington Publishing Corporation

Dawn in Damnation

Clark Casey

LYRICAL PRESS
Kensington Publishing Corp.
www.kensingtonbooks.com

First Electronic Edition:
eISBN-13: 978-1-5161-0496-3
eISBN-10: 1-5161-0496-X

First Print Edition: October 2017
ISBN-13: 978-1-5161-0498-7
ISBN-10: 1-5161-0498-6

Printed in the United States of America

Many thanks for the support and advice of Jennifer Brinsdon, Daniel DeCicco, and my mother, and also for the copyediting of Patricia Abramo, Susan Forste, and Debby Schwartz.

Dedicated to my father.

May he find a cozy saloon in the afterlife where he can play cards.

"Total liberty for wolves is death to the lambs."
—Isaiah Berlin

Chapter 1

Fre...

"What happened?" asked the young man with a nickel-sized bullet hole in his temple.

"Well, what's the last thing you remember?" I asked him.

"Was playin' cards with some cowpuncher. Drew a flush, and he 'cused me a cheatin'. So I reached for my Colt. Reckon he did the same."

"My guess is he was faster."

The newbie had that stunned look they all got in their eyes when they first arrived. He was hardly old enough to grow a proper beard. Just another cowpoke born in a shitty little town who'd rustled some steer, made it with a few whores, then died over a two-dollar pot.

"So's this hell?" His voice quavered. Probably already browned his britches with fear shit.

"Not quite," I told him.

"Purgatory then?" He tried to put on a brave face.

"Kinda... the opposite, 'spose you could say."

"Huh?"

"Well, imagine if you was like a stone in a creek bed. After you die, a panhandler scoops you up with a bunch of other muck and runs you through his sifter. All the stuff that falls through goes straight to hell. The rest gotta be cleaned off to see if it's worth keeping. So you might say you're just here till the panhandler finds out whether or not you got any shine to ya."

"Is this hell's sifter?"

"Folks call it Damnation."

"Who's the panhandler?" he asked, "God?"

"Dunno." I shrugged.

He gave the room a squinty eye, trying to reckon if it wasn't all just a dream. The Foggy Dew had the same creaky chairs and sticky tables you'd find in any other saloon, though a little less flair perhaps. No trinkets on the mantel, just a simple dusty place to drink. Some cried when they found out where they were. Others were overjoyed they hadn't ended up someplace worse. The kid didn't look too impressed.

"What's there to do 'round here?" he asked.

"Drink, play cards... wait."

"For what?"

"Till you go to hell, of course."

"How's that happen?"

"Get yourself shot again, you'll likely find out. Otherwise, you could be here a spell."

"How long?"

"Fella in the corner was at Valley Forge with General Washington. Most don't last a year. Some don't make it an hour."

"Anybody ever come back from hell?"

"Not that I've seen."

"How ya even know they got there?"

"Hmm... Have to ask Sal that one, when he's got a moment."

As the suppertime crowd shuffled in, Sal was busy filling glasses. The bar was lined three deep with bullet-ridden outlaws. One thing you couldn't kill was a man's thirst.

"Say, you got any whores 'round here?" the kid asked.

"Whores go to heaven."

"Ain't what churchgoers say."

"Got some of them here." I pointed to the neatly dressed folks playing gin rummy in the corner. "Least the outspoken variety."

While we were chewing the fat, a short fella in a big fancy hat moseyed up beside the newbie. The brim of his Stetson cast a shadow over his face. All that showed was a whiskerless chin and a mouth that wasn't smiling. He paced back and forth impatiently. The newbie turned to see who was shadowing his backside. Must've figured he was the older of the two, 'cause he gave the little fella a mind-your-own-business smirk. The pacer lifted his face, and I recognized him. Jack looked like he was itching to put a lead plumb in somebody. It had been about a week, so that made sense. He was always taking flashy accessories off those he shot, shiny belt buckles and such. The hat must've been a recent acquisition. If it weren't so big, I'd have recognized him sooner and cleared out as fast as I could.

He pushed his duster over his hip real gently, showing a pearl-handled pistol in a greased black leather holster. I inched my stool away and shielded my face. Then, at the last second, the preacher burst through the door shaking his fists in the air all willy-nilly, hollering with the energy of a much younger man.

"I've had a premonition from the Lord!" he bellowed. "The end is nigh upon us!"

"The end done happened already, Preach," Fat Wally snapped back. "That's why you're here."

"A man of great girth will come from the dust, then fire will rain from above!" the preacher roared even louder. "The streets will muddy, and the seed of Satan will be born unto a woman beyond the grave. For that's how the devil canst reach where the Lord hath delivered us. The hounds will seek to destroy the demon spawn, but the portly pistoleer will protect it!"

"Good one, Preach," Wally laughed. "A dead gal wearing the bustle wrong—and with the devil's baby to boot! Now I've heard it all."

"I have seen it!" he hollered fearsomely. "The flying minions will multiply, and Damnation will grow in head and breadth! The light of the Lord will shine upon us all once more. Then weeds will sprout from the barren dust, but by then it will be *too late!* Once this domain is fattened like a calf, *the evil one will slaughter us all!"*

Jack, for one, had heard enough. He doffed his oversized hat and leveled his gun with his winking boyish face. The shot ripped through the side of the preacher's throat. The old coot gripped the wound and doubled over, then flopped back into a chair, sucking short, quick breaths from the hole as blood gurgled between his fingers. Jack reholstered his weapon, happy to have put a bullet in somebody, and he slowly wandered out of the barroom for a breath of dusty air. The newbie had no idea how close he'd come to getting a lead necktie.

"That preacher fella gonna go to hell?" he asked.

"When he bleeds out," I answered. "Reckon so."

"Ain't there some way of gettin' outta here, aside from goin' to hell?" the kid fretted. "Can I get to *heaven*, mister?"

"Some think so," I told him. "They reckon if you last a whole year in Damnation without shootin' no one, the Lord'll forgive whatever you done. After twelve months without sin, the gates of heaven open up."

"Anybody done it?"

"Record's six months. That fella wasn't right in the head though. Didn't leave his room for four of 'em. Came out to tell us all he was Christ. Then the preacher shot 'em in the gut just to prove he wasn't."

"You're tellin' me there might be a chance a gettin' to heaven if you don't shoot nobody for a year, and the only one to try it was some loon who thought he was Christ."

"Well, truth is I'm fixin' to give it a go myself," I told him. "I already got more'n two months under my belt."

"Is that all?" the kid sneered. Just then, a gust of wind pushed the swinging doors open, bringing in a cloud of dust. A figure in all black followed the dirty breeze into the barroom. The load of hay on his skull fell to his shoulders. It was combed back real neat like a girl's, with a gob of pomade. He wasn't real tall or thick, but looked powerful just the same, like a diamondback whose every muscle is made for striking. Otherwise, you might've took him for a tenderfoot with soft hands and fancy clothes.

The men at the bar all hot-footed out of his way. Sal placed a bottle of gin in front of him, then retreated to the far side of the bar. Most folks drank bathtub whiskey or flat beer, but he had himself an educated thirst for the juice of juniper berries. Some of the newer fellas let their eyes linger a little too long, so he hissed like an angry cat.

"What's that? Some kinda vampire?" the kid asked with a nervous giggle.

"Yup."

"You shittin' me? They're real! Thought they couldn't come out during the day—least that's what the storybooks say."

"Can come out at dusk, and it's always dusk in Damnation."

"*Always?*"

"Long as I been here, and that's nearly fifteen years."

"That vampire drink folks' blood?"

"Nah, everybody here's already dead. Blood's as cold as a crocodile's. That's why he's so ornery."

"Can he fly?"

"Leaps real far, almost like flying. Fast as a bugger, too."

"Any more like him around?"

"Nope, just the one. Musta done something halfway decent to end up here instead of hell. Don't think he appreciates it much though."

"Next, you gonna tell me there's werewolves, too," he laughed.

"They drink down the road at their own saloon."

"Does everyone who don't go to heaven or hell wind up here?"

"Ain't seen my dead Uncle Joe," I said. "And he didn't seem ripe for neither place. Can't speak for the rest. It's a small town, though."

The kid eased back and took a gulp of the coffin varnish that passed for whiskey. Some folks were so relieved they ended up short of hell that they got a little cocky. Reckoned there wasn't much else to be afraid of. "Don't seem like such a bad place," he said.

"You just gotta watch what you say 'round here," I warned him. "Folks draw real fast. They get sick of being here. Puts 'em in bad spirits, and they'll draw if you so much as brush against a fella's sleeve."

"Like Dodge City."

"Worse than that. You risk getting sent to hell every time you leave the rooming house. But it gets more boring than church if you don't stretch your legs once in a while."

"Let me get this straight. If you get shot, you go to hell forever. But if you don't, you can hang out here long as you like, play cards, and maybe have a go at them old churchgoing ladies."

"That's about the size of it," I told him.

"Sounds like you need a sheriff," he said.

"Keep your voice down!" Sal hollered. "Somebody set this boy straight before Jack hears him and shoots up the whole bar!"

"What'd I say?" the newbie blathered.

"Pipe down!" Sal ordered. "No more of your lollygagging—that is if you're hoping to last the night." He stormed off, leaving the kid moping over an empty glass.

"Jack don't like to hear no talk of… *ahem*, law enforcement," I explained

"Who's Jack?"

"Member that short fella in the Stetson who kilt the preacher?"

* * * *

When he had first come to town some ten years earlier, Jack Finney was the measliest pipsqueak who'd ever darkened the doorstep of the Foggy Dew saloon. He needed a boost to get on a barstool. Hadn't made it all but two steps into the room before the betting began on how long he'd last—and nobody wagered a dime past suppertime.

Back then, the quickest gun in town was a sheriff from Lexington, Kentucky, named Jeremiah. He was a good old boy with a righteous streak. He might've taken a few bribes when he was alive, but he kept the peace and went to church every Sunday. He'd been the sort to give everyone a fair shake till they crossed the line, but the way he had met his end changed all that. He was scouting for rustlers, and a couple of two-bit thieves dressed as priests got the drop on him. They gut-shot him and stole his horse and guns, leaving him to die in the woods. It wasn't the bullet wound that did him in, though. They only shot him with a .22, but the pain kept him from walking. Couldn't even crawl to a creek for water. He went four days without anything to eat or drink. He was so parched his tongue blew up as big as a bullfrog's, and he began seeing things that weren't there. Reckoned it best to end his suffering while he could still think clearly. Didn't have no knife, so he widened his wound with his fingertips, trying to bleed out faster. Eventually his heart gave out. After he arrived in Damnation, the stretched-out bullet hole in his belly didn't mend properly, so bits of food and whiskey sometimes leaked out when he laughed. He claimed the spillage was the reason why he was always so damn hungry and thirsty.

Jeremiah wasn't officially appointed sheriff of Damnation. He just happened to be wearing a star when he died. Then he shot a mess of people right away, so folks quickly deferred to him. His suspicious nature wasn't helped any by having been gunned down by phony clergymen. He didn't like to go at anyone head-on who hadn't been tested. He preferred to see them show their stuff against someone else first.

Even someone as scrawny as Jack needed to be tested, and Jeremiah watched him closely as the boys bullied him. It gave them no small joy to hear the kid squeal. Just a few hours after he arrived, a Comanchero who had only been in town a couple of weeks stepped to Jack. He was a half-Mexican bandito who had made his living by stealing goods and livestock from gringos and trading them with Indians. His occupation had cost him an eye at some point, and he wore a black patch over the empty socket. The crosshatch scars on his cheeks and forearms attested to the many knife fights he'd managed to survive. He still had a sneaky way about him, always lurking in the shadows, ready to slit a throat. Now, he stared Jack down with the one good eye.

"My boots could use a shine, boy," he announced. Jack looked around the room, hoping someone'd laugh to let him know it was just a joke, but nobody said a word. "Well, don't just stand there," the Comanchero yelled. "Get down and give 'em a shine!" Jack slowly bent before the dirty boots. They were covered in blood and shit and dribbles of piss, then caked in so much dust you couldn't tell what color they were.

"Give 'em a spit shine!" the Comanchero ordered. Jack's eyes grew tearful. He puckered his mouth to offer a gob of spit, and sure enough the boot crashed into his face. The whole room erupted in laughter. Jack rolled over on the floor, moaning and wishing he'd never died. A ribbon of blood leaked from his lip over his chin.

Jeremiah had been keeping a keen eye on the Comanchero ever since he'd arrived. Didn't trust a man who traded with Indians. The one-eyed bandito had already knifed a couple of fellas over card games. Nobody'd seen him shoot yet though, so there was no way of knowing how fast he was. He carried a greased Schofield revolver, which split in the middle so you could load all six chambers at once instead of one at a time, like the older Colts. It was a soldier's weapon, good for extended battle, but he seemed to prefer slashing throats by surprise. Jeremiah reckoned this would be a good chance to find out if his pistol work was as worrisome as his knife play.

"You don't gotta take no more ribbing today," Jeremiah told the boy as he tended to his lip. "Long as you outdraw somebody. And since Cyclops here is so keen on you, might as well be him. Winner gets free drinks and grub for the rest of the day."

The Comanchero glared at Jeremiah, but it was difficult for him to express himself properly with just the one eye. "In the land of the blind," he said solemnly, "the one-eyed man is king." Then he turned and headed outside.

"Well, shit... Good thing we ain't all blind!" Jeremiah laughed and shoved Jack toward the door.

Mostly out of boredom, ten or fifteen men wandered out in front of the saloon. The sky was always an ashen yellow, no brighter than dusk. The clouds never lifted but streaks of orange and violet broke through in spots. It was pretty, only it never changed. I reckoned the living were so keen on sunsets because they didn't last. Even the prettiest lady in the world would get tiresome if you were stuck staring at her for eternity—especially if there was no chance of giving her a poke.

Most of the fellas didn't consider the gunfight worth vacating a stool, particularly if you had a good one near the fire. Most newbies didn't last their first week, and a skinny teenager like Jack didn't inspire any wagering. As a matter of duty, I went out to document his getting sent to hell. They stood in the center of the road as we lined the rotted-out boardwalk. Sal handed Jack an old Colt and a single bullet. The weight of the gun nearly caused him to drop it.

"Is that all I get?" Jack's voice cracked in disbelief. "Just one bullet!"

"Jeremiah don't want you gettin' no ideas. This way, if you take a shot at him, one of his men'll get you for sure."

"But what if I miss?" It was a fair question. The scared hand of the newbie could easily empty a six-shooter before hitting his target.

"Then I suppose the half-breed can take his sweet time returning fire," Sal answered.

They lined up back to back. Jack's head didn't reach the Comanchero's shoulder blade. On Jeremiah's mark, they each began marching in opposite directions. At the count of ten, they both turned. Jack's slight frame made him more nimble. His hips swiveled squarely in place, slightly ahead of the bandito's. He proved to have naturally quick hands, although they trembled with the weight of the giant Colt. His itty-bitty finger struggled to squeeze the rusty trigger. The bandito caught up with the steady arm of a practiced killer. The missing eye was a big disadvantage. He had to wait until he was fully turned around to take proper aim. Jack managed to get off a lucky shot, but it only winged the bandito's right arm. As he gripped the wound, tar-black blood spilled between his fingers, and the gun slipped from his hand.

They both looked at each other for a cold second. With no bullets left, Jack had two choices: stand there and wait to die or attack with everything he had. The little fella let out a blood-curdling shriek, then charged. The bandito debated for a split second whether he should pick up his gun with his left hand or pull the knife from his belt. Neither were necessary. He could have just knocked the kid down and stomped on him, but the moment of indecision cost him. Jack closed the distance between them and was on him like a saddle sore. Still hollering like a loon, he swung a wide haymaker with the rusty Colt clenched in his fist, braining the bandito above his ear. The edge of the cylinder ripped out a silver dollar-sized chunk of scalp. The Comanchero's eye stilled after the blow. Tears were running down Jack's cheeks. He was only seventeenand had never murdered anyone before—let alone a dead man.

Those who hadn't bothered to come outside and watch the fight would hear the retelling of it for months afterward. The skinny teenager kept smashing the bandit's skull, fearing that if he let up for even a second, he'd be done for. First, the left ear shredded, then the flesh from neck to forehead scraped off. Hairy clumps of scalp clung to the gun barrel like leaves on a rake. Jack sobbed with one swing, then screamed with the next. Some of the noises didn't even sound human, more like a coyote's yelp. When he finally tired, there was no more casing left to hold the brains together. A dark porridge spilled onto the ground like chuck-wagon stew. Jack collapsed on the body and lay there twitching and panting in exhaustion. When they pulled him off, he was as bloody as the bandito. He went back in the saloon and sat in the corner, still shaking as he nursed a beer. Sal gave him a couple of pork chops, and he wolfed them down hungrily. Everyone left him in peace for the rest of the day.

The next morning, Jack skulked into the saloon at breakfast time with dried blood still on his cheeks and hands. He looked like an Indian in war paint. Since he'd proven himself the day before, he wasn't expecting any trouble—at least not before he ate.

"You only earned a pass for one day, kid," Jeremiah announced. One of his men handed the boy the same rusty blood-stained Colt with a single bullet already in the chamber.

"Any volunteers to draw against this hayseed? Winner gets free drinks and grub for the day."

A cowboy with some experience stepped forward. He wasn't a trained gunfighter but had survived four or five draws since he'd arrived two months earlier. He didn't have much of a knack for cards, so he supported himself with his pistol work. Found it easier to spot a fella with a mess of chips in front of him, wait till he drank too much, then pick a fight. The winner typically claimed the loser's possessions.

Jack and the cowboy headed out to the road, and this time half the saloon followed. The rest still didn't consider the action good enough. The payout on the cowboy wasn't very good because nobody thought the newbie's luck could possibly last another day.

They stood back to back and walked off ten paces. This time, Jack was a little smoother and more deliberate in his draw. Meanwhile, the cowboy jammed his hand into his holster and plucked up his gun, letting off two screaming shots in rapid succession. Both struck the ground in front of Jack. He flinched but maintained his composure. He had learned it was better to squeeze the trigger instead of jerking it. The cowboy had just leveled his barrel to send the third bullet into Jack's chest when his own shirt reddened like a rose blossoming from his heart. He fell to the dust. Jack went back inside and ate some more pork chops.

Each day, Jeremiah called for a new volunteer, and each day Jack faced him. Wasn't any choice in the matter. With just a single bullet in the chamber, he couldn't raise the barrel at the man who handed him the gun. There were always two men beside Jeremiah who would've gunned him down. His best hope was to keep firing away at whoever they put in front of him. The first few men weren't very good, but it gave him a chance to learn. The best living gunfighters had upward of thirty kills under their belt, but those were spaced out by months and sometimes years. Jack had the advantage of drawing every single day, which allowed him to fix his flaws while they were still fresh in his mind. And since he had just the one bullet, he put every bit of his concentration into aiming it.

At first Jeremiah was glad to be able to test folks out and separate the wheat from the chaff. He could see their weaknesses when they drew against the kid, and note if someone dipped their shoulder before they pulled. He figured he'd get the upper hand on whoever gunned the kid down. The thing was that nobody could, so all that information went to waste when they fell. Also, Jack learned something new every day. His hand got steadier and quicker. He didn't even bother asking for breakfast.

Just marched straight up and stuck out his hand for the gun and the bullet, then he waited outside to see who'd follow. It didn't escape Jeremiah's attention that he was making a bona fide gunslinger out of the boy, who'd likely be even harder to control.

Everyone else found it a nice change of pace to start out the day with a gunfight. Gave folks something to look forward to, a reason to get out of bed. We all gathered beside the road each morning, even a few of the Indians who camped out in the dusty plains surrounding the town. People started to root for the little fella, and eventually the betting pool swung to favor him against the hardened outlaws who were just in it for free grub and drinks. After a few weeks, Jack gained a lifetime's worth of experience. Then the day came when there were no more volunteers to go up against him.

"All right, boy, you ain't gotta go against no one today," Jeremiah announced. "Drink and eat as much as you like. Nobody'll hassle you. But tomorrow, you go against me."

Everyone was itching to see the matchup. Jeremiah had been studying Jack for a month, but Jack had been practicing every day of that month. Wasn't even the teensiest bit nervous anymore. His aim was dead on and his hand as steady as a post. But Jeremiah didn't intend to get hoodwinked by another thief dressed as a priest. He had found one weakness that he could use to his advantage.

Jack was only given the one bullet each day, so he couldn't risk aiming at his opponent's head, where a couple of inches in either direction might miss it entirely. And he couldn't fire off a quick shot at a fella's legs, since a wounded man might still overpower him. He always shot at the center of the chest, where the target was the widest.

That afternoon, I overheard Jeremiah telling the blacksmith to mold him a sheet of tin. The next morning at breakfast time, Jeremiah was sitting at the bar with his back to the door. He was all by himself, carelessly gobbling down a plateful of beans. A glint of metal shined from under his collar. He'd gotten up early so he could have the blacksmith fit it in place while everyone was still asleep. If it succeeded in stopping Jack's first bullet, he'd have all the time in the world to aim, and since he knew right where the bullet was going, he had extra metal layered in the center. Probably wouldn't stop a buffalo gun, but it'd do for a rusty old Colt. It was a pretty good plan... till Jack came through the door an hour earlier than usual.

The boy was through playing by another man's rules—that much was clear. He grabbed the sheriff's hair from behind and yanked his head back, exposing his neck to the ceiling.

"Ain't gonna be any sheriffs parsing out the bullets no more!" Jack said as he pulled out the Comanchero's knife. He must've pocketed it the first day he'd arrived, when he killed the half-breed and collapsed on top of him. We thought he was just twitching with fear but he was really fleecing that knife from the body. Ever since then, the boy had been biding his time, trying to stay alive till he got close enough and no one was by Jeremiah's side. Jack ran the blade across the sheriff's throat before he could say a damn thing.

By the time Jeremiah's men arrived, Jack had already helped himself to his pretty pearl-handled pistols. He smiled at them tauntingly. They wouldn't have pulled on him if he only had two bullets, let alone twelve. The next week, Jack shot one of the men for fun. The week after, he shot the other. He had learned from Jeremiah not to trust anyone, but also not to grow soft. He made a point of going up against someone at least once a week to keep sharp—and he wasn't too fickle about who. Unlike Jeremiah, he had no problem with shooting untested newbies. Felt it kept him on his toes. And the bullying he'd endured didn't make him sympathize with the misfortunes of others. He turned into the meanest son of a bitch in town, so nobody ever mentioned sheriffs around him again.

* * * *

"I still say you need someone to uphold the rules around here," argued the newbie with the nickel-sized bullet hole in his temple.

"Oh, and what rules would you suggest?" I asked.

"Well, no shootin' each other for one. You fellas are playing for keeps here. Ain't like before when we wasn't sure what happened after you died. This is *it!*"

"So, what if someone accuses you of cheatin', like the fella you said put that bullet in your head?"

"Could wrestle," he suggested.

"And if a fella ain't much for wrestlin'?"

"Well then, he shouldn't call nobody a cheater. And if somebody calls him a cheater, he could just go to the sheriff."

"Sounds like you got it all worked out," I said. "Lemme ask you another question—how's a fella get a bullet in the side of his head from an argument at a card table? Weren't you lookin' at the man when he called you a cheater? Or did he somehow sneak up beside ya?"

"No. I mean yes." He fidgeted nervously. "I guess I kinda turned away when he shot me."

"Is that so?"

"It happened real fast."

"Thought you said the last thing you remembered was that you drew and reckoned he done the same. You telling me you drew your pistol and looked away before you even pulled the trigger?"

"I dunno! What ya want from me, mister?"

"Why'd ya do it?" I pressed him.

"Do what? I tole ya, mister. He 'cused me a cheatin'. Then he shot me 'fore I could shoot him."

"Did he do it real close, or was he sitting across the table?"

"He was across the table," he blubbered. "We was sitting as far apart as them two fellas over there."

"Interesting." I nodded.

"How's that?"

"'Cause that bullet hole's got a ring around it like a hot barrel was pressed to your head. You know what I think? I think you pulled the trigger yourself and you're ashamed of it, so you cooked up a story about an argument over cards. And I'm damn sick of pissants like you coming in here and making stuff up. What I wanna know now is *why you done it?*"

Looked like his face was going to shatter from holding it all in. Finally, he broke down. "I had the sadness, sir. I always had it—long as I can remember. My pa had it before me and, from what I heard, his pa before him. Couldn't be helped. It made me do lots a bad things, and it weren't never gonna go away. So I done myself in."

"All right then." I scribbled down a note. "Sal, get this fella a drink on me."

"Thanks, mister. I appreciate it," he smiled. "And just 'cause I done myself in don't mean I'm wrong in what I'm sayin'. Matter of fact, killin' myself made me realize things."

"Oh?"

"Like how special stuff is. Even breathin' this dusty air and sittin' here in this dark saloon talkin' with you. It's all special! If y'all only knew what was good for ya, you'd stop shootin' each other this very day. Just think," his voice lifted, "if what you were sayin' earlier's true, then a year from today the whole darn town could march straight up to heaven together!"

Some sodbusters at a nearby table burst into laughter.

"Shit, boy, when's the last time you seen a fella do what's best for him?" I asked. "You think if you pluck a man from his life and stick him in a one-horse town with a hundred other rotten bastards he's gonna act *better?*"

"That's why you need somebody to keep 'em in line, *like a sheriff!*"

"Keep it down!" Sal scolded. "You say that word again, and I'll send ya to hell myself."

"Just out of curiosity," I asked the kid, "who you reckon might be capable of stopping these bored and hateful men from shootin' each another?"

It was a subject I'd given a fair amount of thought to. The last time I had preached pacifism, some old-timer tried to gut me, and I had to shoot him—much to everyone's amusement. That's when I took to practicing it instead of preaching it. Everyone could go on blasting one another over nothing. Hopefully, I'd slip between the cracks right into heaven. Sure, every so often a newbie'd come at me for asking the wrong questions, but I'd gotten a knack for avoiding them. Hadn't even heeled myself in a month.

The kid was still giving the question serious consideration. He peered down the bar to where the vampire was drinking by himself. "How 'bout that fella?" he suggested. "Looks like he could uphold rules well enough. He's gotta be quicker than Jack or any other man."

"I expect he is," I agreed. "And he probably could whip this town into shape real quick, if he was inclined to. And if anyone was compelled to ask him."

"Well, dang! That's exactly what I'm gonna do." The kid sprang to his feet and walked straight over before I could stop him. Wanted to show he was more than a cowardly suicide. Strutted up with the gumption of a mayor on Election Day. Didn't even seem to notice the yellow glow in the vampire's eyes growing brighter as he approached. He stuck out his hand real friendly-like and said, "Howdy, pardner. My name's Fre...!"

Didn't even get out his full name. The vampire snatched the outstretched hand like an apple from a tree and pressed the boy's wrist to his lips. Yellow fangs sprang from his gums and pierced the soft sunburnt flesh. He clamped down on the bone without swallowing the blood that was pouring out. With one yank of his neck, the hand tore clean off. The kid screamed like one of them lady opera singers, so high and loud I thought the chandelier'd shatter. The vampire tossed the hand to the ground with the fingers still twitching like a daddy longlegs. Then he spat out some blood in disgust. The kid gripped his stump in shock. Then for some reason, he started scooping up the veins and muck dangling out. Tried to put them back inside like he was stuffing a sausage. Suppose he thought it could be mended somehow. All the while he kept screaming.

"Aw, come on, Sal," Fat Wally complained from the poker table. "Hobble that measly cowpoke's lip. Some of us are trying to play cards here. Can't concentrate with all his yellin'. Shit, I think Red's finally got himself something better than a pair of bullshit," he said, and the others laughed.

Sal moseyed to the end of the bar in no particular hurry. Wasn't the type to break a sweat if he didn't have to. He wiped his hands off on his

Clark Casey

apron, then grabbed the scattergun from the umbrella stand. He came around the other side of the bar and pressed the barrel against the kid's chest to avoid any buckshot spray. He pulled the trigger, and the boy was thrown five paces backward onto the floor with a wet thud.

"*Goddamnit!*" Red hollered. "You stood too close again, Sal. Done shot the guts clear out his back. Got it all over my dang cards. I call *re*-deal!" The other players grumbled and mucked their cards, arguing that Red probably didn't have shit anyways.

"He could've at least got sent to hell like a man, instead of a little girl that seen a bug," Fat Wally remarked. "When your time comes, boys, whatever you do, don't go out like a '*Fre...!*'" Wally clutched his wrist, imitating the boy's shock at seeing his hand torn off. The fellas laughed good and hard at that one, and from then on anyone who left Damnation in a cowardly manner was referred to as a "*Fre...!*"

The Chinaman who tended to the pigs came and dragged Fre's body to the pigpen. The preacher had bled out by then, so he took him, too. The pigs chewed the cold corpses to bits. There wouldn't have been any trace that they were ever in town if I didn't remember to write down a few words about them. On account of all the gunfights, the swine were always plump and juicy. Most folks agreed that the best thing about Damnation was you could eat all the bacon you'd ever wanted.

The vampire finished his drink, then left without a word. A little while later, Jack came back in and scanned the room to see if anyone else needed shooting. Those were the last of the simple days when everyone knew their place, and there was still peace between us and the wolves. Then, just like the preacher had preached, a new gunfighter came to town and stirred up a real shit storm.

Chapter 2

Jack

I slept in the day he first arrived. Sal's giant halfwit barback came round to fetch me at the rooming house. We called him Stumpy because his hand had gotten mangled in a threshing machine. The stump proved useful for washing out narrow glasses that Sal's swollen knuckles couldn't reach inside. He still had the other good hand to pull a trigger and back up Sal, but the stump was the main reason why he'd gotten the job. Stumpy could sooner explain the mysteries of the universe than tell you why he'd ended up in Damnation. Might've pulled the arms off a man thinking he was just a bug. For his part, he was just happy to no longer have a nickname relating to his unusual height after all those years of being called Stretch and whatnot. He was so tall he couldn't tell when his feet were cold. As I opened my eyes, his long skinny frame was lurching over my cot. Though he measured over six and a half feet tall, he didn't weigh any more than me at two heads shorter. Admittedly, I could've stood to lose a pound or ten.

"Please get up now, Mr. Thomas," he pleaded weakly, his pointy stump nudging me like a dull cattle prod. "There's someone real important at the Foggy Dew. Sal says you should interview him for the newspaper right away."

It was hardly a newspaper really, just a one-page leaflet I printed in the back of the general store on an old woodblock press. Rearranging the letters was tiresome work, so I kept the news short. Strictly kept track of who came and left with a few words about what they'd done when they were alive. Called it *The Crapper* on account of that was where folks read it.

"Hurry up!" Stumpy hollered as I slowly roused.

"Why?" I barked back. "Ain't like he's gonna get any deader."

"That ain't it. I don't think. Sal says the man ain't gonna last long the way he's boasting. You know how Mr. Finney feels about blowhards."

"Is Jack there?" I looked at my watch.

"Nah, but Sal says you'll need time to get his story straight before he comes."

"Hell, it ain't even noon yet. Jack never comes in before three."

"The new man's real thirsty. Drank up two pints of whiskey already. Sal don't think he'll make much sense if you don't talk to him soon."

I slid on my trousers and grabbed my cane. The dozen or so cots on the top floor of the rooming house were only half filled with soiled men, but the whole building stank to high hell of whiskey and decade-old boot sweat. It was enough to drive a man to drink ten minutes after he woke—and most did. Some nights I slept on the floor in the back of the general store just to avoid the mingling of so many bad odors under one roof.

"One of you bastards got gangrene?" I called out.

"Red probably yanked his pecker off in the night," Fat Wally cracked. "Left it rottin' beneath the sheets."

Covering my mouth with a handkerchief, I hobbled to the door. Stumpy shadowed me down the steps one at a time, knowing Sal'd scold him if he came back alone.

"If I'd a known it was gonna come to this..." I grumbled. "Racing to interview some dead man before he drinks too much and gets himself sent to hell... Well, shit! I'd a stayed alive!"

"Really?" Stumpy said in his childlike way, as if it was just a simple matter of choice. "But then who'd write the paper?" he asked.

Even with a limp, it was barely a two-minute walk from the rooming house to the Foggy Dew. Damnation consisted of two long roads bisected by three short roads, making twelve blocks of rickety wood buildings. You could see the whole town from end to end in the time it took to smoke a pipe. Each structure was more lopsided and rotted out than the last. The roofs were shedding shingles like a lamb's coat in the springtime. A narrow boardwalk lined the storefronts, but it was more of a hazard than a convenience. With all the missing and broken planks, you had a better chance of tripping and getting a splinter in your face than reaching your destination unharmed. The only use for it would be keeping folks out of the mud, and there wasn't any rain to make mud. Nobody remained from the time of Damnation's construction to tell why it was even there. The builders must've been a peculiar lot. Some reckoned they had special powers, for they somehow managed to construct the entire town without a single level surface. Every windowsill, doorjamb, and floorboard was as crooked as a dog's hind leg.

Across from the Foggy Dew, the vampire was sitting on a rocking chair up on his balcony, looking bored as usual. He had the whole third story of the hotel to himself. It was the tallest structure in town, but didn't offer much of a view on account of the brown dust cloud around the perimeter of Damnation. Dead men and animals came in on a single road that vanished into the dust. If you tried walking out, you just came back again from the other direction.

Most days, he sat looking down in quiet disgust. Could've wiped the lot of us out any time he wanted, but then it'd be just him and the wolves and the dust. The men often brought their arguments out in the road and that offered a little entertainment. There wasn't much to do except drink, play cards, and watch the occasional gunfight. The vampire hawkeyed me, probably wondering how a cripple managed to last so long. Truth was I had a better chance than most of making it a year without getting caught up in a gunfight. I didn't have many personal ties that'd draw me into conflict. It was my nature to watch from the sidelines and listen. And sooner or later, every sorry bastard wanted someone to tell their stories to.

Stumpy noticed the vampire glaring at me. "Don't mind him, Mr. Thomas. He's just jealous. Knows he could never last as long as you without tearing someone up."

"Some folks got a taste for killing that never goes away," I said. "No matter what's at stake."

"How long's it been now?" Stumpy asked.

"About two and a half months. Kinda feel like I got a target on my back these days."

"Ah, nobody'd shoot you, Mr. Thomas. If they did, wouldn't be nothin' for them to read," he said simply. Of course, the wolves weren't fans of my writing, but there had been a relative peace between us and them—so far.

In the Foggy Dew, the new fella was sitting at the bar drinking whiskey with a tequila chaser. Had a mess of dark curly hair like a buffalo hide and the sallow skin of a longtime drinker. A round table muscle sagged over his belt. His eyes were just bloodshot slivers between swollen lids. Most of his scarred cheeks were covered by a patchy beard, except a trail of pockmarks that crept toward his temples.

"Came through the dust an hour ago, and he's already stinking drunk," Sal complained. "Figured you'd wanna make a record of him before Jack shoots him. Claims to be kinda famous."

"Kinda?"

"You'll see."

Rope marks wrapped the fella's neck, and he was gasbagging about how he'd been hanged for robbing a stagecoach then killing a posse of men. Got caught near the Mexican border coming out of an outhouse. I dipped my pen in ink and started scribbling a few notes. Some folks got shot before they said anything of much interest. Left me trying to recall their name and where they came from. Others kept repeating the same nonsense over and over, so I didn't write anything down, thinking they'd never shut up. When they got sent to hell, I forgot what they were going on about. So I found it best to collect whatever facts I could up front, then clean it up later. I ordered a beer and restricted myself to one sip for each sentence I wrote, which proved a fair incentive.

"If I didn't have the backdoor trots from eatin' so many dang Mexican strawberries, they never woulda got me," the newbie chuckled loudly. He might've been uglier than a new-sheared sheep, but it didn't bother him none. He was a jolly killer. "They gave me a proper Texas catwalk," he continued. "I tell you this. The best thing about being hung is I ain't never gotta go back to Fort Worth!" He broke into a fit of knee-slapping laughter.

"Hey, ain't you Buddy Baker?" one of the newer boys asked him. "I hearda you. You shot Jared Nichols in Kansas City—he was fast."

"Not fast enough." Buddy scoffed. "I bet you didn't know I shot more men than William Bonney. And that's a fact!"

"I ain't never heard that."

"That's 'cause there weren't no witnesses to a mess of 'em. Damn journalist got in the way, so nobody recorded it. Ain't my fault a man can't hold a pistol and a pencil at the same time."

"You boys hear that?" Stumpy said. "Buddy here shot more men than Billy the Kid!"

"Lemme get some more of that pork belly and a splash of that there bug juice," Buddy said to Sal. "You say I don't have to eat no more now that I'm dead?"

"Ain't gonna die of starvation." Sal raked his fingers over the ends of his handlebar mustache and filled Buddy's glass. The lamplight glimmered eerily on his bald head. Sal looked more like a mortician than a bartender. "You'll still get hungry something awful. More outta habit, I 'spose."

"Ain't you got nothin' 'sides pork?" Buddy asked.

The dead animals appeared from the dust with blackened eyes and ice-cold blood in their veins. Sal cooked up the pigs for us. Indians got the chickens since they had the fewest to feed. Werewolves took the cows on account they had the biggest appetites. The vampire could eat whatever he wanted, but he wasn't hungry for anything in Damnation—that we knew of.

The divvying up of the animals had been decided long ago by the werewolf pack leader, Argus. In wolf form, he stood as tall as a Shetland pony and was quick as a jackrabbit. Could tell him from the others by his white coat with specks of gray. Argus reckoned it was better to give us the smaller animals than to worry about us picking off any of his pack. He told Sal and the chief so. The chief was the oldest dead Indian. Kind of a grumpy fella. He wasn't too happy about getting stuck with the chickens, but he was used to not getting his way. Some joked that the chief was at the very first Thanksgiving in Plymouth and didn't get nothing but the gizzard. Others said he was the one who traded Manhattan away for a handful of beads, and that's why he was so bitter. When the chief got stuck with the chickens, he told Sal and Argus that next time he'd barter with a tomahawk. Sal said there wasn't no need to worry though—unless a whole mess of Indians came to Damnation in a hurry.

"Just pork," Sal told Buddy. "They serve beef down the road, but I don't expect you'd be welcome there."

"Do I still need money here?" he asked.

"More of a formality," Sal explained. "But an important one. I'll run you a tab, and you can pay it when you win in cards. Eventually everybody gives their money to the blacksmith for bullets, and he's lousy at cards so he redistributes it back a hand at a time."

Buddy didn't seem to mind being dead since he'd probably be doing the same thing if he was still alive: drinking, telling stories, and teasing the younger fellas. He couldn't figure out why he ended up shy of hell.

"Thought for sure I'd done enough killin' to earn a nonstop ticket," he smiled. "But I don't mind hanging out with you boys while they stoke the furnaces for me."

He was knocking back the whiskey at a furious pace. A lot of fellas hit the bottle hard to wash away the sting of those final fears of death. Buddy might've been mourning something else though, some simpler life he never got a chance to live. Every rotten son of a bitch figured he'd get a chance to repent and go straight before he died. Then they ended up in Damnation, never getting the pretty wife and the house with a picket fence and a yard full of youngins.

Sal didn't usually extend so much credit, but he couldn't cut the man off without causing a fuss. The boys crowded around to hear how Buddy had robbed a stagecoach dressed as an Indian, then joined the posse to hunt down the thief. He could spin a good yarn, but his speech was slurring some, and the gap between fact and fantasy was getting too large for anyone to swallow.

At half past two, Jack Finney sauntered into the saloon. It was easier for him to sleep in since he didn't bunk at the noisy stinking rooming house with everyone else. Had his own room in the hotel, just below the vampire's. He wasn't donning the big hat today. He wore all black except for the colorful stitching on his fancy lizard-skin boots, which he had taken off a tinhorn he shot for having an uppity look. Jack rubbed a hand over his smooth chin, wondering what to make of the new fella. For once, Sal was relieved to see Jack, figuring he'd send Buddy to hell before he ran up too big of a tab. Sal was a frugal man. Some said he'd died just to avoid further taxes.

Jack sat alone at the end of the bar eyeing up Buddy. Judging by his sourpuss, the fat man didn't rank very high in his estimation.

"One time, I took on four men in San Antonio," Buddy boasted. "Only had a single-shot derringer, and they was all heeled with fancy Remington six shooters. Had to reload after every dang shot!"

"Did you get 'em all, Mr. Baker?" Stumpy asked.

"I'm still standing, ain't I? Well, I guess I'm not anymore!" he cackled. "But them boys ain't the ones that got me. Hey, maybe they're here. Seen any shot-up Texans with stained shorts 'round here?"

Jack stood, and the room silenced. He wasn't the sort to put off shooting a man. On the way to the latrine, he ambled by the chubby newbie and knocked against his sipping arm. Some whiskey spilled over Buddy's hand, but he didn't make a big to-do of it, like most would. Barely pausing in his storytelling, he licked his knuckle so as not to waste any gut-warmer.

"What's he, *yella*?" Sal whispered. "Thought he was supposed to be some kinda big-shot gunfighter."

"Maybe gun fighting ain't as important to him as telling tales and drinkin' prairie dew," Fat Wally said.

On his way out of the latrine, Jack lingered by the faro table, though he wasn't the gambling sort. He stood beside the banker, watching the cards come out of the shoe and glancing over a punter's shoulder toward the bar. After a short while, Buddy stood, hiked up his pants, and staggered lazily to the latrine. Jack made a beeline for the bar to intercept him in his path. Buddy was nearly twice his size but Jack hardly gave him a foot to squeeze by. As they passed each other, Jack stiffened his elbow at the last moment and bumped hard against Buddy's gut.

"Watch where you're going!" Jack hollered.

"I was watching just fine," Buddy replied. "Better learn some manners, son."

There were a few gasps of surprise around the room. Nobody would ever dare to address Jack that way. He still looked seventeen, because that's how old he was when he died, but he'd sent hundreds of men to hell in the ten years since he'd arrived. It stuck in his craw to be called *son*, but he didn't show it.

"If you're gonna address a man like that in Damnation, I expect you're ready to draw," Jack said calmly.

Buddy was in his mid-forties—old by outlaw standards—and he showed his age, but he acted like a goofy kid and thought everything was a game. "Shit, boy!" He looked down at Jack. "I wanted to draw, I'd a got me some pencils instead of pistols." He laughed good-naturedly, but Jack kept eyeballing him without so much as a blink.

"Ah, you'll understand when you're older, sonny."

"Quit your jawing and pull!" Jack showed a rare flash of anger.

"All right, if you're set on getting yourself shot, how 'bout high noon tomorrow?" Buddy suggested.

"Ain't no such thing as noon here," Jack said. "It's always dusk."

"Oh yeah?" Buddy shrugged and took a gulp of his drink. "Guess we might as well settle it now then." He seemed more put out by the interruption of his drinking than anything else.

"How about you boys settle this outside." Sal tried to sound stern, but he wasn't. Jack must've been in the mood for some fresh air though, because he obliged him.

Buddy staggered drunkenly toward the door, knocking over a spittoon on the way. He cursed at it for jumping in front of him, but then went back to give it a heartfelt apology.

The whole saloon emptied into the road to watch, except Sneaky Jim. The greasy weasel liked to steal sips from other men's drinks while they were in the commode. After a good gunfight, you could expect every glass in the room to be lessened by two sips, and for Jim to be lying in the corner with a bellyache.

"We ain't seen anyone semi-famous get shot in quite some time," Red remarked.

"I reckon the fat man won't even clear leather." Fat Wally waved a five-dollar bill to wager.

"Ain't that the pot calling the kettle black," Red said.

"All right, boys!" Sal interrupted, "I got two-to-one odds that the new man heads south without showing metal."

"I'll take some of that action," I said, having a suspicion Buddy might show some gumption. "He might not win, but I reckon he'll get sent to hell with a gun in his hand."

The vampire was up on his balcony across the road, smoking a pipe with his feet propped up on the banister. He surely enjoyed himself a gunfight. Seemed the only time a smile crossed his pale face was when some loudmouth got a lead plumb in the gut. Looked on it like a type of vaudeville.

As the two men lined up back to back in the center of the road, Buddy's large round body shadowed Jack's lean figure like a carnival tent beside a stake in the ground. The heft on his hips looked like it might hinder him from lifting a sidearm, whereas Jack's trim waist gave no such obstruction, and his arms were coiled tight as a spring.

At Sal's signal, they each began walking in opposite directions. At the count of ten, they turned and stood for a moment. Jack locked Buddy in a cold glare. He could look at a fella like there wasn't nothing else in the world, but at the same time he was aware of everything going on around him—always ready in case some upstart in the crowd decided to pull.

Normally, Jack'd wait till his opponent made the first move. Then he'd gun him down so it looked like it was the other fella's idea and he was just finishing it. Only this time it was taking too long. Buddy didn't see any reason to pull, or maybe he'd forgotten why he came out into the road to begin with. He swayed drunkenly in the wind, covering one eye with his left hand to keep from seeing double.

"Looks like your money's as good as gone," Sal whispered.

Finally, Jack got fed up. His right shoulder popped forward in its socket as his wiry arm collected the pistol in one swift motion. Buddy must've woke from his stupor at that particular moment, because he had the good sense to draw as well. And he was surprisingly fast.

They say steady is more important than fast, because then you only have to shoot once. But when you're steady *and* fast, there's no wasted motion and everything else seems to stand still. Jack's gun slid out of its holster, and the shine of the metal brightened. He cleared leather with a whip of his wrist and leveled the barrel. Jack always looked as though he moved in slow motion because he was so calm, even though he was really moving quicker than runaway mustangs.

This time though, Jack looked even slower on account of how quick Buddy *really was* moving. Drunk as he was, Buddy cleared leather and squeezed off three shots before Jack could pull the trigger once. One bullet hit the ground between them, another ricocheted off a rock into a horse. The third caught Jack Finney in the face, just below his left eye. A drape of blood spread across his smooth cheeks. There was a loud braying in the distance, then the horse and Jack both dropped at once.

The crowd was stunned to silence. Then the vampire laughed from his balcony above.

"Shit!" Sal cussed. "Guess you gotta be fast when you drink too much to aim properly."

The Chinaman came and lugged away both bodies. Jack was hardly a speck of man, all bone and muscle, and the Chinaman hauled him off by the ankles. Then he hitched the pony carcass to the back of a two-horse carriage and hauled it to the pigpen. Its heft, along with Jack's bit of sinewy muscle, would later be appreciated as thick white stripes in the bacon. That evening, Buddy moved into Jack's room in the hotel, just below the vampire, and Damnation had a new top gunman. The paper was a little longer than usual that week, but I suppose it was good practice so my hand wouldn't cramp up later on when the bodies really started piling up.

The Crapper

Comings: *Buddy Baker, originally of Louisville, Kentucky, was orphaned at the age of eight by a fire that took his mother, father, and baby sister. In order to keep himself alive, he took to thievery. At the age of ten, he murdered a man who tried to deprive him of his take in a pick-pocketing, which he makes no apologies for. From then, the list of crimes goes on and on, but Buddy prides himself on having stolen only what others could get along without and never killing anyone without trying real hard not to. In all, twenty-three men were sent to their graves by Buddy's swift arm and discerning trigger finger. He does not regret a one of them neither, unless any member of the posse he gunned down included orphans, like himself, who never had anyone to teach them right from wrong. When I questioned him about his remarkable speed with a sidearm, Buddy replied, "I had to shoot real fast if I wanted to swallow another breath. Guess I was just hungrier for air than them others."*

Goings: *Many will sigh with relief on hearing that Jack Finney of Topeka, Kansas, left town yesterday by the hand of Buddy Baker (his first beyond the grave and just four hours after his arrival). Jack had been the fastest gun in town for a decade. He came to Damnation at the age of seventeen, after losing his first and last earthly gunfight to a man who had called him yellow. When questioned throughout the years on his (until now) unmatchable speed, Jack always responded, "Fuck off, pencil pusher." Since Jack only had the one gunfight before he came to Damnation, some reckoned his hankering for killing was fueled by his anger at never getting a chance to grow up or, as Red phrased it, "'cause* *he died with no hair on his balls."*

Before he left, Jack finally got around to shooting the preacher in the throat. The old coot had been a little too vociferous in sharing his latest vision of fiery skies, a muddy earth that sprouts weeds, and the son of the devil himself being born here to vanquish us all, after the town grows some. Though the preacher was a tiresome man, his colorful banter did help to pass the time. It's been rumored that he hailed from New Hampshire, where he had succumbed to frostbite while being a Peeping Tom.

Oh, and some newbie got his hand taken off by the vampire, so Sal put him out of his misery with his scattergun. I didn't get a chance to find out where he was from, but his name started with the letters F-R-E. He had the sadness.

Chapter 3

Ms. Parker

One evening a couple of weeks after Buddy arrived, a young lady walked into the Foggy Dew wearing a white wedding dress and sopping wet, which was odd since it never rained in Damnation.

Every so often, a woman would turn up. Usually, she'd have killed her husband for cheating, then got hanged for it. One lady had killed her sister for sleeping with her husband. Another had smothered her baby with a pillow just so folks'd pity her grief. Womenfolk never lasted long. Right away, the men started quarrelling over them. Often, a woman would promise herself to one man then go off with another. It was easy for them to get mixed up since there wasn't no Bible to follow, and they didn't have to worry about their reputations no more. Seldom did any of them have shooting or card-playing skills. Wasn't much else to prize in Damnation, so the only thing of value they had was beneath their skirt. Usually a woman got shot within a week, and a lot of the fellas'd say it was good riddance on account of the headaches she'd caused.

We never had any women as proper or as pretty as Ms. Parker though. Shivering in the doorway, her wet dress clung to her body revealing the shape of her slender frame. Her round dimpled cheeks were as pale as moonbeams. The men all glared at her. It must've been shock that caused it. She swooned and sort of drifted to the ground like a feather. Even her fainting had some grace to it.

"Get her to a chair!" Sal ordered.

A couple of sodbusters carried her over to a poker table. After a sip of coffee, she wanted to know where she was.

"Tell her," Sal said to me.

"I don't wanna," I said. She couldn't have been more than twenty-four, and I didn't want to be the one to crush her spirit. When she woke up that morning, she had her whole life ahead of her. Now, she was in a sunless afterlife full of unsavory types. "Why's it always gotta be *me*?"

"You're the dang reporter," Sal said. "Now *report!*"

"Seems like more of a booze clerk's job to break bad news," I argued. "Or what about that preacher fella?"

"Jack shot 'em in the throat for yapping about the end times, 'member?"

"Maybe she's better off not knowing," I offered.

"She's gonna find out sooner or later," Red said.

"Maybe not." Sal smirked.

"You know I can hear you?" the lady reminded us.

"Well, ma'am," I explained. "I'm sorry to say, but you ain't among the living no more."

She pressed her hands against her face and began to weep softly. Then she cried out loudly, "*Oh, Henry! Please forgive me, Henry!*" It must've hit her then that she wasn't ever going to see her sweetheart again. The poor girl collapsed on the table, burying her face in her sleeve.

Sal poured some whiskey into her Arbuckle's to take the edge off. Stumpy fetched an old blanket from the storage room upstairs to warm her up, while I filled her in on the particulars of Damnation, much as I knew them. She sat blank-eyed and listened. It ain't easy hearing that the God you've been praying to all your life deserted you in the foyer to hell with a vampire, some werewolves, and a mess of lecherous card players. She took it pretty well, considering. Then she began to unburden herself about the last day of her life. It had been her wedding day, and she got caught in a compromising position with another man.

"I didn't do anything improper—I swear! I just couldn't push him off me quick enough," she explained. "My father owed the man money, and he was threatening to take our grocery store. Henry, my fiancé, saw us together, then ran off before I could explain." She began to weep again. The sight of her dimpled cheeks awash in tears softened the coldest of the dead hearts in the saloon.

"The scoundrel came after me again, so I stuck a knitting needle in his arm and ran away. I figured my father'd lose the store, and I had already lost Henry. I had nothing to live for, so I went to the lake. I'm not a strong swimmer, you see. Couldn't doggie paddle more than a few feet. I rowed to the center and jumped in, then pushed the boat away."

"Can't see why you'd end up here," Sal said wiping the mist from his eyes. "You didn't kill that man, and even if you did, he'd a deserved it. Far as I can tell, all you did was kill yourself, and suicides don't usually end up here—unless they done other bad stuff."

Her eyes widened as she just remembered something, then more tears came. "I might as well tell you since it doesn't make any difference now," she explained. "I didn't exactly wait until my wedding night." She blushed. "I was expecting when I jumped in the lake."

The room grew silent, and the Christians bowed their heads and crossed themselves.

"I don't get it," Stumpy whispered.

"It was murder," Red said in a hushed voice. "She kilt the child when she kilt herself, and that's why she's here instead of heaven."

"Don't worry, little lady," Sal told her. "I'm sure that baby of yours went straight to heaven."

Ms. Parker smiled on hearing it. Of course, nobody knew for sure what happened to babies when their mommas drowned. She was the first woman to come in that condition. The tiny corpse could've still been inside her. They put Ms. Parker up in the hotel in the room beside Buddy's. After she left, folks debated the issue at some length.

"Course it went to heaven," Sal argued.

A confused look came over Stumpy's face. "So God separated 'em when she drowned?" he asked.

"How could the baby even drown?" Red asked. "It's already swimming in its momma's belly."

After a few rounds, some folks expected the baby might just crawl up into the saloon looking for its momma.

"All this talk of dead babies gives me the willies," Fat Wally confessed.

"You're in a room full of dead men, and a harmless baby scares you?" Sneaky Jim teased.

"But you can reason with a man, or shoot 'em. A dead baby could crawl up and smother you in your sleep."

"Why would it wanna do that?" I asked.

"Revenge, I expect," Red said. "Jack Finney was madder than a wet hen 'cause he never got to grow any hair on his balls. Wouldn't you be cross if you got killed before you was even born?"

The men continued playing cards, but every so often their eyes drifted to the door. Couldn't help but wonder where that kid might've gone. A few candles burned out and Sal didn't bother replacing them, so everywhere you looked was a dark corner a dead baby might crawl up in. Amidst the speculating, the doors suddenly swung open and the room silenced. We expected the child *really was* going to come crawling in. Then the Chinaman appeared in the doorway and everyone laughed.

"Ah fuck you, cowboy asshole!" he grumbled then walked over to the bar so Sal could give him his wages for hauling away bodies and tending to the pigs. Then he went straight to the poker table and lost it all in half an hour. Afterward, he sat back at the bar and had a few drinks on credit.

The Chinaman had been in Damnation long before me, so I never got his story for *The Crapper*. Seemed like a nice enough fella, but I usually called it a night before he came in and never had the opportunity to shoot the breeze with him.

The boldness of a few whiskeys took hold of me, so I turned and asked him, "What did you do to get here, anyway?"

He looked at me kind of funny. He knew some English but didn't seem to understand what I was getting at.

"Where were you before you was here?" I asked.

"Ohio," he said hesitantly. "Work at pig farm. One night I feed pig, then fall... Hit head. Wake up here. Not know how get." He sipped his drink nervously like maybe I was the one who took him.

"You mean to tell me you fell down in a pigpen and bumped your head, and you think you got shanghaied and brought here?"

"No from Shanghai," he said angrily. "From Manchuria."

"Did you ever do anything bad?" I asked. "You know something that might keep you from going to heaven?"

The Chinaman looked a might bit upset. I felt sorry for bringing up bad memories, but with him not knowing English so well, I reckoned it could help him understand how he wound up in Damnation. He took another sip of his drink. I don't imagine he confided with many people, so he probably had some desire to unburden himself.

"Left family in China long time ago," he began. "Work on railroad to send money home. Then begin drink sometime. Then gamble sometime. No more send money home long time." He looked both ways to make sure no one was listening. "Also kill brother."

Sal placed a small stack of chips in front of the Chinaman and told him it was an advance on next week's wages. He took it happily and headed over to the poker table.

"You know, I don't think the Celestial even knows he's dead," I informed Sal. "Nobody ever told him, so he thinks he's still alive! He fell in a pigpen. Probably got torn to pieces!"

"No shit, Tom! Don't tell him though," Sal scolded. "If he finds out he's dead, he ain't gonna wanna work no more. Then there'll be nobody to haul them bodies away and tend to the pigs. As is, he still hopes he might win a bundle at the poker table and be able to pay for his family to come to America."

I scowled at Sal for his rotten four-flushing ways. "It ain't right," I declared. "If there's one thing a man deserves to know, it's that's he's dead. Can't go on deceiving him just to get cheap labor."

"You think it's just for me? Look at him!" Sal said. The Chinaman's rosy cheeks were raised in a broad smile as he picked up his cards. "He's the happiest dang man in the room. He likes working with them pigs, too. And when he gambles, it actually means something to him. Ain't just a distraction like for the rest of these stiffs. He's the only one in Damnation with any hope. Hell, if I could trade places with him, I'd do it in a heartbeat. But if you wanna tell him he's dead and there ain't no chance of him seeing his family ever again, *be my guest!* Not sure what good it'll do though."

I had to think on it some. The Chinaman went on a roll and won a few hands. He soon doubled his money, but he didn't know how to stop when he was ahead. The drink went to his head and he started chasing bad hands with good money, giving it all back just as fast. When it was all gone, he just shrugged and headed for the door. I still wasn't sure if it was better to let him hope for something that wasn't ever going to happen. I decided to turn in not long after. As I turned the corner outside the saloon, the Chinaman was down on all fours on the boardwalk. He had spotted a coin that had dropped between the planks and was trying to fish it out with a couple of sticks.

"Pardon me, sir," I said and he stood with a start. As he turned, he already had an itty-bitty derringer drawn.

"There's no need for that," I told him with my hands skyward. "I got to tell you something, sir. I'm not sure if you wanna hear it, but I feel it's every man's right to know. You ain't among the living no more, friend."

A bewildered look came over his face.

"You're dead," I said plainly.

His round cheeks lifted in a strange smile. "No shit! Me no stupid." He giggled playfully.

"Oh, Sal told me you weren't aware."

"Don't tell him," the Chinaman said worriedly. "Me like work with pig. Only friend in town. If Sal know I wanna work, he pay less."

Seemed they were both satisfied with their little arrangement, so who was I to spoil it. Besides, I didn't know any better way.

Chapter 4

Red's Dead Men

Ms. Parker scurried across the road trying not to make eye contact with anyone. Her long brown hair was tucked beneath a bonnet she had fashioned from an old gray pillowcase, but it wasn't possible for her to *not* attract attention the way she was dressed. The whole town wanted to get a look-see at the dead bride scrambling to get her rations. She had to hold up her long white dress to keep from tripping in the mud. As a result, bystanders were given an unintentional peek at her naked ankle. Just the prospect of seeing those few inches of silky flesh was enough to lure the dirty men to the boardwalk each morning.

A less flattering gown might've helped her blend in, but all the women who came before her were fed to the pigs in their garments, so there was nothing to be found. To her credit, she didn't pay the men's whooping and hollering no mind, and she almost made it across the road untouched. At the last second, a cowpuncher whistled loudly then caught the tail of her dress, cackling wickedly as she spun and fled from his grasp.

They got more riled up with each passing day. A hundred drunken outlaws yearned for the dainty figure they'd seen the night she arrived, all soaking wet with little hidden. It was burned in their minds, and no amount of whiskey or bacon could make them forget it. Just a matter of time before someone took things too far, then shot her for complaining about it afterward. And everyone knew it.

She raced into the general store and slammed the door shut behind her. As she paused to catch her breath, the old-timers gave her the up and down. Those who had grown tired of the riffraff at the saloon sat on storage barrels, chewing the fat to pass the time. They'd all lost their nerve long ago and were considered easy prey. Out in the street, newbies would gun them down to show their grit. Folks called the general store the chicken-shit saloon.

The shelves stocked dry goods taken from wagons that'd come through the dust. Ms. Parker browsed the canned beans and dried pork jerky as if there was some great debate about what she was going to get. She had her pride though. Finally, she selected the same stale crackers and cold tea that she got every day—the cheapest items in the store—then placed them on the counter.

The clerk looked them over and said, "That'll be two dollars—in addition to what you already owe."

Ms. Parker nearly wept having to say the words. A day couldn't pass without a reminder of how her father's debts had gotten her into this situation. If he hadn't borrowed against his store, his creditor wouldn't have been so bold in his advances on her, and she never would've been driven to stab him and jump in a lake. "Put it on my tab, please," she said softly.

"Getting mighty steep," the clerk remarked disapprovingly. "How you aimin' to make things square, ma'am? If you don't mind me askin'?"

"Don't worry. I'll make good on my debts," she said.

"Mighty hard to come up with that kind of money 'round here." He eyed the pale bosom peeking out from the ruffles of her dress. "'Specially if you ain't got no skills, like me having a head for sums or Thomas here having a knack for letters. But maybe something could be worked out," he added, and the old fellas sitting on the barrels snickered.

"I said I'd make good on my debts," she replied firmly.

The clerk opened the ledger like he was St. Peter presiding over the gates of heaven. Resting his glasses on the bridge of his nose, he made a discerning scribble in the margin. Despite his showboating, it wasn't even his store. He ran it for Sal and had no real authority over how and when folks paid their debts. The temptation to humiliate a pretty lady was too much for him to resist though. She didn't pay him no mind and began thumbing through the old issues of *The Crapper* that sat in the corner.

"How much for these?" she asked.

"Them's old. The latest issue's on the rack. It's a nickel."

"But how much for the old ones?"

"What ya want 'em for? Lotta them folks already got sent to hell."

"Just something to pass the time," she said casually.

"Gotta ask the man who wrote 'em then, I guess. Tom's right behind you, ma'am."

"That's all right," I spoke up. "The lady can have as many as she likes. Nobody else's gonna buy 'em anyway."

"In that case, I'll take them all," she said brightly.

"Well, that'll keep you busy," I said. "There's several years' worth. It'll catch you up on everyone in town, I suppose, and quite a few who ain't no more."

Sal only kept the clerk around because no one else wanted to sit in the stuffy shop with the old-timers and add up sums in a ledger. Nonetheless, the clerk prided himself on his diligence and wasted no opportunity to remind folks of it. That evening in the Foggy Dew, he announced loudly that Ms. Parker's debt had exceeded what was permissible. Money was more of a formality, but it still meant something. And it meant the most to those who had none.

"Why's she get to eat for free?" a cowboy asked.

"Ah, leave the woman alone," I said. "She's just a child."

"How come I gotta play cards for my drinks and dry-as-hay pork, and *she don't?*" the cowboy squawked.

"Mind your business!" Sal hollered. "And you, just sit in the damn store and don't tell me how to run things, or I'll let these cowpunchers have at you."

Sal kept wiping down the bar, acting as if he'd already decided on the matter, but after the clerk and the cowboy cleared out he dropped the hardcase act. "The clerk's a ninny, but he's right," he admitted. "If I let her off scot-free, soon nobody's gonna wanna pay for nothing."

"Why they gotta pay anyway?" Stumpy asked. "Could just give it to 'em for free."

"Think about it," Sal said. "Why would folks play cards all day if they didn't get nothing for their winnings. And if folks stopped playing cards, they'd get bored and start shooting each other over nothin'. Probably start with you and me. They need a distraction, and I'd much rather be trading coins than dodging bullets."

"But what you expect Ms. Parker to do for money?" I asked. "She don't seem like a card player to me."

"She could sell her wares," Fat Wally suggested. "I'd give two bucks for a poke."

"Hell, I'd pay five!" Red added.

"A lady like her ain't ripe for that line of work," I said.

"Well, it ain't my problem," Sal argued, "so long as she earns somehow. *Everybody earns!* That's the rule."

Later that evening, before Sal had a chance to approach Ms. Parker about her debt, she crept into the Foggy Dew looking as nervous as a cat in a room full of rockers. Must've sensed her time on the dole was coming to an end.

"What can I do for you, ma'am?" Sal asked. Every man in the room was watching her. She looked like she wanted to turn around and run but was forcing herself to stand her ground. Kind of reminded me of my wife. Consumption had taken her at the tender age of twenty-four, not long after we had settled in the Dakota Territory. Ms. Parker probably reminded a lot of fellas of their wives in their early days, dressed as she was.

"I want to learn how to play cards," she piped up with some resolve. "I don't want to be indebted to no man. My father borrowed against our store, and that's what got me in this mess in the first place."

There was no shortage of volunteers to teach her. Red was the loudest and most enthusiastic. The big Irishman made room for her beside him at the poker table. He explained the rules of five-card stud, and she proved to be a pretty quick learner. Red offered her whiskey, but she didn't want none. Just kept quizzing him on every move he made.

Red wasn't much of a card player. In fact, that was what got him killed. He tried to bluff a large pot he couldn't cover, and they shot him in the mouth for lollygagging. Had a hole in his tongue to prove it. Liked to wag it at the newbies to taunt them. The reason why he ended up in Damnation was because he was an asshole. Bullied women all his life. As Ms. Parker studied his card playing, he was eyeing her bosom. He threw his cards down after a glance and put his hand on her thigh. She just moved it away.

"Why'd you fold that pair of tens?" she asked. "Nobody's had better than a pair of sevens in four hands."

"Don't you fret yourself over my strategy, little lady." This time he slipped his hand up beyond the hem of her dress. His fingers quickly traveled north. Ms. Parker screeched and shot up with a start. The boys sitting at the table all laughed. There was one man at the bar who clearly wasn't amused though. He was an older farmer who had only been in town a couple of weeks. He rose from his seat, rearing to stick up for the lady.

"Better let her be." Sal caught him by the sleeve.

"I don't abide the disrespecting of women," the farmer said. "And I ain't afraid of that carrot-topped heifer."

"Simmer down there, alfalfa desperado," Sal told him. "Ain't Red you should be afraid of. It's them other micks that got his back. See those clover munchers at the dice table and that fella up on the catwalk with half a face?" The gruesome-looking man was holding a Winchester repeating rifle. From the internal balcony above the bar, he could cut anyone down before they got within ten feet of Red. Seeing he was out-gunned, the farmer wisely sat back down.

"Better for her to learn her place now anyway," Sal advised.

Ms. Parker took a lonesome look around the room. When she saw that nobody took exception to a man getting fresh with her, she quietly scooted over to the other side of the table.

"I thank you for your instruction, sir," she told Red. "It's been very informative, but I think I'm ready to play a few hands by myself."

"Suit yourself," Red huffed.

In an odd moment of generosity, Sal staked Ms. Parker the ten dollars she was due on her first arrival, even though her debt now far exceeded that. He wanted to at least make it look like he had done all he could for the lady before she inevitably turned to trading her wares.

The cards were dealt and Ms. Parker barely glanced at hers. "I bet five dollars," she piped up. Her brazenness gave the other players pause. One by one they folded, except for a soot-covered fella in the corner. Either he had a good hand or little faith that a woman could draw better cards than him. He raised her ten.

"I don't have that much," she said softly.

"Guess you'll have to fold," he replied blankly.

"My wedding dress is worth thirty-five dollars," she said. "I'd wager it against whatever you have there in front of you."

Whistles and catcalls broke out around the room. There was more than fifteen dollars in front of him, and he was certainly in a position to haggle, but the prospect of seeing Ms. Parker without her dress was too tempting—especially with the fellas egging him. "Okay," he said and tugged his ear blushingly. "But you have to put the dress here on the table first. And you ain't walking out of the bar with it if you lose."

The catcalling rose to a frenzy. He reckoned he had her either way. If she folded, he'd take the pot. And if she took off her dress, there'd be little chance of her making it out of the saloon. At the very least, the spectacle would give him the opportunity to grab his money back.

"Agreed," Ms. Parker said and pushed back her chair back. As she stood, every beady eye in the room was watching. She hopped up on the table without removing her garment and sat directly on top of the chips.

"Pot's square," the dealer declared. The crowd laughed, and the man reddened in anger for how she'd outwitted him. Begrudgingly, he flipped over his cards showing a pair of fours. Ms. Parker laid down a pair of sevens, then climbed off the table to collect her winnings.

It would cover her debt, but more importantly, it showed that she could earn without resorting to anything unrespectable.

"Neither of those hands were anything to write home about," I said to her. "Why'd you go all in?"

"I reckoned they'd all think I was too scared to bluff," she smiled. "When someone went in, I was petrified I'd lose it all."

"You could've folded and still had nearly five dollars for the next hand. How'd you know that fella was bluffing?"

"Well…" She hesitated to answer. "I guess I can tell you since it's *you* who told me, in a way. I noticed the coal dust on his clothes and figured he was a miner. He also had the initials *TJ* stitched on his coat pocket. I remembered one of those old issues of *The Crapper* had mentioned a miner named Tim Jerkins. It said that he had died of an allergy to peanuts. Earlier, when he was offered some nuts, he got real fidgety and tugged on his ear, but he didn't want to admit that he had an allergy. He probably thought it would be taken as a sign of weakness by the others. That's when I figured it was his tell. He touched his ear every time he had something to hide. I noticed he scratched his ear when he raised me ten dollars. And then he nearly tore his earlobe off when I raised him with my dress."

"Glad to see somebody profited by my writing," I told her.

By way of thanks, Ms. Parker paid for my next few drinks. Those old issues of *The Crapper* might've given her some clues, but she was plain good at reading folks. After all, I wrote the paper and still had no idea the fella's cards were shit.

Not everyone was willing to give her credit. Red came out of the latrine, and while he passed he took the opportunity to goose Ms. Parker's behind, then called out cheekily, "There's a big winner! See what I taught ya, little lady?"

It must've been a gut reaction. She turned around and smacked him clean across his saggy red cheeks. The room fell silent.

A fella might've laughed off a woman smacking him when he was alive, but in Damnation it was looked on as a sign of weakness. Wasn't much use in trying to win a lady over since everybody was going to have her eventually, or nobody was because she'd be sent to hell. If you let a lady boss you, some newbie might think you didn't have any grit. Then he'd shoot you to set an example so people would think twice about coming at him. Red did the only thing he could. He smacked Ms. Parker right back.

Everyone knew she'd learn her place eventually, but it had been a nice change of pace having a real lady around, and a spunky one to boot. It reminded folks of what it was like to be alive. Like seeing a tulip in the early days of spring. You knew it was going to wilt soon, but you wanted to hold onto it as long as you could. Tulips need sunshine to grow though, and it was always dusk in Damnation. Ms. Parker wept from the blow, but when she saw that nobody was surprised that he struck her, she wiped her tears and put on a brave face.

There was one other person in the room who hadn't been around long enough to tolerate the hitting of women.

"*Hey!*" Buddy shouted from the doorway.

"Mind your business, newbie," Red said.

"I just decided my business is making sure no ladies get hit today."

"If you want a piece of her, wait your turn," Red snarled. "It'll come soon enough."

We learned then that Buddy wasn't the waiting type. He marched up to Red and backhanded him across the cheek, knocking him clear to the floor. Red reached for his gun, as did the rest of his gang, but Buddy had both his pistols out with the hammers cocked before any one of them cleared leather.

Red rubbed his swollen cheek as he got to his feet. "You may be fast enough to beat Jack Finney," he said, "but you ain't gonna take out six of us."

"Shucks," Buddy said with a playful smile. "Can't say I much mind going to hell. Just stopped off here for a drink anyway. To tell the truth, I'm kinda curious what the place looks like."

Everyone else scattered as Red's men surrounded Buddy with their pale knuckles gripping holstered guns, waiting for an excuse to pull. Buddy kept both his pistols trained on Red.

"Killing me ain't gonna stop the rest of these boys," Red warned. "And after they gun you down, they'll all have their way with the lady. By the end of the week, every man in town'll have a go at her, 'cept maybe the pencil pusher and the halfwit."

"Not him." Buddy nodded to the man beside Red. "Nor him." He locked eyes with the fella just beyond that. "Eh, maybe he'll survive." Then Buddy shifted his gun. "On second thought, I'll start with him. My record is five men without a scratch on me. Course, I was dead drunk then and I'm cold sober now. Hell, I bet I could shoot six of you before your ugly friend up there with the coward's stick hits me." He motioned to the faceless man on the catwalk above the barroom. An oval of raw skinless meat squinted down, with one eye atop the barrel of a rifle. Much of Red's courage for intimidating folks came from having a fellow Irishman up there. Since he was the only one of them born in America, they deferred to him as leader of the gang. At Red's signal, he would pick off anyone in the room. Even Jack Finney left Red alone, so he never had to test his speed against the sharpshooter.

"Then again, I could just peel him off first." Buddy raised one of his pistols to the second floor. The other six men had yet to pull their weapons.

It wouldn't be easy for them to hit a moving target through the gun smoke of Buddy's first shots. "Yeah, come to think if it, I might be able to get all seven of you." Buddy smiled with genuine pleasure. "Then when we're all in hell, I'll shoot y'all again and you can see where they send you next." Buddy laughed loudly, which made the gang uneasy. None of them seemed keen on going to hell over a woman—even one as pretty as Ms. Parker. Red could tell their confidence was slipping. He slowly backed out of the door, and his gang followed, including the man on the catwalk with no skin on his face. Up close, you could make out the gnawed muscle and ligaments webbing his jaw bone. On his way out, he flashed an eerie smile that gave me the willies.

"By God, you backed 'em all down!" I said.

"Guess so." Buddy said plainly.

"I ain't never seen no one back down seven men before."

"Ah, half them was just sodbusters. Probably couldn't shoot worth a piss anyhow."

"I don't expect that'll be the end of it," Sal warned. "A man can't last long in Damnation after getting backed down in front of half the town."

"Suppose not." Buddy smiled, sounding almost cheerful about the prospect.

Just then Red burst through the door with two pistols already drawn and firing in our direction. He must've given his boys a pep talk because all six of them were lined up single file right behind him. The second man's Winchester leveled over his shoulder and the other five pistols were waving in the air, trying to take aim on Buddy. Looked like a many-armed God of guns coming at us. A bullet struck the faro dealer in the face and he fell, spilling chips and cards on the ground.

I dove to the floorboards and crawled beneath a table for cover. Much as I wished I was the courageous sort, I found myself better suited for dodging fights. Whenever any action started, I prayed for it to be over as soon as possible. I'd shot my share of men who came at me head on—one every month or so when I first arrived. But eventually I learned it was easier to let the troublemakers sort each another out.

There was a pause in the gunfire, so I lifted my face from the sawdust to see if Buddy had been shot, along with the faro dealer. A cowpuncher was lying beside me with a fresh bullet hole in his head just beside an older one, but Buddy was nowhere to be seen. Then I looked up to see a strange sight. Instead of following the conventional wisdom of ducking from the hail of bullets, the chubby gunslinger was standing straight up and turned sideways to make himself a wee bit narrower. His belly still hung out, but he was less of a target. The bullets whizzed by him. One struck the chandelier, and the room dimmed, leaving just a few candles to see by. Buddy calmly raised his pistol and fired, striking Red just above his heart. As he fell, Buddy was already adjusting his aim on the heart of the man behind him. This time he struck the fella right in the ticker. One after another, they dropped to reveal the man behind them, like they were all lined up to go to hell. If Red had cleared the doorway and let the others take aim before he began shooting, it might have been a different story. As the sixth man dropped, Buddy drew his other pistol and shot the seventh man in the forehead. The heap of bodies blocked the door, and nobody could get in or out. Without wasting a second, Buddy reloaded both guns. It was the only thing Buddy was diligent about. Putting off reloading for even a sip of whiskey could leave him clicking empty in the next gunfight.

"By golly, you got a new record now!" I told him.

"Guess so." Buddy shrugged.

A moan came from within the pile of shot-up Irishmen. Among the dead limbs, a pale freckled hand stirred. The poor bastard wouldn't shut up, so we lifted the corpses off him one by one. They were heavier than wet sacks of grain. As luck would have it, the moaning man who was still clinging to the afterlife lay at the very bottom. A bullet had pierced Red's shoulder but it wasn't anything he'd bleed out from.

"Better kill him now if you wanna sleep sound tonight," Sal advised. "When he heals up, he's sure to come at you again."

"Nah," Buddy said, slapping his pistol lazily into his holster. "I like having somethin' to look forward to."

Chapter 5

Jams O'Donnell

"You sure ask a lot of questions," Ms. Parker told me between bites. Her plate was piled high with scrambled eggs and bacon strips. There wasn't any toast on account of no wheat grew in Damnation.

Now and again, supplies rolled in on wagons with dead men at the reins. Sometimes, there were beer kegs or whiskey barrels in the back. After the drivers got shot up by bandits or Indians, they came through the dust cloud with their goods still intact. But mostly we just ate the dead animals that wandered down the road. If you were a vegetarian in Damnation, it wouldn't be worth it to shoot you since you'd already be in hell.

"I used to work for a newspaper before I died," I told her. "Now I write *The Crapper* to kill time—pardon my language. I get a nickel a piece. I ain't much of a card player, so it pays for my drinks. Also gives me a reason to talk to folks and see how they're getting along."

"Well, I'm getting along fine," she said cheerfully. "Damnation's not such a bad place once you get used to it. Where else can a girl wear her wedding dress every day? And I can eat as much as I like—though I might not fit into my dress soon." She patted her belly. Breakfast was a never-ending plate. Sal kept piling on the food till you pushed it aside. Ms. Parker put away two full plates without letting up. "Henry loved bacon," she said. "He would have liked it here. Aside from all the shooting, of course."

Ms. Parker had put on some weight since she'd arrived, which was unusual. Folks didn't change much in Damnation. Of course, women didn't usually last long enough to tell. And nobody'd ever seen a small-framed girl like her put away so much food.

"How did you get into the newspaper business, Mister...?"

"Just call me Thomas, ma'am," I said. "My mother was a school teacher and my father raised steer. I broke my leg falling off a horse when I was a boy and it didn't mend proper. That's how come I got this limp. Wasn't much work for a crippled cowhand and I was pretty good with my letters, so I guess you could say I fell into the business. My grammar ain't what you'd call top notch. I just say it how I see it, ma'am, but I can put a bit of flourish into my words when I'm moved to."

"So how did you, um, end up here, if you don't mind me asking?"

"No, I don't mind, ma'am. I've done bad things. Ain't gonna deny it. I worked for a newspaper in the Dakota Territory that was owned by a man named George Hearst."

"The senator?"

"Did he become a senator? Well, he ran a mining company when I was still alive. They were prospecting in the Black Hills and found some gold—only a lot of it was on land Mr. Hearst didn't own. He told me to report that the Indians were coming back and the homesteaders should all clear out. I rightly refused to do it. Instead, I reported that the army had the Indians on the run and Mr. Hearst had a keen interest in the land. In response, he sent some gunhands out to scare the homesteaders off. They probably would have left, too, if I hadn't already told them their land was worth fighting for.

"When Hearst couldn't scare them off, he sent some real rough men up there and they killed all the homesteaders. Butchered five families and made it look like the Indians done it. Then Hearst bought the newspaper I worked for and said I could write up the story his way or find another job—if I made it out of town alive. Well, I wrote it up like he told me, blamed the Sioux even though there wasn't no Sioux within a hundred miles."

"You didn't?" Ms. Parker gasped.

"I did and I got what I had coming to me for it," I said. "A couple of years later, a young man no more than sixteen came into my office. Said he had survived the slaughter of the homesteaders out in the Black Hills. He was confused because first I told his parents to stay put since the Indians weren't coming. Then after his family was killed by white men, he found out I blamed it on the Indians. He asked me for an explanation, and when I could not provide a satisfactory one, he gut-shot me." I lifted my vest to show her the hole in my shirt that went straight through my belly.

"I died there on the floor of the newspaper office. Can't really blame the boy though. Hearst had already left town by then. If he did become a senator, I guess the kid never caught up with him."

"I don't see why you should end up here." Ms. Parker started working herself into a tizzy. "You had no choice! It was all Mr. Hearst's doing."

It must have reminded her of her own straits and how she wasn't to blame neither. I'd already had plenty of time to consider why I ended up where I was though.

"I reckon it was on account I told people to take a stand, but I never did so myself," I explained. "I got a nice raise from Mr. Hearst for writing them stories and I never tried to leave town. I wrote lots of things he told me to that weren't true." Ms. Parker stirred her eggs with her fork, trying not to judge me too hard nor show disapproval. "But if I had it to do over again," I added, "I'd just shoot the sumabitch the first time I laid eyes on him—pardon my language, ma'am."

"And you would be right in doing so," she agreed. "Some people don't deserve to be born in the first place, and it's no sin in seeing to it that they don't harm anybody else."

"Interestin' way of looking at things, ma'am."

"So I heard you think it's possible to get to heaven by refraining from shooting anyone."

"Ain't me that come up with it, but I suppose it helps to believe something."

"And you're the only man in town who doesn't carry a gun because of this belief?"

"Yes, ma'am."

"It's beyond me how nobody has managed to test this theory by now." She shook her head in disbelief.

"There ain't been many women who lasted long enough to try, ma'am. As you may have noticed, the men here usually ain't much concerned with the long term, being as how they're more preoccupied with the day to day."

"Well, I've never carried a gun in my life," she said. "And I don't intend on doing so now. So if I do last a year in this place, you can rest assured I won't have shot anyone. Then you'll know if it really gets you into heaven."

"I can appreciate your conviction, ma'am, but a man such as myself has less to protect than a lady such as yourself. Plainly speaking, I ain't got nothing these fellas want, but a lot of them ain't had relations with a woman in a long time—if ever." I nodded to the wily-eyed cretin at the end of the bar who was openly gawking at Ms. Parker. When I interviewed him a few months back, I learned that he had worked in a slaughterhouse and died from an infection after a chicken pecked his hand. I wrote it up in *The Crapper* and folks started calling him the Chicken Choker. He seemed to begrudge me personally for the nickname. A man like that didn't have nothing to lose. Even with Buddy looking out for Ms. Parker, he'd try to have his way with her the first time he caught her alone.

"It'd be advisable for you to take some precautions," I warned her, "in case you ever have to defend yourself at close range." I lifted the wood-handled steak knife from her table setting, wiped its blade on my handkerchief, and handed it to her beneath the bar. "There are worse predicaments for you to worry about than prolonging your stay."

After a moment's hesitation, she slipped the knife into a small handbag she had fashioned from old linens. The vampire walked into the saloon just then and sidled up to the bar. He ordered a cup of coffee but then caught sight of Ms. Parker. His fangs showed and he made an angry hissing noise, then walked straight out. Ms. Parker was nearly brought to tears.

"Now why's he gotta do that?" she asked. "I didn't do anything to him."

"Ah, he's just grumpy. Don't worry about him, ma'am. He don't usually bother no one 'less they bother him first."

"Seems like every time I walk into a room, he storms out. And if he comes in and sees me, he flashes his fangs like that."

As the vampire was walking out the door, Buddy happened to be coming in. Still groggy from the night before, he didn't even bother looking up and their shoulders crashed directly into each other. The whole room silenced, waiting for blood to spill. Although the vampire had a much smaller build, the run-in didn't cause him to budge an inch. He stood dead in his tracks, looking curiously at the pudgy gunslinger. Buddy was wiping the sleep from his eyes and muttered politely, "Oh, excuse me there, fella." It was as close to surprised as I'd ever seen the vampire. One eyebrow dipped in confusion, then he continued on his way.

"I'll be!" Sal remarked. "Seen a heap of men torn up for less."

"*A lot* less," Fat Wally conferred.

"Why you reckon he let Buddy go then?" Stumpy asked.

"Seemed like he just didn't want to be delayed from leaving," I said.

Buddy moseyed to the bar, still in the cloud of his hangover and entirely unaware of how close he had come to never eating breakfast again. "Hen fruit over easy and a whiskey," he called out. "Make it a double."

He must've been used to the bite of strong drink first thing in the morning because the first sip didn't cause him to wince. Likely, he'd been a bachelor all his life, with no steady work or a sweetheart to keep him from doing whatever he wanted. Ms. Parker went over to thank him for coming to her rescue against Red. He flushed while fumbling to take off his hat and brush the crumbs from his mustache, not sure how to comport himself around a lady. He kept bowing like Ms. Parker was the Queen of England.

After breakfast, they played poker together. Buddy tried to give her some tips, but she already knew what she was doing. In fact, she had more of a knack for the game than he did, since she never got frustrated and threw away money on mediocre hands. Also, she always seemed to know if a fella was bluffing. Her winnings would be plenty to keep her fed and housed. She could keep the room in the hotel beside Buddy, and just below the vampire.

"I don't suppose any man's gonna get fresh with her now that Buddy's taken a shine to her," I said.

"Maybe not." Sal replied. "But there's more to worry about in Damnation than just men."

Suddenly, Old Moe burst through the door. He'd been in town the longest by quite a spell and had seen every kind of dead outlaw. It was surprising to see him move so hurried. "You fellas gotta see this!" he hollered. "Hurry up'n get outside!"

Knowing that Moe didn't impress easily, we all quick-footed it out to the road. I expected to see the gunfight of all gunfights going on, but there was nothing except for a few tumbleweeds blowing around. Moe stood on the boardwalk, pointing up at the sky. "Lookie there!"

The same old dreary gray blanket was hovering above with ashen yellow swirls and specks of violet. Then a flickering of light brightened within it, showing some depth to the sky. For the first time, you could see there was something beyond the cloud cover. There were layers. And still more layers beyond that. Must've been some ten seconds later when a low rumble sounded in the distance. The sound wasn't just above us. It was far afield, stretching beyond the dust cloud border surrounding Damnation.

Those who hadn't followed Moe outside now came to investigate the noise. For a moment, it was like I was back on my pappy's porch, watching a storm brewing in the distance, counting the seconds between the flash and the thunder to figure out how many miles away the storm was, and how much time there'd be to batten down the hatches and secure the livestock.

"Ever seen anything like that before?" I asked Moe.

"As long as I been looking up at that rotten muck of a sky, there ain't been a peep or a blink. Just the same old scraps of a dead sun."

"What ya suppose it means?" Sneaky Jim asked from the doorway. It had been enough of a spectacle to interrupt his prime sip-thieving time.

"Maybe it's God," Red slurred drunkenly. He hadn't gathered the nerve to go up against Buddy yet. Kept saying he would as soon as he sobered up. To avoid it, he started drinking first thing when he woke and didn't stop till he passed out.

"Yeah," Fat Wally added. "He knows Tom's got his sights on heaven. Wants to let him know the inn's all filled up." Everyone laughed, grateful for a distraction from all the seriousness. All except the Chicken Choker, who'd been eyeing Ms. Parker. Now his crazy eyes were locked on me. It was the first time he heard I had my sights set on heaven, and it rubbed him the wrong way.

"What ya think yer better'n us, pencil pusher?" he hollered drunkenly.

"Easy there, Choke," Sal said. "Don't go misinterpretin' those flashes in the sky for your own brilliance."

"No! I say if Tom don't wanna be here, we should send him off *today!*" He pulled a pistol from his hip to gesture with. With a nickname like Chicken Choker, there was little chance of him lasting more than a few months. Too easy for folks to pick on him and draw him into a fight. He didn't have the speed to win many draws. It was plain dumb luck that he'd managed to stay north of hell this long. But if he shot someone of note for no good reason, the story might give folks pause before they pulled on him. Could extend his stay some.

"Gunfight!" one of the cowboys called out. Some others joined in on the chant. The thunder had attracted a good-sized crowd from the rooming house, and they were all itching for some entertainment. As much as Sal or Buddy might've wanted to step in, it was past the point where they could.

"He ain't heeled!" a high-pitched voice screeched from the crowd. Ms. Parker was standing on her tippy-toes just beyond the Chicken Choker's shoulder. Her pale cheeks reddened in protest.

"Well, he shoulda got heeled before he done put himself up above the rest of us," Choke said and raised his gun.

With my bad leg, he was well beyond the range where I could've rushed him. All I could do was take the bullet calmly and not go out like that newbie Fre who had bawled his eyes out. As the barrel leveled a flash of white suddenly sprang out from the crowd like a cloudburst. Choke got knocked down just as he pulled the trigger. The bullet struck the ground, and he tumbled over in the dust. There was a wood-handled knife buried in his back. The bundle of white rolled over as well, and I could see it was Ms. Parker who had delivered the blade.

The Crapper

Comings: *Ms. Sally Parker of Peoria, Illinois, joined us after an unfortunate incident that I will briefly relate here, once and for all, so everyone can stop pestering her about it. She was put in a compromising position by a man her father had owed money. Her fiancé, a luckless and no doubt regretful man named Henry, mistook the situation and ran off before she could explain. Ms.*

Parker bravely fought off her assailant, wounding him with a knitting needle. Seeing as how she had lost her sweetheart and her family's farm in the same day, Ms. Parker fell into despair and took her own life by drowning. Sadly, she was with child at the time. Please do your best to make the young lady feel welcome. There are six men who recently left town that probably wish they had done so.

Goings: *Six Irish boys from Red's gang were sent to hell by the hand of Buddy Baker. Two were the Kelley brothers from Westmeath. They fled their homeland to escape the potato blight only to die of influenza in New York City after brief careers in pick-pocketing and burglary.*

Also felled was Jimmy McReadon, a prospector in Comstock Lode. He had been kicked in the head by a pack mule in a Utah mining camp. Folks teased that he was giving the beast a poke at the time. Jimmy believed he ended up in Damnation for failing to send for his baby sister, as he had promised to do when he departed from Cork.

Sean O'Malley was also among those who took aim on Buddy. Just before arriving in town, he had been shot by Pinkertons in Duluth for stealing a horse. He didn't show much surprise at ending up in Damnation, though he never gave any specifics of his other earthly transgressions.

Frank O'Reilly was a crack shot with the Winchester from his days as a hunter in the northern territories. A bear had mauled him in Yukon, earning him the nickname No-Face Frank. He was always shy about his wounds and preferred to do his drinking alone, stationing himself up on the catwalk where he could pick off anyone who messed with one of his countrymen. His aim didn't do him no good this time when he couldn't clear Red's shoulder quick enough.

The sixth man shot by Buddy spoke no English and was only fluent in the Irish language. I'm told that he hailed from County Sligo on the West Coast of Ireland. His name was Jams O'Donnell, and I struggle to recall a tale as sad as his, so I will relate it here at length as it was told to me. Just after his birth, his father was jailed for pinching a loaf of bread to keep his family alive. His mother was a gypsy traveler who died of bad blood when O'Donnell was ten. Shortly after, he was evicted from the family home by Protestants who had no rightful claim to the land.

Since O'Donnell was part gypsy, the townspeople wouldn't take him in. The travelers wouldn't claim him neither, since he knew no trade and was just another mouth to feed. The boy wandered the frigid coastline, digging up potato spuds where he could find them and sleeping in caves so damp that the clothes rotted from his body.

Shy of his twentieth birthday, he met a lass in similar straits, the unwanted daughter of an Irish maid who'd been raped by an English soldier. The two briefly took comfort in each other's company and had a child that filled their poor hearts with joy. Unfortunately, the potato blight worsened and both wife and daughter died within a year from sickness caused by malnourishment. O'Donnell's only chance for survival was to feed on the flesh of his departed family, which was likely his only sin and the reason why he ended up in Damnation instead of heaven.

Next, the miserable O'Donnell wandered south to the Port of Galway, where he was offered passage to America in exchange for shoveling coal in the engine room. The smoke was hard on his already weakened lungs, but he took an extra shift to have some pocket money when he arrived in the New World. He suffered from breathing problems aboard the vessel and lost consciousness before landing in Boston, where he is presumed to have died. O'Donnell came up the road to Damnation just three weeks ago, relieved to find himself in a dusty town so unlike his damp and dreary homeland.

Red enlisted him in his vendetta by claiming that Buddy was a Protestant land grabber, like those who stole his family home. Since O'Donnell had been too small to fight against the British invaders as a child, he felt obliged to defend this arid patch of afterlife. If anyone had explained to him what he was really fighting for, he probably wouldn't have taken up arms since he had never fired a gun in his life. One can only hope that when Jams O'Donnell arrives at his next destination, he finds himself in a place less deceitful than Damnation and more hospitable than Ireland.

Also shot during the crossfire was a cowboy from West Texas named Steve and the faro dealer with the handlebar mustache who everybody called Hoss.

Oh, and I would be remiss in my duties if I did not record for posterity that the Chicken Choker got knifed by Ms. Parker. She came to my defense when the crazy bastard drew on me, while I was unarmed, after we all saw those mysterious flashes in the sky. I believe he was from Arkansas.

Chapter 6

The Gunfight of a Century

"Who knows?" Spiffy speculated. "Maybe we're still on earth after all." The wiry cowboy was trying to remove a piece of pork gristle from between his teeth as Sal collected the lunch plates. We called him Spiffy on account of him getting killed in his Sunday best. He'd been caught fiddling with another man's wife after church and received a bullet in the heart for it. His clothes were still pretty dapper except for the blood stain on the lapel. "Maybe we're just shrunken down real small," he continued. "So small that the whole town could fit on the head of needle."

"You reckon that's possible?" I egged him on. It passed the time to hear folks chew the fat about where we were.

"Sure, that lightning coulda just been some fella striking a match to light his pipe after supper."

"He musta ate beans," Red played along. "And that thunder was a big ol' fart."

"Hell, if we're still on earth, we should figure out a way out of here," Fat Wally suggested. "Then I can go see my sweetheart."

"Ah, what'd be the use?" Sal shook his head. "If the whole town's the size of a needle, you wouldn't be able to climb one of her cunt hairs, let alone give her a poke."

"Well, I could crawl up inside her," Wally said with a laugh. "Wiggle around in her and show her a good time."

"Shit, she probably wouldn't feel nothin' even if you *was* full sized," Red teased.

"I can't believe I have to listen to this shit," Sal griped. "What ya make of that thunder'n lightning, Tom?"

"Don't know," I said. "But there's definitely something above us. Judging by the echo of it, might be somethin' beside us, too. For now, I'm sticking to my plan of trying not to get shot or shoot nobody, and see what happens."

"If there was a heaven, you wouldn't get there by not killin' nobody for a year," Fat Wally argued. "They just tell ya that 'cause it's impossible to do."

"If he wants to believe it, let 'em," Sal defended. "It's better'n waiting around to get shot with nothing else to look forward to."

The doors swung open, and a skinny farm boy crept in with his head down, trying not to make eye contact with anyone. Both cheeks were red and swollen like a chipmunk's. As he came to the bar, the candlelight showed welts on his arms and neck. Hardly an inch of him was without some sort of bruise. He looked up and asked shyly where he was. A pair of purple shiners rounded his mopey eyes.

After Sal broke the news to him, he began crying. He missed his damn mommy and his farm and the stars overhead in the Wyoming sky, and some fat hussy he was hoping to marry. He went on and on for so long, not only did you no longer feel sorry for the beating he'd taken, you nearly condoned it.

"Hey, churn-twister, what's your name?" Fat Wally asked.

"Petey."

"Well, dally your tongue or we'll have to call you Whiny Pete," he told him.

The boy had been shooting at tin cans that morning, practicing to be a gunslinger. Didn't know there was a herd of steer nearby. The gunshots set off a stampede that trampled a bunch of schoolchildren. His pa found out and beat him to within an inch of his life. Then the father of one of the dead kids beat him the rest of the way. He sat at the bar screaming, *"The children! All the dead children! Their bodies were crushed!"*

Sal begrudgingly gave him some whiskey on credit. "Not sure why I bother," he said. "Ain't like he's gonna be around long enough to pay it off."

The drink settled Petey down some and he stared out at the never-ending dusk, watching the wind toss handfuls of dust against the window pane like a farmhand spreading chicken feed. An hour or so passed, then he suddenly started screaming, *"I wanna go back! Just one more chance! Please Lord! Send me back!"* Even the Christian folks snickered some.

Fat Wally had heard as much as he could bear. He marched over and struck the boy across the face, sending him to the floor for a mouthful of sawdust. "Man up now, boy!" he told him. "You're in Damnation. Not your damn pappy's farm. Them kids prolly went to heaven anyway. Least they don't have to listen to you whine all day. And if they do show up here and start crying, I'll send their damn asses to hell myself."

Petey's big bruised cheeks grew redder with rage. "You bastard!" he hollered and lunged for Fat Wally. For a large man, he was surprisingly nimble and managed to step aside in time, letting the angry boy fall to the floor. Not seeing any point in mustering a second attack, Petey lay there weeping, but much quieter now.

Wally's luck improved with the silence, and he began winning in poker. To celebrate, he had a few drinks. Then he started losing, so he had a few more drinks in sorrow. By early evening, he was so sozzled that he had to squint in order to make out the cards in his hands.

"Ah, shit!" he swore after mistaking an eight for an ace, and staggered to the latrine, leaving a near-full beer on the bar. Sure enough, Sneaky Jim spotted the unattended mug and raced over to empty it. Wally returned just as the suds were vanishing down his throat.

"You measly sip stealer!" he yelled, and fired his pistol. The shot missed by several feet, striking the wall as Jim fled the saloon. While Wally was reholstering his weapon, Whiny Pete crept up behind him and cracked a broomstick over his head. All three hundred pounds of him sank like an anchor. Wally wasn't knocked cold though, and he rose a little starry eyed. As soon as he realized what had happened, he grabbed the boy by the neck and began smashing his head into the side of the bar till pieces of wood splintered off. Finally, Sal fired his scattergun into the ceiling and yelled, "I ain't cleaning up your mess. Go outside and draw!"

"I ain't got no gun," Pete said.

Sal placed an old rusty Colt on the bar. It was the same one Jeremiah Watson had given Jack Finney way back when he first arrived. The handle was still stained with the Comanchero's blood, only this time it was fully loaded.

Pete picked it up and peered down the ancient rusty barrel. "But the sight's crooked!"

"If you wanted a better gun, you shouldn't a caused a stampede that killed them children."

No one was willing to loan the kid a better gun since Wally might claim it. Not that Wally was much of a shot, even when he was sober. In truth, the odds didn't favor either man. There wasn't anything else to do, so twenty or so of us gathered out on the boardwalk to watch. Nobody wanted to wager on the kid since they were hoping to be rid of him and his whining. And nobody bet on Wally since he was shitfaced.

They stood back to back in the middle of the road, and at Sal's signal started walking in opposite directions. Wally wasn't so good with his numbers. He must've forgotten that ten came after nine because the kid turned around and shot while he was scratching his head. The bullet struck the ground, which cleared up Wally's counting problems. He quickly turned and fired five shots in succession. Meanwhile, Pete emptied his gun in a panic. Both of them must've had their eyes shut because even though they stood only twenty paces apart, neither had a scratch on them.

"This could take a while," Sal remarked.

"Ah, let's just call it off," Wally offered. "I'm too damn drunk to shoot straight."

Whiny Pete was not of the same inclination though, and he made haste in reloading. "I'm gonna send your ass to hell, you fat bastard. If them children do show up here, I don't want you hurting 'em." With trembling hands and tears in his eyes, he fired and caught Wally in the leg. He shouted out in pain then raised his gun, reckoning he still had a bullet left, but it clicked empty.

"Damn! I wasted a bullet on that measly sip stealer," he recalled and got busy reloading. Pete's next shot caught him in the arm, but Wally had already managed to drop a couple bullets in the cylinder.

"Goddamn that hurts! Will you just send me to hell already?" Wally limped forward, swinging his pistol closed with a click. His arm was shaking from the wound and he missed twice more. Fed up, he hurled the gun at Pete's head, which knocked him out. Then Wally fell on top of the skinny kid and began squeezing his neck like a stubborn jar full of jelly.

"Probably the only way Wally could win a gunfight in his condition," Sal remarked matter-of-factly.

Pete woke with a gasp just as his windpipe was about to be crushed. He tried to throw Wally off him, but it might as well have been two anvils pinning his shoulders down. Fortunately for him, he had landed right on top of his gun when he fell. He must've felt it beneath his leg because he quickly recovered it and pointed the barrel at Wally's side. The bullet ripped through his beer-and-pork gut but didn't strike nothing important. He went on choking the blue-faced boy as if the shot wasn't nothing but a pinprick. Pete re-aimed the barrel at Wally's chest this time and struck him right in the ticker. Wally slumped over on top of him.

"That oughta do it," Red said. "I got dibs on Wally's stack."

"*Help!*" Pete bellowed from beneath the corpse. "I'm suffocating under here."

"Been here nearly a hundred years," Sal said, shaking his head in disgust, "and that's the worst damn gunfight I ever seen."

Chapter 7

The Vampire

In the evening, the Foggy Dew could get hotter than a whorehouse on a nickel night. After supper, I often fancied a stroll about town to stretch my legs and cool down. A steady breeze blew from the flatlands beyond the buildings, where small whirlwinds of dust formed. Looked like tiny tornadoes, but they could barely blow your hat off. It was all we had as far as sights to see. Not exactly the Grand Canyon, but watching the spirals of dancing dust could take your mind off things if you were losing in cards or missing your sweetheart.

The dust could get in your eyes, but if you kept your head down while you walked, it wasn't unpleasant. The sky was the same old gray mop with yellow and violet swirls. No flashes of lightning showed, nor could any rumblings of thunder be heard. The dusk always made me miss the warmth of sunlight on my cheeks. The dimness played tricks on my eyes, and I nearly ran into Ms. Parker and Buddy before I recognized them out in front of the wolves' saloon.

"They sure are loud in there," Ms. Parker remarked. "How many werewolves are there anyway?"

"Not as many as us," I told her. "Maybe one for every five men. They're a rambunctious lot, so it sounds like more. Quick buggers, too—not as quick as the vampire, but you'd be lucky to shoot one before it got you, if it was so inclined."

"Do you need silver bullets to kill 'em?" Buddy asked. "Like in them storybooks."

"Nah, regular ones'll do. They die like dogs. And they stick together in a pack, so if you send one to hell, the rest'll chew you to bits." Ms. Parker shuddered and took a worried step back. "Ah, they don't have much use for us, ma'am. They prefer a warm-blooded meal, same as the vampire. If they can't get one, they'd much rather have a cow than a cold, bony human."

"Speak for yourself." Buddy patted his belly playfully.

"I've never seen a werewolf before," Ms. Parker said. "What are they like?"

"They change in and out of human form as they please, ma'am. When they turn into wolves, some are bigger than lions."

"What's with the sign?" Buddy pointed to the bones hanging from a post at the end of the road.

"It's the remains of a couple a newbies," I explained. "Their first night in town, they lost all their money and got kicked out of the rooming house for causing a ruckus, so they cold-crouched it in the flatlands outside of town. They hadn't been around long enough to know hunger wouldn't kill them. It kept gnawing at them. Didn't know who had claim on the cattle neither, so when a steer wandered down the road, they figured they'd cut it up for rib eyes. They knocked it down and splayed it open with a sharpened stone, then hacked out hunks of meat and cooked them over a fire.

"Argus, the wolf pack leader, smelt the meat burning. Like I said, wolves don't care much for the taste of men. We're too salty and skinny, worse than eating crow, I suppose. But Argus raced out and chewed them two newbies to bits anyway. He ate them real slow, like a kid swallowing brussels sprouts with a sourpuss. Could hear them crying for hours. Eventually, they bled out. Argus licked the bones clean and made that sign saying *cows* with the arrow pointing toward the wolves' saloon. Pretty good incentive for folks to order pork, I'd say. Since then, relations with the wolves been somewhat shaky, but they ain't bothered us none."

Just then, a large brown wolf wandered out the front door of the saloon. He searched the sky for the moon. Not finding it, he sniffed the well-traveled planks of the boardwalk. His haunches were nipple-high on a short woman and he was thick as a boar. He turned to us as he caught our scent and his eyes glowed red like hot coals. Suddenly, he began running straight toward us. Before we knew what was happening, he sprung into the air and landed on top of Ms. Parker. Buddy drew as quick as he could, but a smaller gray wolf came from behind and clamped down on his wrist, shaking the pistol from his grip. The big wolf sniffed at Ms. Parker's belly, snarling like it was hungry for whatever she'd eaten last. The weight of his paws pressed her to the ground, so she couldn't squirm away.

My flimsy cane wouldn't have done much damage, so I looked for a loose plank to strike the mutt. Just my luck, it was probably the only stretch in town where the boardwalk wasn't rotted out. Buddy's pistol lay on the ground nearby, so I hobbled over to pick it up, wondering if it was even worth it. Shooting the beast would just attract more of them. It'd also be trading the possibility of heaven for a lady who probably wasn't going to last the month anyhow. But if my wife had come to a place like Damnation, I certainly hoped someone looked after her. Surely Ms. Parker hadn't hesitated so long in stabbing the Chicken Choker to save my worthless hide. I raised the gun to the wolf's back and pulled the trigger. It misfired. On hearing the click, the wolf swatted me to the ground with one paw.

Its teeth were about to pierce her stomach when a burst of wind roared down the road with the strength of a full-sized twister, sending loose wood and shingles through the air. Then a dark form swept down on the wolf and tossed it across the road like a tumbleweed. The vampire stood in the middle of the road with his fangs out, hissing like a cat defending a saucer of milk. The smaller wolf left off tussling with Buddy to jump at his back with teeth bared, but the vampire turned just in time and caught it by the throat. Lifting the beast in the air with ease, he heaved it through the window of an abandoned storefront.

The bigger wolf was on its feet again and lunged for the vampire's leg with teeth as long as sheep shears. The vampire stepped back but wasn't quick enough and his calf got punctured. He looked more surprised than pained, like old folks who are shocked when their bodies don't move as quick as they used to. He swung his other leg angrily at the wolf's ribs, causing it to yelp. While it lay panting and wheezing, he gripped its hindquarters and heaved it through the window of another abandoned storefront, shattering the dusty glass. Both wolves were cut up pretty good. Bloody shards of glass were sticking out from their fur as they ran off whimpering.

"Thank you for saving us," Ms. Parker said after she caught her breath. "Mister..?"

"Nigel," he replied curtly.

"Thank you, Mr. Nigel."

"Just Nigel, ma'am."

He had a funny accent, sounded real proper-like, which caught me off guard knowing he'd torn a man's hand off just for introducing himself. Then again, the pigs we ate probably didn't reckon we were too sophisticated neither. As Buddy got to his feet, he eyed Nigel up warily.

"They would've killed us for sure if you hadn't come along," she said.

"Ah, they might not have," Buddy grew a tad defensive. "I was just about to get the upper hand on that wolf. Once I got my gun back, I woulda plugged that other mutt. But thanks for the assistance n'all."

"I thought werewolves didn't attack people," Ms. Parker said.

"I ain't seen it happen before." I shrugged. "'Cept them boys who took a cow. They usually leave us alone 'less we get between them and a meal."

"It is not you that they were after, ma'am." Nigel limped closer while bracing his wounded leg. "It's what's inside of you."

"*Inside* of me?"

"There is warm blood in you, ma'am."

"But she's dead like everyone else in Damnation," I told him. "Drowned herself in a lake—pardon me for saying, ma'am."

"Oh, that's all right. It's true," she admitted. "I'm as dead as can be."

"You may be deceased, but there is a heartbeat in you still. I believe you are with child, ma'am. And I assure you that child is still alive."

"But my baby drowned," Ms. Parker cried. "How can it be?"

"I do not know how it transpired," he said coldly, "but I am certain there is a living heart inside of you, and it pumps warm blood." His fangs still showed between his pale lips. Despite his polished manners, he had the hunger of a starved animal. "I could smell it the first time I saw you." He gazed at Ms. Parker like he was trying to charm her, but his bloodshot eyes and long yellow teeth only gave her the willies. She clutched her tummy, then her eyes suddenly widened in surprise.

"I think he's right!" she said. "I can feel something moving around in there. I figured it was just indigestion from all the food I've been eating, but I have been sick the last few mornings."

"The werewolves can smell it," Nigel warned. "And they shall return. I imagine they are as famished for warm-blooded nourishment as I am."

"Well, we'll just have to kill them mutts before they come back." Buddy plucked his gun from his holster. "We can start with whoever's left in that there doghouse saloon."

"I assure you that you are no match for a pack of wolves," Nigel warned. "Go on into their den if you like. While I'm certain I will eventually be sent to my proper place in the cosmos—wherever that is—I am not so eager to venture there tonight. I'll be taking a nightcap at a slightly more civilized establishment," he said, kind of snooty-like.

Chapter 8

Drinking With Nigel

We took a table in the back corner of the Foggy Dew and everyone gave us a wide berth. Sal set down a bottle of gin and glasses, then backed away. Nobody had ever survived a conversation with the vampire before.

"So why'd you end up here instead of hell?" Ms. Parker asked directly. She wasn't the type to beat around the bush. When he didn't bite her hand off, I reckoned he must've liked that about her.

"You may consider it a reprieve," he replied in his fancy way of talking, "but to me it is a far worse punishment. There is no palpable nourishment here, very little entertainment, and you'd be hard-pressed to find anything resembling stimulating conversation."

"But you done something worth saving your hide for, ain't ya?" Buddy asked.

"I really couldn't say." Nigel sipped his glass of gin without much interest. "I'll tell you what... You can listen to my story and judge for yourselves. If nothing else, it will at least pass the time."

"Fair enough," Buddy agreed.

"I was born in London in 1635 and spent a century slaughtering thousands of people to slake my thirst. Then I stowed away on a cargo boat to the New World, where I killed a thousand more. I was the only vampire on the entire continent!"

"Sounds kind of lonesome," Ms. Parker remarked.

"Indeed," Nigel admitted. "I had not spoken to a soul for more than fifty years when the frontiersmen began building their crude sod houses in the interior. One day a woman scolded me for poaching her livestock. Her hubris amused me, so I chose not to feast on her. She had been widowed during the colonies' revolt against England, but she was determined to stake a piece of land for herself. We lived together as man and wife for five years before she became with child."

"Wuz it yours?" Buddy blurted out.

Nigel lifted an eyebrow in offense. "You don't mean to take me for a cuckold, sir?"

"So vampires can have children with regular women?" I asked.

"Certainly."

"So does that make the child a vampire, too?" Ms. Parker asked, looked oddly worried.

"Very rarely, perhaps one in a thousand, and the child would only become a full-fledged vampire if it consumed warm blood."

"Oh, good," Ms. Parker said.

"But say it was one of them one-in-a-thousand types, and it happened to drink some blood," I asked out of curiosity. "Would it wanna feed on people, even if it was half a one itself?"

"Indeed, and most voraciously," Nigel answered. "You would not care to cross paths with a mixed-breed. Throughout the ages, vampires have survived by being discreet in their feeding. Mixed-breeds know no such discretion. Their appetites are too great to control. In the Middle Ages, they destroyed entire villages, which the vampire community went through great pains to cover up. Eventually, unions between vampires and humans were banned altogether to avoid such problems."

"So you was breaking vampire law by having a baby with that lady," Buddy pointed out. "Like some kinda vampire outlaw."

"Yes, I suppose you could say that," Nigel replied dryly. "But as I said, there was only a one in a thousand chance of my child inheriting the vampiric traits. Even then, he would've had to consume warm blood to trigger it."

"As if the wolves weren't enough to worry about!" Ms Parker said.

"No need to fret about that now, ma'am," Buddy told her. "Ain't no half-breed vampire gonna get here. Prolly go straight to hell for killin' its own kind!"

"So what did happen with your child?" Ms. Parker asked Nigel.

"It is not a story with a happy ending, I'm afraid. My two brothers had grown bored in England, so they tracked me down. My older brother Ian was a strict follower of vampire law and very much opposed breeding with humans. When he discovered that I kept house with a human and she was with child, he tried to kill her. Since I was well nourished from the blood of natives and Ian was still weak from his journey, I gained the upper hand. My younger brother always had a skittish temperament. He was torn by watching us fight, and he ran off when I proved the victor."

Nigel had not exchanged more than a few words with anyone in nearly a century. Now he was gabbing on like a schoolgirl. His taking a shine to Ms. Parker must've provoked it. We listened quietly and kept nodding, hoping when it was over he wouldn't find a reason to send us all to hell.

"While we were fighting," he continued, "the townspeople became convinced that we were all witches. As I was recovering from my wounds, they captured my wife. I offered to trade my life for hers, but once they had me shackled to a tree, they burned her at the stake." Nigel's eyes moistened. "My unborn child perished with her."

"How horrible!" Ms. Parker gasped.

"Indeed." He quickly regained his composure, then a wicked smile came over his face. "I was to have my revenge though. They intended to burn me, but I caught my guard unaware and used his finger bones to pick my shackles. I slaughtered the townspeople, only sparing the women and children, since they had no part in the decision to kill my wife."

"But why didn't you just turn your wife into a vampire when you had a chance, so she wouldn't die either?" Ms. Parker asked.

"Despite the tales you've heard, a human cannot become a vampire through a bite any more than a pig can become a man from the ample portions of bacon you consume. Vampires are born of vampires."

"Ain't it true that you need a wooden stake to kill 'em?" Buddy asked.

"No, a bullet will suffice, though you'd be hard-pressed to shoot quickly enough. Otherwise, we can expect to live as long as five hundred years before expiring of old age. Nothing lasts forever."

"How come we didn't know about none of this before?" Buddy asked.

"For the expediency of our feeding, we have always kept our identities secret. If your livestock could comprehend your language, you would not inform them of your intentions, would you? Sure, encounters have been reported now and then, but they were usually considered little more than folklore."

"So if the townspeople didn't get you, how did you die?" Ms. Parker asked.

"My younger brother allowed the vampire tribunal to know that I killed Ian, and it is strictly forbidden to kill another vampire. So they sent a hunter named Luther after me."

"Your own brother tattled on you?" Buddy shook his head in disapproval.

"There was no need for that. Vampires can read thoughts. All Martin had to do was be in the presence of another vampire for it to become known."

Ms. Parker shuddered as if she'd seen a ghost.

"Are you feeling okay, ma'am?" Nigel asked.

"Oh, why yes. I suppose the morning sickness is coming in the evenings," she said. "Is that the name of your brother? I knew a man by that name, but it couldn't have been the same man. Martin is a fairly common name, after all."

"So can you read our thoughts?" I asked Nigel, trying not to think of anything unpleasant about him.

"Dead men don't offer them as freely as the living," he said, "but the silence is welcome after centuries of listening to prayers for sex and money."

"And what happened with that hunter vampire they sent after ya?" Buddy asked.

"Luther did not know the territory as I did. I might have evaded him for decades. Alas, he played upon my sympathies. He collected the town's women and children, including some of my wife's kin, and locked them in a barn, then threatened to burn them alive. I knew it was a trap, but I no longer cared. Rather than see more needless death, I let Luther kill me. Then I ended up here, though I don't know why."

Nigel emptied his glass of gin in one gulp. He might've been a few centuries old and had eaten a mess of people, but he still looked like a heartsick schoolboy.

"You sacrificed yourself for your wife and then for those women and children," Ms. Parker said. "That's why you've been sent here! You've been given a second chance."

"Damnation is not a second chance," Nigel said with some annoyance. "I have never seen a single soul escape this town. There is no heaven and no redemption. There are only varying degrees of hell—not the least of which are boredom and solitude. At least you have food that you can eat here. For me, there is no substitute for warm blood. I am continually hungry and bored."

"Well, it looks like you got yourself some excitement now," Buddy pointed out. "Them werewolves'll be back."

"So do you know what happened to your younger brother Martin?" Ms. Parker asked shyly.

"I suppose he might still be wandering around America. If you'll excuse me, ma'am. I think I should spend as little time in your company as possible. I'm afraid I might not be able to withstand the lure of the warm blood inside of you." As Nigel headed for the door, Ms. Parker braced her tummy in fear.

"Don't worry, ma'am," Buddy told her. "Ain't no vampire gonna eat you or your baby while I'm around."

We walked Ms. Parker back to the hotel to be sure the wolves didn't double back for her. As we crossed the road, the wind picked up. The normally unmovable clouds parted for a brief instant, and a faint beam of light shone down from the corner of the sky. For the first time, a pale circle was visible beyond the embers of dusk. Some howling sounded in the distance, then more joined in. Soon the entire pack was calling at once. A moment later, the clouds converged. Dusk resumed, and the wolves were silent.

The Crapper

Comings: *Whiny Pete's probably already chewed the ear off every man in town about the stampede he caused and the children he killed, so I won't waste much space on him here, except to say that I don't expect he'll last more than a month, and when he reads this and starts whining about the prediction, it may shorten that time considerably.*

Goings: *Fat Wally hailed from Mississippi where his momma was born to a proper family. His pa owned some land, but Wally had a wild streak that couldn't be appeased by farming. He ran off to pilot steamboats when he was fifteen and eventually got involved in managing sporting ladies, which became his lifelong career. He loved his pork, even before he wound up in Damnation, and considered bacon a main dish and eggs just a side. Some five years ago, he joined us after his heart gave out in a brothel in New Orleans, where he was spending the money he had fleeced from a banker.*

Wally was considered by most to be amicable company at the poker table and his constant ribbing of the newbies provided a welcome distraction. He couldn't abide jabbering whiners like the one who pressed a pistol to his breast during a botched gunfight that turned into a wrestling match. But fair is fair, and the man who ain't smelling sulfur is the victor. One thing that can be said about Fat Wally's departure is that he won't have to listen to Whiny Pete no more. Unfortunately, the rest of us will.

Though not really a new arrival, I would like to share some recently learned information about one of our oldest residents. The vampire's name is Nigel. He introduced himself after he saved Ms. Parker from a couple of wolves. He came from England originally. Had himself a human wife in America, and they're not supposed to do that according vampire law. Nigel had to kill his own brother to protect her, and then another vampire hunted him down and held his wife's kin hostage. Nigel sacrificed himself so that they could live. He don't seem like such a bad guy after all, though I wouldn't test him on it. Also, he thinks Ms. Parker is still with child, and she's pretty sure she is, too.

Oh, and I think we saw some kind of moon-like thing in the sky last night when we were walking her home.

Chapter 9

A Dandy from the Dust

"So if y'all saw the moon, then I reckon we gotta still be somewhere on earth," Whiny Pete speculated.

"Not necessarily," Spiffy put in. "Coulda been just lookin' at it from some other planet. Or it coulda been a different moon entirely. Like one of the moons of Jupiter, for instance."

"You sayin' there's more'n one moon?" Stumpy asked. "I only seen the one—unless they come out at different times."

"Ah, that don't mean we're on Jupiter," Red argued. "Or that we're anyplace at all. Coulda just been made to look like a moon. And we're somewhere between heaven and hell."

"Maybe Jupiter's between heaven and hell," Spiffy suggested.

"So let me get this straight," Sal wiped his hands on his apron. "You're saying God put our dead souls on Jupiter? That's the most ridiculous thing I ever heard!"

"Gotta put 'em somewheres." Spiffy shrugged. "Why not Jupiter? Nobody's ever gone there, so who's to say the whole planet ain't filled with dead souls."

"Ah, I don't give a piss where we are so long as there's whiskey to drink!" Red interrupted.

"I can't even say for certain it was a moon we saw," I told them. "It was just a round bright thing. Only saw it for a second or two."

"Did it look larger than the reg'lar moon?" Spiffy asked. "'Cause if we're shrunken down smaller than a needle, it might appear that way."

"Ah, enough with your shrunken-smaller-than-a-needle nonsense!" Sal hollered.

"If it was a moon, would that make the wolves friskier?" Pete chewed his fingers in worry. "I heard full moons get 'em all riled up. They was howling somethin' awful last night."

"Wolves don't need much to get 'em going," I said. "But if it was a moon, then it was a full one, and that probably don't weigh in our favor. Least from the stories I read."

The speculating was cut short when a new sharpie walked into the saloon. He wore a bright white suit with a string bowtie. His skin was as smooth as a lady's, and you might've took him for one if it weren't for his tall frame and wide jaw. Most folks came to Damnation looking a little ragged, whether they were sent by a bullet or a blade or the hoof a stubborn mule. One lumberjack arrived with a hatchet still wedged in the side of his skull. Said he'd gotten into a fight with another man over the ugliest whore in Montana. I'd never seen anyone come through the dust as clean as this man.

"Shit, Spiffy, he's dressed even fancier than you," Sal said. "Might have to give 'em your name."

Before we could start a betting pool on his cause of death, he turned around, and that resolved the matter. A mess of bullet holes dotted his back like freckles on an Irish lass.

"Ain't many folks singing my graces," Sal remarked. "But you gotta be *really* sore at someone to unload on 'em, then reload to shoot 'em some more."

"Musta been woman problems," Red decided.

"Why's that?" I asked.

"Nobody'd waste that much lead if you just steal their horse."

"It's true," Spiffy agreed. "In some parts, a dozen bullets cost more'n a horse. Of course, a cuckold wouldn't be concerned with pinching pennies. Seen it myself!" He pointed to the wound on his breast. "It's a professional risk for us Casanova types," he bragged, though Spiffy hadn't had many conquests. It was rumored that the woman he'd been caught with had taken a roll in the hay with half the town.

Regardless, Spiffy swaggered over to the newbie like he was too big for his breeches and bought the man a beer. "Damn back shooters!" he said by way of commiseration. "They're the lowest scum of the earth. Can't stand it when a man won't come at you head on."

"Oh, I believe he intended to," the newbie said with an evil grin. "But I was on top of his wife at the time and having too good of a time to oblige him."

Spiffy chuckled. "Another man's wife, huh? I thought so. Rode that horse before myself. Did she even tell you she was spoken for?"

"She didn't do much talking, though I suppose she would have if not for the gag in her mouth." The sharpie snickered.

"So you're a rapist?" Spiffy was dumfounded.

"Among other things," he answered without shame.

"Then I say you got what you deserve!"

"I guess I did." He nodded with his creepy grin.

"Well don't you even wanna know where you are?"

"Does it really matter? The last place they called earth and said I came out of my mother, though I don't recall the event. I suppose they got a name for this place, too."

"Damnation's what they call it. It's kinda like a sifter for hell, but I guess you don't care much about that."

"Very well. Damnation it is." He lifted his glass with little interest. "When I was a kid, a nun in the orphanage told me to behave or I'd burn in hell for all eternity. I raped her and cut her throat and have been doing my utmost to misbehave ever since. It seems I didn't end up in hell after all, so why should I believe you know any more about Damnation than she knew about earth?"

"'Cause you done died, mister!"

"So it seems." the stranger shrugged. "And since I lived so wholeheartedly, I've been rewarded with the chance to keep doing what I enjoy."

Ms. Parker came through the swinging doors while gripping her belly in discomfort. She had been getting larger of late, and had to let out her wedding gown on account of it. The soft glow of fertility suited her. There was a rosy shine to her cheeks that none of the other dead women had, and her bosom had swelled. The stranger looked at her, like a wolf watching a lamb.

"Who is that delightful creature?" he asked.

"You mean Ms. Parker?" Spiffy said. "She wouldn't interest you none. She's wearing the bustle wrong. First pregnant woman there's ever been in Damnation. Still not sure how it happened."

"You say this is hell's sifter." He smiled, "But I do believe it's heaven."

The dandy swaggered across the room like he was accustomed to women looking favorably on him. As he approached Ms. Parker, he doffed his hat with a courteous bow, showing a mess of wavy yellow hair, then flashed his bright white teeth. Your average outlaw wasn't too easy on the eyes, so the pickings in town were pretty slim, but this fella would've stood out among any gussied-up sharpies.

"I do believe we are birds of a feather," he announced. "A man in white and a lady in white. All we need is a chapel and a priest. My name is Malachi."

"Pleased to meet you, Mr. Malachi." She blushed at his chivalry.

"Just Malachi, ma'am. Would you care to join me for a glass of lemonade?" She accepted his arm, and he led her to a table in the corner.

Buddy came in while they were shooting the breeze and sat at the end of the bar watching them. Looked like he was aching to put a lead plumb in the fella, but he had to concede that she wasn't averse to his company. Buddy wasn't slender, nor smooth of cheek. And just because he could outdraw any man didn't mean the prettiest girl in town was going to go weak in the knees for him. He nursed his beer, surely wishing he could trade some of his speed to be as handsome as the man in white.

"Who's the greenhorn?" he asked.

"He's a bad egg," Spiffy explained. "Kilt and raped a nun in an orphanage. Prolly kilt and raped plenty of women. You gonna let him sit with Ms. Parker?"

Hearing that the man was an orphan hit a tender spot with Buddy. As an orphan himself, he was less inclined to shoot someone who didn't have a family to teach him right from wrong. Not that he could abide the killing and raping of a nun. He was more concerned that Ms. Parker might not take a shine to his meddling in her affairs.

"I ain't her pa," he replied. "I can't tell her who she can and can't drink lemonade with."

"That Malachi fella's worse'n Red and his boys you shot up. He doesn't even care that he's been kilt. Says he's just glad he's got a chance to rape some more."

Buddy just grimaced and kept his eyes peeled for anything that would warrant his interference. Spiffy didn't press the matter any further, and nothing more was said till Nigel came through the door. He scented out Ms. Parker right away. Seeing her in the company of the stranger, he headed straight to their table, but Buddy blocked his path. It was the first time anyone ever tried to stand in his way.

"Don't worry about it," Buddy told him. "I got this one."

Oddly, Nigel didn't tear off any of Buddy's limbs. Must've had his reasons for keeping him around. "I don't think you realize how dangerous that man is," he said. "His lust for killing approaches that of a vampire."

"Sure, he's a real bad egg. I got that," Buddy said. "But he's just a man and I don't need no backup for a man—'specially a dead tenderfoot. Soon as the lady shows any sign of displeasure, I'll be sure to relocate him to his 'proper place in the cosmos' or whatever you call it."

"It could be too late by then. I can smell his bloodlust. And she's pregnant! No, this won't do at all. If you hope to raise a child here, I dare say you have to be a tad more picky about whom you allow to remain. There could never be any sort of harmonious society with men like *that* in the population."

"Well, I can't shoot him for what he done on earth," Buddy argued. "Nor what you think he might do in the future. There's a code among men. He's gotta actually do something here. But I'll have words with the lady."

Buddy walked over and greeted Ms. Parker, then nodded to the stranger in white. They looked pretty cozy together, which made Buddy fidget nervously.

"There's a couple a free chairs at the faro table if you'd care to join me, ma'am."

"Thank you, Buddy, but Malachi and I were just about to take a stroll around town," she replied. "This afternoon, he walked in on a holdup in Chicago and bravely shielded some children from gunfire. He was hit in the back. Isn't that just horrible?"

"Lotta bullet holes just for crossfire." Buddy stared into Malachi's cold eyes.

"Yes, it's remarkable the cruelty some people harbor toward the innocent." Malachi returned the stare. He looked like the sort of kid who'd pull the legs off a bug for fun. Couldn't fault Ms. Parker for not noticing though. Many a man bought a murdering widow's story just because she had a nice pair of legs. Ms. Parker seemed stung by Buddy's insinuation.

"Well, I'm sure Malachi wouldn't know so much about gun wounds since he's not in your line of work," she replied with some venom.

"Oh? What line of work you in, friend?" Buddy asked

"Sales," he replied. "The good book of King James."

"You tellin' me you're a bible thumper?"

"Most popular book of all time. It practically sells itself. I just filled the orders for those in need."

"If you'll excuse us, Mr. Baker. I'm going to give him a tour of the town now. The twilight skies are endearing till you begin to miss the fullness of the sun."

"Yes, ma'am." Buddy dipped his hat as they strolled out arm in arm. Then he cowered back to the bar.

"Well, get after them!" Nigel ordered.

"I can't be right on their heels," Buddy argued. "Ms. Parker'll think I'm spying on her."

"You are."

"I don't want *her* to know that."

He insisted on waiting a full minute before following. They were strolling along the boardwalk in no particular hurry and had just reached the edge of town. Buddy might've been good with a gun, but he wouldn't have made much of a Pinkerton, unless he was trailing a blind man. I watched from the doorway as he zigzagged up the road. Every time Ms. Parker turned around, she was sure to see a post with a pot belly or a large body diving behind a rotted-out barrel. Malachi must've noticed, too.

As they were taking in the mini dust twisters on the flatlands, Buddy let out some cooing noises meant to mimic an owl. He was trying to distract them in case they got it in their heads to do some smooching. It wasn't very convincing since there weren't any birds in Damnation. They turned and headed back, taking the long way to avoid going by the wolves' saloon. Malachi went into the latrine, and Ms. Parker took the opportunity to give Buddy a piece of her mind.

"I do appreciate you looking after me, Mr. Baker, but this has got to stop," she fumed. "I didn't mean to mislead you..."

"No, ma'am," he sulked.

"Now hear me out. I don't intend on having my every move watched."

"But ma'am, you don't know what kind of man you're keeping company with."

"Neither do you."

"But ma'am, he told Spiffy—"

"Yes, I know all about it. Malachi told me that he was a sinner when he was alive. He told me plenty... How he was disrespectful to women and broke the law, but coming to the other side has changed him, and he regrets what he's done."

"But you don't understand, ma'am. Even the vampire says he's real bad. Smells the evil on him."

"Oh, you mean the vampire who avoids being in the same room with me because he's afraid he'll eat my baby? And this coming from a murdering train robber. The first time a decent man comes to town you all try to scare him off. Frankly, I don't care what Malachi might have done when he was alive. Doesn't he deserve a second chance? Ain't that why we're *all here*?" she said in a huff.

Malachi returned with his bible salesman's smile and Buddy scampered off. Nigel also left for fear Ms. Parker would trigger his thirst for warm blood.

"Watch 'em," Buddy told me on the way out. "If anything happens, get the vampire. And if the vampire looks like he's getting hungry, come get me and I'll send both their asses to hell."

On account of my limp, I reckoned I wasn't the best choice for a job that entailed a lot of running around. Ms. Parker was liable to get raped or eaten before I fetched anyone who could help. Not to mention, if Malachi tried something when no one else was nearby, I might be forced to shoot him, which would preclude my chances of getting into heaven.

Chapter 10

Hardin

"First, it's the thunder'n lighting, then there's a dang moon in the sky," Sal griped. "Now, we got a dead pregnant gal who the wolves wanna eat—and the vampire's soft on her, to boot! What's next?"

"Could start snowing," Red joked.

"Ain't cold enough for snow," Spiffy said in earnest.

"If there's snow in hell, then why couldn't it snow here?" Stumpy asked innocently.

"Come again?"

"When ya'll sat down with the vampire, Sal said you got a snowball's chance in hell of surviving. Since ya'll survived, there's gotta be snowballs in hell, right?"

"Enough of that now, Stumpy. Run along and collect some glasses," Sal ordered.

A man with a bowler hat and a long soup-strainer mustache walked into the saloon. He was tidily dressed, but not in a flashy way like Malachi. His dark frock coat had no bullet holes or blood stains, so Sal started the betting on the cause of his death with arsenic for insurance money. I bet a buck that he was choked by a thief.

"This heaven or hell?" he asked straight away. He didn't show any surprise at being dead. Must've seen it coming.

"Kind of in-between," Sal told him.

"Fair enough." He scanned the half-empty room. Most of the men weren't up yet. A lot of folks kept regular hours even though it was always dusk. The clock above the bar let you know when chow could be expected. Breakfast was at ten, lunch at two, and supper at half past six. Otherwise, folks'd sleep all day and Sal'd be up all night cooking breakfast whenever they woke. Having regular hours also made it easier to get a card game going. There were already a few men playing stud.

"Got any dice?" the new man asked.

"Dice usually don't start till later," Sal told him.

"Damn it all! I was on roll. Woulda made a bundle if that sheriff hadn't a shot me."

He took his hat off and laid it on the bar. Four bullet holes dotted the back of his head. He must've been shot at close range, because the gunpowder singed the hair around the wounds.

"Saw the bastard in the mirror," he said. "I woulda shot his ass first, but I had twenty dollars on the line and was fixing to roll an easy eight to win."

A couple of sodbusters had bet the man died by gunshot, with gambling as the reason, so they split the pot. In most cases, it was the safest bet, but folks liked thinking up odd ways of dying. Weren't many other opportunities to exercise your creativity in Damnation.

"Hey, ain't you John Wesley Hardin?" one of the two-bit thieves asked.

A hush fell over the room. There hadn't been anybody really famous in town since a vaudeville actor came and got shot the very next day for tap dancing too early in the morning. Except Buddy, of course, and he wasn't near as well-known as Hardin.

"I saw you kill Jim Bradley in Towash, Texas," a man said. "You cleaned him out in cards, and he said that if you won one more hand, he was gonna cut out your liver. I'll be damned if you didn't win the very next hand. Jim didn't even clear leather before you put a bullet in his face, then two more in his chest.

The men gathered around the famous gunslinger, asking for stories of his exploits. He had killed his first man when he was just fifteen. A freed slave had challenged him to a wrestling match. Hardin beat him badly by scratching out one of his eyes. The next day he returned with a stick, so Hardin shot him dead. Three soldiers were sent to arrest the boy on charges of murder, but he got the jump on them and killed all three with a buffalo gun. Over the years, he earned a reputation for sending Texas lawmen to the bone yard.

"Looks like you got some competition, Buddy," Sal chided.

"Him? How many men he kilt?" Buddy asked.

"They say forty-two, not counting Indians."

"Shit, I shot more'n that."

"Yeah, but you only killed twenty-three when you was alive. Hell, even the Christian ladies shot forty dead men. They practically jump in front of your gun in Damnation. Harder to pull the trigger when it ain't some sorry sodbuster looking to eat lead outta boredom."

"They say Hardin killed more men than them Earp boys and Doc Holliday combined," Whiny Pete said.

Buddy sat stewing in the corner. Ever since Malachi arrived, he'd been in a sour mood, and the arrival of a new hot-shot gunslinger didn't improve it any. He looked on Hardin in much the same way Jack Finney had looked upon him when he first arrived and was full of boasts. Hardin wasn't averse to letting the boys paw on him either. Nor did he easily tire of talking about himself.

"Is it true that you once got the jump on Wild Bill Hickok?" someone asked.

"Ah, Bill's a good ol' boy," he replied. "I was just a hayseed at the time, but it's true. I'll show you how I done it. Lemme see that there pistol, amigo." Hardin held the Colt backward with the butt out like he was surrendering. "I offered my gun to him like this. Now reach for it," he said, and as the man did, Hardin spun it around his fingertip till the barrel pointed out. "Gotcha! Curly Bill Brocius taught me that one," he said with a laugh, but he didn't give the gun back. Buddy watched from across the room as he slipped it in his coat. There were two reverse holsters rigged to his vest. The handle pointed inward so he had to draw cross-armed.

"They call that the Road Agent's Spin." Hardin kept chewing the fat so the man wouldn't think to ask for his gun back.

"Mighty dangerous having a man like that armed," I said to Sal.

"Could keep Buddy in line," he said. "Knowing he ain't the only stallion around."

"Sooner or later, they're gonna lock horns," I warned. "Buddy's got his wild side, but at least he's fair. I don't know about that Hardin fella. Heard lots of stories about him. He don't seem like the type to hear a man out before he starts shooting. He could turn out to be worse than Jack Finney, and nobody wants to go back to how things were when he was around."

Sal adjusted the toothpick in his mouth while debating the matter. He hadn't lasted just shy of a century by betting everything on the wrong horse. "Have to see how things play out."

Hardin finished up his credit's worth of whiskey, then Sal rushed over to fill his glass, making sure to knock his knuckle loudly on the bar. "This one's on me, Mr. Hardin."

"I know," Hardin said with a queer smirk, as if Sal wasn't nothing but a pissant drink fetcher.

Sal returned to the topside of the bar shaking his head. "You might be right about him."

The boys kept clamoring for more stories from the famous outlaw.

Hardin must've had calluses from patting his own back so much.

"Ah, they make up lots of stuff about me." He waved his hand to dismiss them. "They say I killed a half dozen men just for snoring. Ain't true though. Just killed the one. Shot him though the wall. He was snoring something awful."

Chapter 11

Mabel Starr

Just a few days after Hardin arrived, a new lady came out of the dust. She was a little flashier than Ms. Parker, though not quite as polished. She arrived in the evening while things were in mid-swing. Wasn't too bothered about being dead. Just ordered a whiskey, took her ten chips, and doubled them at faro.

"Two in less than six months," Spiffy remarked. "That's a lot of women for Damnation!"

"She a whore?" Whiny Pete asked.

"Relieved plenty a men of their banknotes, I reckon. Just didn't satisfy 'em."

"Too bad," Whiny Pete said. "'Cause I'd a paid my last chip for a poke."

"Ah, you prolly died with no hair on your balls," Red teased. "A woman like that needs a real man."

Calling Mabel Starr a colorful character was like calling a porcupine pointy. She was hard to miss, with her shock of red curly hair and low-slung tits like a bull. Her voice let you know from across the room where the fun was being had. She moved from table to table with an easy smile and a wink. Made everyone feel like they might have a chance with her. The greasy outlaws combed their hair with dampened sleeves and sucked in their guts—all on their very best behavior.

"Well, she managed to make it through the night without getting shot or raped," Sal said as he was closing up. "That's more'n you could say for a lot of women."

Sal put her up in a room in the hotel beside Ms. Parker, and the next morning I interviewed her for *The Crapper*.

"Look out, boys. Got me a hot date with a reporter," she said as she came in. "I guess I might as well spill the beans to you before people go makin' stuff up about me."

Mabel was a plain-spoken gal, despite her blue-blood upbringing. Her family came from old money in Philadelphia but had lost it all in the stock market, so she struck out on her own when she was fourteen and fell into the racket of hustling speculators. She conned prosperous folks into investing in a silver mine by showing them a hunk of ore worth a thousand dollars and saying it was just the teensiest bit of what was below the surface. Then she'd milk them for equipment and wages. Eventually, she came across a ranch boss who figured out the scheme and shot her. Dying hadn't hurt her figure though. She was still a fine-looking woman—even with the bullet hole in her bosom.

"A hundred cowboys in this town and only a couple of gals!" She laughed mischievously. "Don't sound so bad to me."

She ordered the house special: whiskey and eggs with a side of bacon. Mabel wasn't dainty with all her curves, and she had the appetite of a half-starved tree humper. Sal got some exercise walking back and forth to the kitchen refilling her plate.

"You're tellin' me I ain't gotta worry about getting fat or looking old?" she asked on her second helping. "And I can drink as much as I like?"

"You'll still ache some the next day," I warned. "But nobody's gone to hell from drinking too much, yet."

"Can I get pregnant like that other gal?"

"Ms. Parker was with child before she arrived. The pigs don't even get pregnant here."

Mabel's sunny disposition briefly darkened. "I'm pretty sure I couldn't have kids anyhow. Had me an operation in New York City. Ain't been the same since," she said bluntly. "Sad to think there ain't no more chance of me having a youngin' though. Always wanted to raise one of my own someday." She took a mournful gulp of whiskey, then regained her usual gusto. Some folks kept moping over what they'd lost or what could've been, but the ones who lasted were more keen on how it could be worse. Mabel was about the most optimistic dead gal I ever met.

Buddy soon shuffled in, rubbing the sleep from his eyes and hankering for some breakfast. A few of the boys made room for him at the bar, which made him look like a person to be reckoned with.

"Who's the big fella?" Mabel asked.

"You mean Buddy?"

"Is that Buddy Baker? Didn't he shoot up a whole posse outside of Fort Worth a few months back? Will you excuse me, darling?" Mabel strutted to the other end of the bar, sweeping her hair back to showcase her ample bosom. Buddy perked up some as she introduced herself. It was the happiest I'd seen him since Malachi started courting Ms. Parker.

"How long you think before she gets shot?" Sal asked.

"I ain't betting on this one," I told him. "Mabel could last awhile. Seems like she can handle herself."

"I ain't seen a figure like that last more'n a week in thirty years," Sal said. "I give it till suppertime before somebody gets shot over it."

"Somebody might get shot," I said, "but it ain't gonna be Mabel."

"Why you say that?"

"There ain't been gunfighters good enough to protect a figure like that before. Jack Finney wasn't hardly interested in women, and Jeremiah hated them. Now there are two."

As Sal was clearing away our breakfast plates, Hardin came in looking fresh as a daisy. Two nickel-plated pistols hung from his border-cross rigging. They called it that because they were popular in Mexico where you needed to shoot fast and often. The men at the middle section of the bar cleared out, giving Hardin a much wider berth than they'd given Buddy. Sal made haste in fetching a plate of eggs and a pint of beer for him.

"Say, is that John Wesley Hardin?" Mabel said. She left Buddy blowing in the wind while she strutted to the other end of the bar. The sway of her hips told Hardin all he needed to know before she opened her mouth.

"You may not remember, Mr. Hardin, but we crossed paths in San Antonio," she said. "I'll say, you were a dashing figure then, and the grave certainly hasn't done you no harm." Any man would've been flattered by her attention, even if she hadn't been one of only two young ladies in town. Hardin just nodded smugly. After a lifetime of taking whatever he wanted, he reckoned it fitting that a well-built redhead was waiting for him beyond the grave. Men that'd been dead for twenty years without so much as a speck of womanly affection were eating their hearts out.

"It didn't take her long to figure out who's the fastest gun," Sal remarked.

"A woman like that knows she ain't gonna last long without a man," Red said. "She might as well take the fastest gun before he takes her."

"Ms. Mabel's a real pretty lady," Stumpy added innocently.

Buddy sat by his lonesome, brooding over his eggs and whiskey. As if losing the lady's attention to Hardin wasn't enough, not long after, Ms. Parker came in accompanied by Malachi in his bright white suit. They sat at a table in the corner, needling a plate of scrambled eggs like a couple of lovebirds too distracted to eat. Buddy looked on them with the sourpuss of a broken-hearted kid.

"Must be hell for him," I said. "Being trapped here watching them together. There ain't even another saloon for him to go to!"

"I suspect he'd *rather be* in hell." Sal waved five dollars in the air.

"I'll get in on that action," Red said. "Two bits says Buddy'll get sent to hell by his own hand or Hardin's by the end of the month." The boys piled their money on the bar. Sal tallied up a list, but I was the only one betting Buddy'd last. I covered what I could. Then Sal started a pool on how long Mabel would last. Again I was the only one who gave her more than a month. I covered a few more bets but didn't have the cash to back them up.

"Shit, Tom," Red said, "if Buddy and Mabel both get shot this month, it won't be long before you follow 'em."

It was true. There'd have to be a huge increase in the circulation of *The Crapper* in order for me to cover my end. Unless some war sent a lot of folks to Damnation in a hurry, my only chance was if at least one of them survived. Otherwise somebody'd shoot me for welching. Much as I longed to escape the sad confines of Damnation for someplace better, I preferred it to the prospect of hell.

"Why you suppose all whores go to heaven anyway?" Whiny Pete asked out of the blue.

"I reckon it's just nature's way of correcting things," I said. "Not every man's handsome enough that a woman'd offer him a poke. But with sporting ladies, a man's just gotta work hard enough to earn the money for 'em."

"But they get *paid!* So why should they get to go to heaven, too?"

"If you had to give a poke to a fat bastard like Red, you'd expect to get paid *and* go to heaven, wouldn't you?"

"Guess so."

While Ms. Parker went to the latrine, Malachi headed to the bar for a refill. Mabel happened to be walking by, and their paths crossed. He stopped and dipped his hat real gentlemanly like, with a flash of his toothy smile. Mabel's eyes traveled over his smooth cheeks, and she didn't look disappointed in what she saw. Her freckled skin flushed red as cherries and she half-curtsied. As she dipped, the fellas behind Malachi were given a bird's eye view of her cleavage, which inspired some whooping and hollering.

Hardin was watching the encounter from down the bar, and he didn't look pleased. In his younger days, he might've been able to compete with the good looks of the white-suited sharpie, but age had caught up with him. The flesh below his chin now drooped like a rooster's wattle, and his hair had thinned to a widow's peak. He suffered the same curse many of us had: not dying in our prime.

"This oughta be interesting," Sal said. "That crazy dandy and the gunslinger are after the same gash."

Several moments passed while the two were locked in admiring smiles. Hardin's brow furrowed in anger. If he shot Malachi without cause, it might make him look unfavorable in Mabel's eyes, but he wanted to show his strength. Stumpy came by collecting glasses just then, and Hardin stepped in front of him. The tall lanky barback tried to dodge the gunslinger, but lost his balance. All six and a half feet of him tumbled to the floor, along with a full tray of glasses.

"Watch where you're goin' boy!" Hardin shouted.

Sal came out from behind the bar to try to calm the situation. "Oh, he didn't mean nothin' by it, Mr. Hardin," he blathered meekly. "The boy's just a halfwit."

Stumpy had some trouble getting to his feet. His handless wrist kept sliding uselessly off a chair, and nobody wanted to help him up—for his own good. The safest place for him was the floor. Eventually, his good hand gripped a hat hook below the bar, which he used to pull himself up. He was confused and couldn't understand what he'd done wrong. Kept jabbering on about how there must be some mistake. First, he checked how many glasses had shattered, knowing they'd be deducted from his pay. Then he reckoned he must've spilled some beer on Hardin, so he balled up a rag to wipe the man down. "I'm sorry, Mr. Hardin," he muttered.

Seeing the large figure rise and extend his arm unsettled Hardin.

"You comin' at me, boy?" he said.

"I'll just clean you up good as new, sir." The gentle giant stepped forward waving an oily rag, still stunned from the fall.

Sal tried to grab Stumpy's sleeve and pull him out of harm's way, but there was no putting him off when he was keen on cleaning a mess. Sal looked back to the one man in the room who stood a chance of stopping things from getting out of hand. Buddy was slumped over the bar. He might have had the speed to go against Hardin, but he either lacked the nerve or inclination today. In Stumpy's face, you couldn't see nothing but an earnest desire to clean the man's shirt. Hardin lifted his gun with a crooked smile.

"It'll be right as rain, Mr. Hardin. I promise," Stumpy said cheerfully. Hardin sent three bullets into his gut without so much as a blink. His long bony body staggered forward and collapsed on Hardin's shoulder like a folded quilt. Hardin looked into Malachi's eyes as he pulled the trigger a fourth time. Oddly, Malachi was smiling right back at him, like he appreciated the handiwork. Stumpy fell to the floor. Then Hardin headed for the door. As he crossed the threshold, he let out a snicker.

Sal wailed and collapsed on top Stumpy. His cranky old bartender eyes filled with tears. He tried to stop the bleeding by plugging the wounds with bar rags, but there were too many. The poor halfwit's eyes stilled, and he was no more.

"Fetch my scattergun!" Sal ordered. As mean as he could be, he loved Stumpy like the son he never had. Came to feel like he raised him after all those years of looking out for the boy.

"It ain't worth it," I told Sal.

"Like hell it ain't! Get me that damn gun. I'm gonna shoot that bastard!" Sal swore. "I don't care how fast he is. A spray of buckshot'll slow 'em down." I held Sal in a bear hug to keep him from going off half-cocked. He broke my grasp though, and Red had to throw his weight in the way till the rage passed.

"That sumabitch!" Sal hollered.

"He'll get his in due time," I assured. But the truth was that if Buddy wasn't up to the job, there wasn't anyone who stood a chance against Hardin. The saloon doors were still swinging back and forth from Hardin's exit, and between them a flash of light flickered in the sky.

"You see that?" I asked. Another flash flickered across the saloon walls, and everyone ran out to the road. Bluish bursts were still rippling above, and thunder rumbled just beyond the town.

"That was even louder than the last time," Red said.

"What ya suppose it is?" Whiny Pete asked worriedly.

"Dunno," I said, "but it sounds like it's getting closer.

The Crapper

Comings: *Mabel Starr, John Hardin, and Malachi all arrived recently. Ain't much I can tell you about any of them that ain't already been widely discussed. Mabel's a proud swindler from Pennsylvania, Hardin's a famous outlaw from Texas, and Malachi might be some kind of nun-killing bible salesmen from the Chicago area, but he ain't too forthcoming with the details.*

Goings: *We've all been guilty of dressing down Stumpy at one time or another, for stepping on our feet or spilling our drinks, but an apology and an effort to make amends always followed. In my forty-odd years of life and my fifteen-odd years of death, I've met every sort of fella a couple of times each, but I ain't never met a man of such stature who could disarm a brute with just his own meekness. Few could argue that Stumpy's gentle soul was worth gunning down for his klutziness, though Mr. Hardin saw otherwise.*

Stumpy was not much of a storyteller—I don't think I ever heard him speak more than a few sentences at a time, but there was a simple wisdom to his sparse words. Through the years, he mentioned various parts of his life to different folks, which I've only just begun to piece together. He was born in Minnesota and had little memory of his childhood. Some suggest he had been dropped on his head as a child, but if his kind nature was the result, then we'd all be lucky to take such a tumble. His father was a farmer. When asked of the possible sins that might have caused him to be sent to Damnation, Stumpy once said, "The cows! All the cows we butchered!" Then when questioned about the chickens that were also slaughtered on his farm, he just laughed and said, "Ah, chickens ain't got big enough eyes for sadness."

To be honest, I can't rightly say for sure whether the size of creature's eyes in any way relates to their capacity for pain, any more than I can say the height of man relates to the size or nobility of his heart. One thing that could be said of Stumpy, though, is that when he was around there was always one man in the room head and shoulders above everyone else, who didn't think he was any better than anyone.

Chapter 12

The Blue Men

At first it was hard to put a finger on it, but something was missing in the Foggy Dew. The dank wood walls seemed less cheerful, and the banter over card games wasn't as amusing. Folks just didn't have the same pep as they used to. Even the ribbing of newbies was a joyless task. Then I realized what was missing. The sound of Buddy's laughter used to fill up the whole saloon. Most folks were sad about being dead or worried about getting sent to hell. Not Buddy. He laughed at everything, especially his own jokes, and his giddiness was as infectious as smallpox. Everyone within earshot eventually got it, which made being dead sort of fun.

"Why you suppose he can't shake it?" I asked Sal.

It had only been a week since Hardin shot Stumpy, but Sal was back to his practical way of looking at things. The loss of his beloved barback reinforced his belief in doing whatever he had to in order to survive. If anything, he was colder and more calculating in his figuring.

"When Buddy came to town, he didn't have nothin' to lose," Sal explained. "After he killed Jack Finney, he became the biggest toad in the puddle. Then he fell for Ms. Parker and she was kinda sweet on him as well. Don't ya see? Even when he was alive, Buddy didn't get much notoriety as an outlaw. Hell, he probably ain't ever been with a woman he hadn't paid for. But when he got here, he was somebody. I reckon them first few weeks in Damnation was as good as it's ever been for Buddy. Now, Ms. Parker's sweet on that dandy rapist, and Hardin's the one everybody's clamoring to hear stories about. Don't you see? He lost the girl *and* his bragging rights."

"Think his saddle's slipping on account of it?"

"Maybe Buddy was only fast 'cause he thought everything was a joke. Slows you down when you get to worryin' over stuff."

"How you suppose Hardin manages it?" I asked. "He's as serious as an avalanche."

"Dunno," Sal said plainly. "Takes a real rotten soul to keep up that sort of hatred. He probably never gets bored of killing, whether they deserve it or not."

Hardin ran the dice table most nights. When he didn't feel like passing the dice, he just kept rolling. Mabel stood by his side, batting her eyes and petting his shoulder. Sal didn't dare charge either of them for drinks. And Mabel hardly ever lost, so she was socking away a tidy sum.

"What you suppose she's gonna do with all that money?" Sal asked.

"I wouldn't have any idea," I said. "Ain't worth nothing once you get out the door."

Coins were becoming scarce, and it made folks tense. At least when Jack Finney was around, a man could gamble in peace and scrape by enough to eat and drink. Now, some fellas could hardly afford a beer with their breakfast. Sal feared a revolt and started pouring whiskey into everyone's scrambled eggs to take the edge off.

Late in the afternoon, Buddy skulked in and asked me if he could borrow a pen and ink, of all things. Then he sat in the corner and began scribbling furiously.

"Now I've seen it all!" Sal declared. "The gunfighter who took out Jack Finney has traded in his pistol for a pen."

"What you suppose he's writing?" Whiny Pete asked.

"His will." Sal shrugged.

"He don't own nothing though," I said.

"Maybe he's after your job," Red laughed.

The barroom was already crowded, even though supper wasn't for a couple hours yet. Some railroad workers had come in after a tunnel collapsed on them in Pennsylvania. They'd been trapped for three days before the air ran out. Their clothes were covered in a fine layer of crushed stone, and when they spoke the dust in their lungs escaped from their mouths in little puffs. It was easy to spot them on account of their faces were still blue from suffocation. But they were happy as hogs in shit to be wetting their whistles and stretching their legs.

"Dang!" one of them pronounced. "If I'd a known I'd be able to get away from my wife *and* drink all day, I'd a died a lot sooner!" He'd gotten lucky at the poker table, won a few big hands and was sharing the wealth. They knocked back the bug juice at a furious pace.

Some said that the first drink after you died was the finest. You no longer had anything to fear, no responsibilities weighed you down, and you felt invincible. It was certainly grand to be liberated from all your earthly worries, but it didn't last. Those same folks usually said that the following morning was as bad as you could ever possibly feel. The worst part was having nothing to look forward to. When you died, all hope vanished. So if you were too sick to enjoy a few laughs, then you were entirely sunk. One fella stayed in bed for a whole week. When he finally gained the strength to rise, he picked a fight with Jack Finney just to end his misery. Figured hell had to be better than the hangover.

The blue-faced railroad men were still living high on the hog though. The largest of the three noticed Buddy scribbling away in the corner and decided to give him a ribbing. Men who weren't lettered never liked to see anyone doing what they couldn't. In similar situations, I always wished I could challenge bullies to a spelling bee instead of a draw. Fortunately, not many men cared to pick a fight with a crippled reporter for the only newspaper in the afterlife.

"Hey, Longfeller, you writin' love poetry?" he heckled.

Buddy didn't seem to hear him on account of how hard he was concentrating. He just kept scribbling away. When he finally got up to go to the latrine, the blue man was annoyed at being ignored and decided to block his path.

"Hey, Longfeller, I asked you a question. I asked if you was writin' love poetry over there?" He snickered as if it were the funniest thing ever said. Buddy tried to move past the man but couldn't avoid brushing against his boot.

"You done stepped on my beetle crusher, Longfeller!"

The room grew silent, and those standing behind the railroad worker wasted no time in clearing out.

"Ain't you gonna 'pologize?" He stood so close bits of spit sprayed Buddy's face. The odd thing was that Buddy's arm didn't move. It remained frozen at his side with trembling fingers. It was embarrassing to watch. After a long moment, he mumbled weakly, "Sorry," then stepped by.

"You're yellower than mustard," the blue man called after Buddy.

Hardin had a good view of the action from the dice table. There usually wasn't much that gave him cause to speak, but I heard him ask, "Who's that sad sack?"

"That's Buddy Baker," Mabel told him. "Shot up a posse in Texas."

"He thinks he's some sort a hotshot gunslinger," Red added.

"Somebody oughta put his sorry ass out of his misery," Hardin said and went to get a beer. The huddle of blue-faced men remained stationed in front of the bar like it was a train car and they were checking tickets. After backing down one man, they reckoned they had rule of the roost. Nobody moved an inch for Hardin to get by, but he wasn't the type to go begging anyone's pardon. He pushed straight through without a word and stuck up a finger to signal for a beer. The blue men must not have recognized Hardin from all the wanted posters and newspapers. And none of them had been dead long enough to know the pecking order.

"Hey, boy!" called out the big fella who'd been ribbing Buddy. "You just spilt my drink." Hardin looked from side to side in disbelief. It must have been quite a spell since anyone had spoken to him in that manner. "I'm talking to *you*!" he yelled. "Is every man in this town yellow?"

The room quieted once again. All of the railroad men were heeled with shiny Colts they'd bought with their winnings. Hardin opened his vest to reveal the butts of his inverted pistols, ready for his famous cross-armed draw. He combed his soup strainer with two fingers and glared at them.

"You got my attention now, blueberry boy."

Hardin wasn't the type to bother talking a man down. He preferred to get busy making holes in them. I reached for my pocket watch, fixing to get a gauge on just how fast he was. By the time I had fetched it from my pocket though, it was all over. Hardin raised a pistol in each hand. The guns seemed to float up in the air like helium balloons. He knocked the ear off the man on the right and obliterated one eye of the man on the left. Then he trained both barrels on the blowhard in the center.

His two friends had fallen, but he still hadn't managed to draw. His arm was frozen in place, gripping his shiny gun. The quivering of his fingers made the barrel clatter against his leg. All that fear of death he'd spent the day washing away was back again and even stronger, as a fear of hell. He unclenched his fingers from the handle, then slowly showed a sweaty palm in surrender. There was a hopeful look on his face—a half-smile, like he was fixing to laugh at the situation. He reckoned everything would be all right since he'd surrendered. It was a long moment for him. Probably felt longer than those three days in the collapsed tunnel, waiting for the air to run out. Everything was going to be all right though. Because if a man begs for mercy, he gets it. But not from Hardin.

The first bullet shattered his chin before he could speak. A piece of his gum dangled below his lip with a couple teeth still attached. The second bullet ripped through his neck. He dropped to the ground gasping and clutching at his useless windpipe. Hardin calmly reloaded each gun in turn, then replaced them in their holsters. This time when he stepped to the bar there was plenty of room cleared out and a fresh glass of suds waiting.

"Ah shit!" Buddy called out from the corner. Hardin looked over as

Buddy balled up the page he'd been scribbling on and tossed it over his shoulder in disgust.

"I'd say that proves it," Sal said. "We got a new top gun."

"Not sure," I told him. "Have to see how things play out."

Chapter 13

Malachi

Each night after supper, Ms. Parker and her beau strolled around town like a couple of newlyweds. They took in the gloomy violet and yellow sky, then stopped to watch the mini dust twisters blowing across the flatlands, like they were gazing at the prettiest ocean sunset you ever saw. I followed them just like Buddy asked. Malachi saw Ms. Parker to her door every evening and never did nothing improper while I was watching. He might've been blabbering on about how he was a reformed person and how sorry he was about all the bad things he'd done—though no one knew for sure if he told her exactly what he'd done.

As Ms. Parker's belly grew larger, she appreciated the attention of a handsome man. Perhaps she reckoned it'd be good for the child to have a father figure around, even if he was a dead tenderfoot.

"What's the kid gonna do for schoolin'?" Spiffy asked.

"I didn't have no schoolin'," Red said.

"And look how you turned out," Sal chortled.

"What's he need schoolin' for anyway?" Red argued. "Ain't like he needs a trade here. Just gotta learn how to play cards and drink."

"Kinda dreary for a kid to grow up in a place where everyone's dead," I said. "Imagine never gettin' to play in the grass or see a blue sky. And if it's a boy, how's he gonna meet a nice girl? The women here are already dead—and usually killers to boot."

"If it's a girl, the pickings for men ain't all that swell neither," Mabel added. "Except for you, honey, and you're already spoken for." She pinched Hardin's cheek. He just nodded and collected his beer, then went back to the dice table.

"My first time was with a saddle tramp in Toledo," Red said, shoveling down a plateful of pork and beans. "She might as well have been dead. It weren't so bad though."

"The vampire might have different plans for the kid," Sal said grimly.

"Like lunch," Red added, and a few of the others nodded, seeing it as a reasonable suspicion.

Ms. Parker and Malachi set out on their evening stroll with me at their heels, but at the edge of town, my stomach startled to rumble something fierce. Sal's cooking wasn't always agreeable to a dead man's stomach. The pork shoulder tasted like machinery belting covered in prairie butter. While the lovebirds were gazing on the mini dust tornados, I got a case of the backdoor trots. They were already starting to meander back toward town, so I hot-footed it to the Foggy Dew where the closest water closet could be found.

They were only out of my sight for a couple of minutes. Malachi must've been waiting for his chance though. As I was finishing up in the latrine, a scream came from outside the window. I bolted out the front door and heard another scream, so I turned into the alley, where the white-suited dandy had Ms. Parker pinned to the wall. He was lifting up the layers of her fluffy dress but had not yet reached her bloomers.

"Malachi!" I hollered. "Unhand her now!" He looked up but didn't stop. Seemed pleased even, like he preferred having an audience to his wickedness.

If I had been heeled, my chances of getting to heaven would certainly have been precluded, but I was not. Malachi was quite a bit larger than me, so I gripped my cane and drew back. Ms. Parker's screams excited him and he began unbuckling his pants. I smashed him across the back, but it didn't knock him down, worked up as he was. He turned and shoved me. My bad leg buckled and I fell to the ground. He began working quicker after that. Got his belt unbuckled with one hand while gripping her throat with the other. She screamed out, but he smacked her across the mouth, bloodying her lip, and she quieted.

Whenever my leg went out, it took a while to get it going again. Had to rub it down like an old stubborn mule. There wasn't any way I'd be able to stop Malachi from his evil deeds. Worse still, I'd be forced to watch from the ground. Then I turned to see a something that really got my blood going. Buddy was charging down the alley toward Malachi. For a chubby fella, he could move fast as all get-out when he wanted to. He gripped the fiend by his collar and threw him into a rotted out hitching post. Malachi knocked his head and fell to the ground in a daze. Buddy didn't draw his gun though. Just stood there waiting till Malachi got back to his feet, gritting his teeth in anticipation. Malachi slowly roused. Once he was upright, Buddy backhanded him across the cheek, sending him to the dust once more.

"Growing up an orphan might excuse some things," he told him. "But it don't give you cause for rapin' ladies."

Malachi stood once more. A savage look came over his eyes, like his hunger for violence had been awoken. Buddy looked pretty savage too, sweating and panting like a wild boar. It was reassuring to see him worked up about something again, even if he wasn't laughing.

The boys in the saloon had heard the ruckus and came out into the alleyway to investigate. Even Hardin had left the dice table to see what all the commotion was. He stood in the back with a keen eye. You'd have thought he was readying to draw a picture of the event.

"You heeled?" Buddy asked Malachi.

"No."

"Get him a gun," he told Sal.

"I don't think that would be a wise course of action," said a voice behind me. Nigel stood at the foot of the alley, keeping his distance from Ms. Parker.

"I don't need any of your namby-pamby," Buddy replied. "This here's man's law, not vampires'. I can't shoot a man who ain't heeled. People'll say I'm no better'n a back shooter."

"Don't be daft!" Nigel scowled. "You don't arm your pigs before you slaughter them. Why's he any different?"

"'Cause men are men and pigs ain't got no fingers to shoot with. 'Sides, I ain't plannin' to eat the sumabitch. Now get that man heeled, Sal, so I can send his ass to hell!"

Sal took off his own holster and handed it to Malachi. While Malachi strapped it to his waist, Sal explained the rules. "Both men will stand back to back, then walk ten paces as I count aloud—"

"Hell I will!" Malachi shouted, and raised his pistol.

Buddy was tending to Ms. Parker, so Malachi managed to get off a shot. The bullet struck the side of his gut. He groaned in agony and doubled over. Malachi smiled and took aim on Buddy's head.

"You back-shootin' bastard!" Buddy hollered and drew. His arm moved so quick, it looked like the gun just appeared in front of him. He fired four shots in a flash before Malachi could squeeze the trigger. The softhorn's bright blue eyes broke apart like any other mudsill's peepers. He remained upright as the empty sockets filled with red. One ear clung to his neck by a flap of skin. Buddy stepped forward, holding the wound on his side, and shot twice more shattering Malachi's white teeth. "Take that, you sumabitch!"

Malachi dropped to his knees, then fell forward for a mouthful of dust. He was little more than swine feed now. His white suit was caked in blood. Buddy didn't dally about reloading. Not that there was any fear of retribution from the crowd. To the contrary, they broke into applause, topped off by some hooting and hollering that made the Indians seem quiet by comparison.

"Ain't never seen a gunfighter get a standing ovation before," Old Moe remarked.

Even those who weren't fans of Buddy stood clapping like they heard a mayor's speech.

"Well, he earned it, gosh dang it!" Red admitted.

Buddy moved closer and aimed at the corpse on the ground. Six more shots echoed down the alleyway. The smooth skin on Malachi's cheeks mottled up and split with splinters of bone. Groans of disgust came from the crowd. A few of the newer men aired the paunch at the sight of it. Hardin was watching carefully, like he'd been counting the seconds it took for Buddy's pistol to leave its holster.

"What the hell'd you do that for?" Sal asked Buddy.

"The next place he ends up, ain't no ladies gonna be tricked by his good looks," he said with a chuckle. The sound of his laughter made the shadow of Hardin shrink some by comparison.

Ms. Parker rushed over and hugged him. Buddy winced as she squeezed his side, but didn't stop her.

"Damn waste of bullets!" Sal remarked.

Chapter 14

Wounded Men Get Strange Ideas

It wasn't till midday when a small crowd began to shuffle into the Foggy Dew, some of them so hungover they thought they were going to die, again. Most just ordered coffee, not being able to hold down anything solid. Wasn't much to celebrate in Damnation, but Malachi had been unanimously disliked, and his departure was like the Fourth of July. Folks that'd been dead eighty years tied one on like they had croaked yesterday.

"Ah, this belly wash'll never fix me up," Spiffy complained.

"Yeah, I'd give anything for a drop a cream to lighten it up," Red said.

Since you couldn't get milk out of the dead cows, you had to drink your coffee black. A lot of folks put whiskey in it so it wouldn't taste as bad after a few sips. Red peeled white paint chips from the wall and stirred them into his cup.

"What the hell you doin'?" Sal asked.

"Ain't like it's gonna kill me." he shrugged. "I like a little color in my Arbuckle's is all. Sure couldn't make it taste no worse."

"Good thing Buddy's a fat bastard," Spiffy said. "Otherwise that bullet wouldn't just winged 'em. If he was skinny like me it mighta hit somethin' important." He grabbed his crotch with a smirk.

"Ain't much chance of hitting *anything* important on *you*," Red teased. "'Specially your pin dick."

"And if he was skinny," I put in, "the bullet mighta missed him entirely."

"Fair enough," Spiffy conceded.

"I just hope Buddy heals up before there's any more trouble with them wolves," Whiny Pete fretted. "They still got a hankering for Ms. Parker's baby, don't they?"

"I wonder why they ain't come back yet?" Red asked.

"Prolly still healin'," Spiffy suggested. "When the vampire tossed 'em through the windows they got cut up pretty good, didn't they?"

"Whatever the reason," Sal interrupted. "We ain't got much in the way of defenses if they do come."

"Nigel's still around," I said.

"Vampire's too unpredictable," Sal said.

"How about Hardin?"

"After what happened with Stumpy? He's about as reliable as a woman's watch. Could shoot one of us just as easily as a wolf. Unless the wolf beat him in dice, of course."

"Can we arrange that?" Red asked.

"You can't roll dice with paws. But that gives me an idea, in case I ever need Hardin to get rid of anyone," Sal said, more to himself than us.

Buddy was recovering in the hotel and couldn't get out of bed. Folks either healed or died in Damnation. Wasn't any doctoring or medicines to give you. You just wrapped a wound. If it started to rot, before long somebody usually shot the man for complaining too much. Buddy looked like he'd mend up with proper bed rest. Ms. Parker brought him his meals during the day and sat playing cards with him. I brought him supper. By evening time, he was nearly climbing the walls out of boredom.

"Want me to fetch you a pen and ink?" I asked him one evening.

"What for?" Buddy asked.

"You seem to take to scribbling."

"Nah." Buddy waved his hand. "I don't need that hogwash no more."

I started to collect the dirty dishes and make my way out.

"Hold it there a minute, Tom. I didn't mean nothing by saying scribbling was hogwash."

"Oh, I know, Buddy. No offense taken."

"No, wait. Lemme explain. It's just that when my spirits were sunk, I thought I didn't have the nerve for gunfights. I figured I needed to be good at something else."

"You wanted to find something else to impress Ms. Parker with?"

"Yeah, but not just that. See a man needs to be good at something. Gives him self-worth, whether it's pouring drinks like Sal, or scribbling like you, or shooting real fast."

"I know, Buddy," I said. "Folks eat lead all the time 'cause they got nothing left, and they ain't good at nothing. Hell, I almost did before I started *The Crapper*."

"Really?"

"Sure, when I first arrived, times were tough. Damnation wasn't the civilized town you see here today."

"You sayin' it was even *worse!*?"

"Shit, there were gunfights almost hourly some days. I couldn't shoot or play poker worth a piss, and cripples didn't stand a chance of lasting more'n a couple of weeks. Too easy of a target for bullies. And everyone had to bully somebody to show they weren't weak. The boys all bet I'd be smelling sulfur by the end of the week. I knew my chances were slim. Worst part was the waiting—like a death sentence with no guarantee of meals or a cot in the meantime. On my third night, I stuck a pistol in my mouth just to get it over with. Then I thought about how nobody would remember I was even here. Struck me as sad. I reckoned there should be some record that a man had come and passed through this dusty town— even if he only lasted a few days.

"That night I wrote my obituary. By the time I finished, I was blind drunk. Had to pinch off a loaf, so I visited the commode. While I was sitting there, I musta pinned it to the back of the door and forgot all about it. Hadn't thought of it at the time, but the location offered a captive audience. Everyone's grateful for something to read while they're doing their business—least the lettered ones.

"Next day, I was still no good at cards or shooting, but some of the fellas saw my obituary in the latrine. They gave me a few coins to listen to their stories and put 'em to paper. Turned out, they were all scared they wouldn't last the week, and they liked the idea of a record of their lives. That became *The Crapper*. I wrote it out by hand every couple of weeks, listing the new arrivals, what they done, and where they came from.

"Every so often, I still had to shoot a quarrelsome drunkard, but most folks let me be. A year later, the woodblock press came down the road on a coach that was headed for a new frontier town. It let me print a mess of copies to sell to each man. Ain't thought about eating a lead plumb since."

"Shit, Tom. Why didn't you tell me that story earlier? It's downright *inspiring!* When I hear it put that way, I ain't sure why I wasted so much damn time sulking and doubting myself. Coulda just pulled myself up by the bootstraps like you done and shot Malachi and them railroad men."

"Guess it's not so easy when you ain't sure if you're gonna make it through the rough patch," I said.

"Ah, I knew I was gonna make it." he blushed. "Just forgot for a spell, is all."

I finished collecting Buddy's dishes and put them on a tray. As I turned to go, he called out, "One more thing, Tom. Scribbling's a lot harder than shooting people. Don't let anybody ever tell you different. I kilt lotsa people, but I couldn't fill one single damn page!"

"I'm sure you woulda got the hang of it eventually," I laughed. "Besides, I filled more pages than I can count, and it don't mean a one of 'em are any good."

"Hmm…" Buddy scratched his whiskers. "Guess that's another thing that's easier about gunfights. Long as they ain't standing, you know you done a good job."

"I reckon so. Anyway, glad to see you got your jolly back, Buddy."

"My jolly?"

"Yeah, some folks reckon that's where your speed comes from. Long as you keep laughing, ain't nobody can outdraw you."

"That so?" He chuckled until a splinter of pain shot through his side and he had to grip it with a wince. "Tom, remind me when I'm healed that I owe you for that pen you lent me. I snapped it in frustration when I couldn't use it properly."

"Don't worry, Buddy. I made lots of money this month wagering you wouldn't make much of a scribbler."

"Is that so?"

"It's the only reason I'm still around."

"Guess we're square." he shrugged. "Say, Tom, there was another thing I been meanin' to ask. You really think you'll get into heaven if you don't shoot no one for a year?"

"Not sure. Gotta have something to look forward to though, right?"

"I suppose. Why you wanna get to heaven so bad anyway? Ain't you like it here, playing cards and drinking with us?"

"It ain't that. There's some people that got kilt on account of some lies I wrote a long time ago. Their lives got cut short. They shoulda had their time. So I reckon I owe them an apology."

"You wanna go to heaven so you can *apologize* to people?"

"Yup," I said.

"Well that's the dangdest reason I ever heard."

"'Sides, nobody around here's had a bath in years. Ya'll smell worse than hogs in the heat of July!"

The Crapper

Comings & Goings: *Four railroad workers from Pennsylvania departed the same day they arrived after unwisely testing John Hardin's patience. I am told their names were Fred, Douglas, Paul, and something else. They all had wives and children and* *bragged of being hard workers. Apparently, they weren't bad sorts when they were on their own, but when the gang came together they got rambunctious in their one-upmanship. As we can all attest, the company of men often brings out the worst in a fella.*

Buddy also shot the good looks off the face of Malachi, who was probably the most unrepentantly evil man ever to set foot in Damnation. Good riddance! He had a long career of killing and raping the innocent, of which he intended to add Ms. Parker to the list. Ms. Parker confirmed that he was from Chicago.

Chapter 15

Lucky

For the better part of a week things were pretty slow. Not even any new Indians came to town. Then two new fellas showed up at the same time. They didn't have the scare in them like most. Just looked hungry. One fella was real large, bigger than Buddy even, and hairier too. His buddy was short and slight with a gray handlebar mustache.

"Where you fellas coming from?" Sal asked.

"Topeka," the little one said.

Sal placed a couple of dust-cutters in front of them and knocked his knuckle on the bar to let them know they were on the house.

"Just getting in today? Looks like them cuts healed up a while ago." There were gashes on their arms that had already scabbed over.

The large fella looked questioningly at Sal.

"Ain't that what done you in? Looks like you two been in a knife fight with each other and you both lost. In case you ain't figured it out yet, you're dead."

"Oh, those are old wounds," the small one replied. "We're miners. Yes, we know we're dead. Our mine collapsed on us."

"Oh? Didn't know there was much mining in Kansas," Sal said casually as he worked his way down the bar wiping up glass marks. The two fellas kept scanning the room, looking over everyone's faces real good.

"How'd they take to the news of being dead?" I asked Sal.

"Didn't faze 'em none."

"Maybe they saw it coming," I said.

"Could be. But something about them fellas don't add up."

"How's that?"

"For one, I ain't never seen miners with no dirt under their fingernails."

"Hmm, me neither."

"Also, they both got cuts up and down their arms, but that ain't what done them in. Their mine collapsed. Only they ain't blue in the face from suffocatin' like them other boys."

"If they ain't miners, who you reckon they are?"

"Not sure, but I don't like the looks of 'em."

The two new men kept scanning the room like they were counting how many of us they could take on before someone drew. With Buddy in the hotel and Nigel staying clear of the Foggy Dew on account of Ms. Parker, we couldn't put up much of a stand. Sal wasn't bad with a scattergun. A few others could shoot, but most of them could hardly hit a slow moving man.

"Go up to the hotel and make sure Ms. Parker don't come down," I whispered to Whiny Pete. As he took off out the front door, the two new men watched him.

"Got any women?" the big fella asked.

"There's some old broads playin' gin in the corner. Don't suppose you'd like to give them a whirl on the dance floor."

"Any younger ones?"

"Just Mabel," Sal said. "The redhead over by the dice table, but she's spoken for."

The big fella trotted over while smacking his lips, and eyed Mabel up real good. Hardin slid his coat back revealing an ivory gun handle. The bearded man stooped down and gave a sniff at her tummy. Hardin's fingertip brushed against the butt, letting him know he was just a wrist-cock away from eating a bullet.

"Lose something, friend?" Hardin smiled.

The big fella snorted, then stood and returned to the bar.

"Ain't her," he told the little guy.

"Who you fellas looking for?" Sal asked. "Maybe I can help."

"Brunette in a white dress."

"Ain't seen any. Did you try the Indians' camp? Maybe she prefers men with feathers on their heads."

They both gulped down their drinks and walked out.

"Them had to be a couple of mutts," Spiffy said.

"Course they was," Red said.

"Chief's gonna have his hands full," I said.

"A couple tomahawks ain't gonna stop them," Red said. "They'll be back."

"They must not've told the rest of the pack about Ms. Parker," Sal added. "The pack would get suspicious if they cause a ruckus with the Indians, then they heard a mess of shooting and howling in here right after. Might buy us some time, but Red's right. They'll be back."

"Hopefully Buddy'll mend by then," I added. "Or maybe Nigel'll lend a hand."

The prospect of getting eaten sobered the men up. Despite being as full as ticks on stagger juice, everyone was a little jittery. A short while later, when the door creaked open, they all flinched like the devil himself had arrived. Turned out to be just a skinny fella with buckteeth and a splash of freckles on his cheeks. He wasn't a child nor quite a man yet, being somewhere between hay and grass. He crept to the bar, looking scared as a whore in church.

"Think he's a wolf?" I asked.

"Nah, too nervous," Sal said.

The kid didn't even ask where he was. Just wanted a line of credit for the poker table.

"What's your name, son?" Sal asked.

"Lucky," he said sheepishly.

"Guess you weren't today." Sal motioned to the bullet hole in his forehead. A few of the fellas at the bar laughed. The kid just nodded blankly, like he was accustomed to being teased. Sal slid a stack of ten chips across the bar.

"Pay back thirty at the end of the day—if you're still around."

It was the only way for the house to stay ahead, since most folks lost their chips and got sent to hell within a couple of hours. Lucky walked over to a table where Red and Spiffy and a couple of farmers were playing stud.

"No new blood," Red told the kid. "It's bad luck."

"Aw, come on now," Spiffy intervened. "The boy's just been shot in the head. Probably gonna lose his stack and get shot again in another hour. Might as well give him a chance. 'Sides, you ain't won a hand in hours."

"I's just pacing myself," Red said.

"Sorry, mister," Lucky said timidly. "I understand your not wanting me to play'n all." He had big watery calf eyes, like his momma got made into steaks before he weaned off her tits. "Truth is, if I was you, I wouldn't want me playin' neither. I prolly will get shot pretty quick. I was just hoping to get in a few hands first."

Red gave in. "All right, deal the cards, but if you bring me bad luck, kid, I'm gonna put another hole in your head."

Lucky had a seat and didn't say a peep as he received his cards. Red took one look at his, then slammed them down on the table. "I get the same damn shitty cards *every* time! You even shuffling 'em?"

The dealer didn't bother responding to Red's gripes. He just placed his finger on the table in front of the next man. The two farmers folded, so it came down to Lucky and Spiffy. Spiffy raised three bucks and Lucky called him.

"Ain't ya even gonna look at yer cards?" Spiffy asked.

He turned over a pair of jacks. They were good enough to beat Spiffy's tens.

"Where you from, kid?"

"Oklahoma."

"My cousin had a ranch outside Fort Gibson," Spiffy said. "His cattle kept getting poached. They took 'em cross the state line to Arkansas to sell. Do any rustlin'?"

"No, sir."

"Ah, you're too small to steal cattle anyway. Probably couldn't rustle a billy goat," Spiffy laughed.

On the next hand, Red took a look at his cards and hollered at the dealer once more. This time Spiffy, the kid, and one of the farmers stayed in. Spiffy got bold and raised five bucks. The sodbuster folded, but Lucky saw it and raised five more.

"Hey, Red, lemme borrow five bucks," Spiffy said.

"I ain't lending you shit."

"C'mon, Red. Look at these cards. I can't lose." Spiffy gave him a peek. Red shrugged and slid the money to the center of the table.

"Pot's square," the dealer called out.

Lucky laid down three eights. "Goddamnit!" Spiffy swore and turned over a pair of kings. Nobody was looking to take over his chair, so he just sat there moping. He had fashioned himself a real Renaissance cowboy. Thought he was good at both gambling and screwing. It saddened him to think he wasn't much good at the one and probably would never do the other again.

"How's it you got that bullet in the head?" he asked Lucky.

"Got shot in a card game," the boy answered.

The cards were dealt again. Red took a look at his and slapped his knee with an all-fired glee he surely was not known for. "By golly, I *finally* got some dang cards!" he called out.

Everyone within earshot reckoned he got bored with the shit cards he was dealt and decided to bluff. "I bet ten dollars," he said while trying his hardest not to twitch or blink. His face looked ready to break apart at any moment. It was a tall bet to match if you didn't already have a stake in the pot.

"The sun even shines on a dog's ass some days," one farmer said and folded. The other quickly followed.

"Not here it don't," Spiffy added. "Ain't got no sun *or* dogs in Damnation!"
"If you ain't got chips on the table, quit your jawin' now," Red threatened.
Lucky didn't have to think on it long. He saw the bet and raised
it three more. Red turned to him with a sourpuss. "Hey, boy, you catch that bullet
for cheatin'?"

"I ain't never cheated in my life, sir," Lucky answered in earnest. "Always
been good in cards. Been beat up lotsa times on account of it. Usually, I
throw down a few hands so the other players don't get too angry. They
hate gettin' beat out right. This afternoon, I was playing stud in Tulsa,
and a big ol' cowboy kept riding me. If you're a skinny kid like me and
you're any good at cards, there's always a big 'ole cowboy riding you. No
escaping it. He said I was a pissant good for nothing. Said my momma was
a trollop and anything he could to get my goat. I let him win a few hands,
but he kept riding me. So finally, I swore I wasn't gonna throw down no
more hands to the bastard, even if he sent me to my grave. The very next
hand I drew aces and eights."

"A dead man's hand," Spiffy remarked solemnly.

"The cowboy went all in with a pair of queens," Lucky continued. "When
he saw my cards, he pulled his gun. Next thing I knew, I was walking up
the road to this dusty old town and this was the first place I come to. I
saw there was a card game going on, and sure enough a big ol' cowboy's
riding me again. So reckoned I musta wound up in hell. Figured I might
as well beat y'all straight out and see where they send me next. It couldn't
be much worse than this shitheel town."

"Enough of your jawin'!" Red broke in and threw three chips on the
pile to see Lucky's bet, then laid down a pair of aces. "What you got, kid?"
he asked smugly.

Lucky laid down three queens, looking as grim and resigned as an
undertaker. Red was flabbergasted. He pulled his gun, pointed it at the kid,
and cocked the hammer back. Lucky closed his eyes and braced for the blast.
To his credit, he didn't beg for his life like a Fre. Didn't even say a peep.

"Well, Lucky, I guess this just ain't your day," Red said after a thoughtful
moment and uncocked the hammer. "I'm gonna let you live—at least what
passes for living here."

Chapter 16

The Miners Who Didn't Mine

"Get Buddy," Sal whispered to Whiny Pete as soon as they came through the door. It was suppertime, and we hadn't been expecting them so soon. Hoped it'd be at least another couple days before the big fella and the little guy with the mustache darkened the doorway again.

"Buddy's still laid up."

"Get 'em anyway. And tell that vampire what's going on in case he cares to help. We're gonna need him."

The two men began crowding the sodbusters in front of the bar. The average farm boy was bold in fighting but had little experience in handling a pistol. They might've used a rifle to scare coyotes away from a henhouse but drawing and aiming a sidearm was another matter. The big fella stepped on the foot of a feisty churn twister who was just minding his own business. "What's the big idea?" he asked, looking cross.

"Where's the woman in white?" His eyes glowed red like hot branding irons. The farmer hadn't been around long enough to know about the werewolves and thought himself brave.

"I ain't seen no woman, but I reckon if there was one she'd stay clear of the likes of you," he replied. "You smell like a wet dog."

Those were the last words the man spoke. The big fella gripped his throat and pushed the balls of his thumbs into his breathing pipe. The farmer gasped and choke in his hands while everyone watched. As the body dropped to the floor, a hunk of his windpipe clung to his finger. He flicked it off, then turned to a cowboy and asked again, "Where's the woman in white?"

The bronc buster reached for his sidearm, but he fumbled the handle while trying to clear leather. Meanwhile, the smaller fella's neck grew half a foot in a blink and a snout popped out of his face. Then a million little hairs pushed through his skin, forming a gray shaggy coat right before our eyes. By the time the cowboy had his gun raised, the little wolf was on all fours. He bit into his wrist causing the gun to drop. The big fella moved in closer and wrapped his fingers around the cowboy's throat. Ms. Parker had been in the powder room, and she appeared at the doorway to investigate the commotion just then. Her scent stirred their hunger. The big fella bolted toward her, transforming into a brown shaggy wolf mid-gallop. His hindquarters kicked over a chair as he scrambled across the room, moving too fast for anyone to take aim. He sprang for poor defenseless Ms. Parker, and there wasn't anyone nearby to save her.

Then a shot rang out and the wolf turned over in the air, crashing into a table. Buddy stood at the doorway with a pistol smoldering in his grip. A bloodied bandage wrapped his gut, and he grimaced from the pain it caused him to stand. The smaller wolf snapped at Buddy's wrist, and he dropped his gun. A nearby sodbuster swung a boot at the beast's ribs. It yelped, then sprang on top of him, chewing his neck till it gushed blood like Old Faithful. Then it leapt on Buddy with its teeth bearing down on his throat. Buddy gripped its jaws, cutting his fingers on the razor-sharp teeth. The wound on his side split open in the struggle and was leaking a fair amount of blood.

Sal leveled his shotgun but couldn't get a clear shot. The only one with a good sightline and a steady arm was Hardin. His hand lingered beside his pistol, but he didn't draw. Looked to be calculating something. Just one throttle could've severed Buddy's head, leaving nothing between the wolf and Ms. Parker—or the rest of us. Nobody wanted to interfere, likely because they were scared of retribution from the rest of the pack. Hardin certainly had the grit, but he still hadn't decided who was the worse enemy.

Suddenly a burst of wind blew through the door, darkening the whole room with dust. The mangy wolf was lifted off Buddy and thrown to the floor. As the dust settled, Nigel stood above him. We had never seen him kill in anger before, only in amusement or annoyance. He bit into the beast's neck and peeled back a strip of furry skin, revealing the muscles on his withers. Instinct must've kicked in, and he lost all control. Maybe some part of him still hoped warm blood flowed in the animal. Mabel covered her eyes, but Ms. Parker didn't look away. The floorboards reddened, and chunks of wolf meat clung to the walls and ceiling. After tasting the cold blood, he spit it out in disgust.

Nigel was tuckered out, and without warm blood to replenish him he could hardly stand. He collapsed in a chair. The larger wolf quietly got to its feet, despite the bullet in its side, and made a break for the door.

"Get him before he alerts the pack!" Nigel yelled.

Buddy scooped his gun up from the floor and fired from the hip but missed. Sal took aim with his scattergun, but by the time the bystanders had cleared, it was already out the door. A few cowboys scrambled out to the road, but their six shooters had no accuracy at a distance.

"If he makes it back, we're all done for," Nigel said. I grabbed a Winchester from the umbrella stand and hobbled to the doorway. My pa had taught me how to shoot duck when I was a kid before I busted up my leg, and I was a fair shot.

"Ain't you tryin' *not* to shoot no one?" Whiny Pete asked.

"That won't matter if them wolves get us," I said and took aim. The wolf was just a few yards shy of turning the corner, where the buildings would provide cover. I had his hindquarters in my crosshairs. Just as I was about to squeeze the trigger, a flash of lighting brightened the sky. Then a jagged blue-white bolt ripped through the cloud cover to the center of the road. Of all the places it could have struck, it hit the exact spot where the wolf was. The beast keeled over and was cooked where he lay. Gray smoke rose from its singed fur. Two cowboys hustled out and carried the carcass back before it was spotted. The smell of burnt hair filled the room.

"Thank you for saving us," Ms. Parker said to Nigel.

His fangs were still sticking out on account of his hunger hadn't been satisfied. "Go away!" he ordered.

"But there's nothing to worry about now that the werewolves are dead."

"It is not them that I worry for. Flee from me before I finish what they intended to do."

Ms. Parker bolted out of the saloon in tears.

"Hey!" Buddy said as he got to his feet. "Why you scaring the lady?" He was unsteady from loss of blood and needed the wall for support. He pulled his gun out and began twirling it around his finger playfully.

"This is none of your business, gunslinger."

"Well, I just made it my business that ladies don't go running from here in tears after they been attacked by wolves—and maybe insulted by a vampire."

Nigel looked at him icily, then shook his head. Buddy kept spinning his pistol around his finger as the blood from his wound darkened his shirt. Then his eyes rolled backward and his knees buckled. The gun slipped off his fingertip and landed on the ground, firing a shot into the base of the bar.

"Ah hell, we'll call it even," Buddy said.

"Get those damn wolves hauled off to the pigpen before the rest of the pack sees 'em," Sal ordered. "And get a damn mop to wipe the guts from the ceiling."

"You think the pack knew they were coming here?" I asked.

"We'll know soon enough."

Chapter 17

The Homesteaders

Time passed in poker hands. The average man could play ten or so an hour, or about a hundred a day. Added up to upward of seven hundred a week. Went by fast if you were winning, slow as molasses if you were losing. The only value a man had in Damnation was how many chips were in front of him or how fast he could draw. Large stacks bullied small stacks into folding, and small stacks waited till large stacks got bored and bet on losing hands. Likewise, the stout picked on the measly, and the quick guns shot the slow.

The town was growing on account of more homesteaders getting killed while traveling west. Every day more Germans, Irish, English, and Czechs wandered out of the dust. They'd crossed the ocean with hungry children for the hope of free land. Packed everything they owned in rickety wagons to stake a plot in the frontier. Then their crops failed, or their livestock got sick, or someone pushed them off their land. They ran out on their families and tried to rob stagecoaches. They got into knife fights at whorehouses or got scalped by Indians. Some just fell off their horses, drunk in the night, and woke up in Damnation with a bump on the head and an emptiness in the gut that wasn't ever going to be filled again. By the time they got to the tables, they had nothing left to lose. They raised like they had aces in the hole and turned over broken straights and missed flushes. When they couldn't get no more to drink on credit, they fought over pennies and blew each other to bits.

Gunfights were more commonplace, but the newer fellas were usually lousy shots. They just kept winging each other till they slumped over and bled out. If nobody spared a bullet to put them out of their misery, they moaned all the way to the pigpen. While their legs were being gobbled up, they'd still be griping about how their cards were shit or their gun had jammed.

Not everyone had the temperament to last in Damnation. Needed a degree of detachment a lot of folks couldn't summon. You could spot them a mile off. They had more expectation than resignation in their eyes and just couldn't let things be. Started eyeing others' possessions or positions of respect. The old-timers knew better than to tangle with those just passing through. And if they tangled with us, Buddy'd usually set them straight. Since Ms. Parker was sweet on him again, he was back to his old jolly self. He'd come in with guns blazing and send a couple to hell at once.

But when Buddy wasn't around, it was a free-for-all. Hardin didn't care much one way or the other. Mabel and the dice games were all he needed. Nobody messed with him, and he didn't mess with nobody, unless they rolled a number he couldn't match. Could tell he was weighing things over whenever a ruckus started though, calculating who was the fastest and who he'd have to go against eventually.

"Why you suppose Hardin ain't gone against Buddy?" Whiny Pete asked. "Think he's yellow?"

"Hardin ain't scared of no man," Red declared.

"Might not be a man he's scared of." Sal winked.

"Interesting perspective," I said. "You think Hardin's scared of Nigel, maybe hoping Buddy'll go against him first?"

"They both seem sweet on Ms. Parker," Whiny Pete put in. "They might fall out over her."

"Ah, Nigel won't even be in the same room with her," I said. "Reckon, he ain't gonna come courting her."

"Maybe he wants to eat her baby, or maybe he wants to court her. I don't know," Sal huffed. "Either way, Buddy ain't gonna like it. So if I was Hardin, I'd wait till one sent the other to hell. Then take out whoever's left. Less work that way."

"Buddy'd be pretty tough for anyone to beat now that he's got his jolly back," I argued. "Maybe even Nigel."

Nigel sat up on his balcony most days smoking his pipe. When there wasn't a gunfight to watch, he stared at the sky. He could go a whole day without moving—just recalling the past, I suppose. When you had a few centuries of wear on your boots, sorting through faces and names could take a while. Eventually, he had to wonder on the meaning of the lightning. Couldn't be a coincidence that it struck the exact spot the werewolf was crossing. Half the fellas reckoned God smote the wolf to protect us. The other half reckoned he was punishing the beast for other stuff. If Nigel had a different take on it, he wasn't sharing it.

"Vampire prolly reckons the devil done it," Red speculated, "since that's who made him. Like how we think God done it since he made us."

"What makes you think the devil made him?" I asked.

"'Cause he's evil. The devil makes all evil stuff."

"How about Malachi? Did the devil make him?"

Red thought on it a moment. "Nah, the devil prolly got in him after he was born, but vampires ain't natural."

"According to your reckoning, if the devil made the vampire, he made the werewolves, too," I said.

"Of course! Wolves as big as lions ain't natural neither."

"If the devil was behind that lightning, why would he strike one of his creations in order to protect another?" I asked.

"Dunno!" Red answered. "Why would God make one man rich and handsome and another man poor and ugly?"

Just then, two of the homesteaders started brawling over cards. A table got flipped over, and the ruckus interrupted the conversation. The newbies who couldn't afford guns often boxed or scratched each other's eyes out. When the fighting spilled out into the street, Nigel was like a bean-eater watching cockfights. Probably would've wagered on them if there was another vampire around. He might've had a soft spot for Ms. Parker, but he still had a cruel streak. Must've got a taste for violence with all the wars he lived through. Never interfered in any of our quarrels though, like the game was better appreciated without his meddling—unless Ms. Parker was in any danger.

One time, a sodbuster drew on a cowboy while she happened to be passing behind him. Nigel had swooped down like a vulture and took his whole arm off before he could shoot. Some folks still insisted Nigel was waiting for her baby to be born so he could eat it. Nobody mentioned it to her though. Most evenings, after she retired, he popped into the Foggy Dew for a glass of gin, but he usually didn't offer much to the conversation.

There was one other subject on everyone's mind. As Ms. Parker's belly grew, everyone got real curious about what would come out. Nothing had ever been born in Damnation before. Everyone came from out of the dust cloud. Some expected the devil might pop out. Christian folks thought it might be the second coming of Jesus.

"Ain't no way Jesus'd show up in this shithole," Sal argued. "He ain't even been back to earth in all this time, and they got sunshine and whorehouses."

"Could be a martian," Spiffy speculated. "They mighta put one of their soldiers in Ms. Parker's belly so they could attack us. Like one of them

Greek toe-jam horses."

"You mean a Trojan horse?" I asked.

"Whatever ya call it." Spiffy shrugged.

"Enough of your outer space nonsense!" Sal hollered.

"Well, if the devil comes out of Ms. Parker, we can all just head to hell and have the run of the place," Red said. "Though I don't look forward to running into Jack Finney again. He sure was an asshole."

"Been a while since them werewolves got sent to hell," Spiffy said. "Think they really didn't tell the others they were coming here?"

"If they had, the baby would make for a small meal divvied up among a pack," Red said. "I know I'd keep it quiet if I was sitting on the last pork chop."

"Good point," Spiffy agreed.

"The pack will eventually figure out those two wolves are missing," Nigel said from the end of the bar. "Werewolves keep track of their own, even if they don't share everything, and they will come looking for them."

"Well, we'll just have to send their asses to hell like them other two," Buddy boasted.

"You talk bold, but you have not faced the fury of an entire werewolf pack," Nigel said. "There are at least fifty wolves in town. I faced ten once while at full strength and barely escaped with my life. In my weakened state, I couldn't take on more than three or four. Remember, I've not had warm blood for nearly a century."

"It's a good thing you got me here then," Buddy said.

Nigel shook his head and sipped his gin.

"We can't trouble Ms. Parker over it," I said. "She could lose the child worrying over them wolves."

"If she did, would her baby go to heaven or hell?" Whiny Pete asked.

"Heaven," Sal answered. "The baby ain't had no chance to do nothin' wrong."

"So what if it grows up here and shoots somebody, then gets shot itself?" I argued. "Does it go to hell? Seems only fair for it to get another chance like the rest of us had."

Nigel's scratchy voice called out with contempt, "This God you dream up, what makes you think he is fair? Humans live eighty years if they are lucky. I was alive for over three hundred years. My child didn't even make it out of the womb. Any god who would orchestrate such disparity amongst his creations certainly is not concerned with the infant offspring of a suicidal woman."

The vampire could get kind of philosophical at times.

Chapter 18

The Inventor

An old man lay on the floor in the corner of the Foggy Dew, moaning for days. He begged for scraps, but nobody gave him any so he ate the crumbs off the floor. Somehow he'd made it to a ripe old age, but he would've been better off dying sooner, with a stronger body more capable of defending himself. Wild-eyed newbies delivered kicks to his ribs on their way to the commode.

No one wanted to waste a bullet on him, figuring they'd need all they had if more wolves showed up. From all his jawing, we learned that the drunkard had died, due to a lack of forethought, by freezing on the open plains. He was born in Boston but had a terrible fear of water that drove him inland, trying to get as far from the ocean as possible.

When he first came in the door, Sal reluctantly gave him ten chips, reckoning they'd be gone in an hour. Sure enough, he drank up five in half an hour, then bet the rest on a single hand of poker. Worst part was he'd didn't even have a pair. Then he laid down in the corner with his back as a mattress and his belly as a blanket and started groaning.

"Should be some sorta rules 'round here," Buddy said. "Can't just let a man starve to death."

"But he's already dead," Sal said.

"Still, shouldn't let him suffer like that. He's a man, ain't he?"

"You kiddin' me? You could send that halfwit to a hundred towns like this one," Sal said. "Give him as many chances as you like. He'd never learn. He'd spend half his money on whiskey, then piss the rest away on the first crappy hand he was dealt. Some people ain't got no sense. There ain't no fixing 'em! Why should the rest of us have to shoulder their load?"

"Should be some sort a help for his kind," Buddy argued. "Not everybody can play cards or shoot a gun or pour drinks like you. They still deserve to eat. Maybe that fella's got a knack for drawing pretty pictures or making music on some instrument we ain't got here. Just 'cause we ain't found a use for him don't mean he should starve on the floor. Musta been some reason why he was sent here instead of hell. Hey, old man, what good you done in your life?" Buddy asked.

He opened his cracked lips and muttered softly, "Had a sister."

"Hear that, boys?" Buddy said. "Probably had a baby sister that he took care of 'cause his parents done run out on 'em. You gonna let a man like that starve on the floor?"

Sal looked cross at Buddy. "What are we supposed to do, find a use for every lost soul that walks through the door?"

"I suppose not," Buddy said. "But I ain't gotta watch 'em starve while you got plenty back there. Just 'cause you cut up some dead pigs that wandered down the road and threw 'em in a frying pan, don't mean you're in charge of who eats." Buddy pulled out his pistol and put it on the bar. "Now I'm telling you to feed that old man or your ass is gonna meet them two wolves we kilt."

"You robbin' me?" Sal asked.

"Nah." Buddy put his gun back in his holster. "Put it on my tab. In fact, put it *all* on my tab. Feed every hungry sumabitch in here. I'm… What ya call it? Redis'buted stuff!"

A mess of stinky bog-trotters all rose from the back of the room and headed to the bar at once. Even those who just ate were lining up for free grub.

"That'd be a mighty large tab," Sal said.

"When you come to collect on it," Buddy warned, "you better learn yourself a knack better'n pourin' drinks and complainin' about poor folk."

Sal tossed a rag angrily on the ground and kicked a barrel. Buddy'd gone too far this time. Sure, Hardin drank and ate for free, but even he wouldn't propose giving food away to *everyone*. Of course, Sal wasn't dumb enough to go against Buddy. Not after he already shot six men who had the jump on him, not to mention Jack Finney while he was stone cold drunk. Even if Sal got off a shot, he might still get mowed down like Malachi did.

"Ain't fair, Buddy. I'm just trying to do right by the system. Wasn't even me that set it up. I used to warsh glasses for the fella who ran the saloon before me. Someone stuck a knife in his gut. Know what his last words were? *Never give nothing away for free.* I start givin' away grub, and the coins'll be worthless. You'll see! Then poker won't mean so much. You damn sure don't wanna see this place when a hundred outlaws ain't got no card games to distract 'em. How you gonna protect Ms. Parker then, huh?" "Dunno." Buddy gave it some thought. "Could stop making bullets." "Um, we tried that," I said. "Pardon me for interrupting, Buddy. After the last blacksmith got shot, there wasn't anybody who knew how to make bullets. Men started beating each other with chairs. There were wrasslin' matches all day long. Hard to maintain order if brute strength rules. At least guns level the playing field a bit. Gives the smaller fellas a chance. When you make two men go out in the road and count to ten before they shoot, it makes an event of it. And when folks line up to watch a gunfight once in a while, they wonder if a thing's worth quarrelling over. Eventually, a new blacksmith showed up. Luckily, he ain't no good at cards so the money he collects gets spread around."

"Hell, if we didn't have no bullets," Red chimed in, "the wolves wouldn't let us have no pigs."

"I guess that's true," Buddy admitted. "Sounds like we need a sheriff." "Last fella with that idea didn't fare so well," I said. "You want the job, Buddy?"

"Seems like a pain in the ass. Lemme think on it a spell."

Sal went to the kitchen and fetched a plate of cold leftover bacon. Then he marched over to the moaning man and dropped it on the ground in front of him. The old fella grabbed a piece and gnawed at it with his sparse teeth.

"Hey, old man, if you was such a dang saint taking care of your baby sister, why the hell'd you end here instead of heaven?" Sal asked.

Bits of gristle collected on his whiskers as he tore into the bacon. "Married her," he mumbled between bites. "And she was a good poke after I broke her in."

In a flash of anger, Buddy turned around and pulled out his gun in one swift movement. Then he stood over the man for a moment, his hand trembling in debate. In the end, he couldn't stop himself. The bullet sent a splash of cold blood back on his gun. He wiped the barrel off on his pant leg, then reloaded the empty chamber with a regretful scowl.

Sal, for one, seemed happy to have one less mouth to feed. He picked up the plate of bacon and brought it back into the kitchen to wash the blood off for tomorrow's breakfast.

The Crapper

Comings: *Lucky's already relieved most folks of some money at the poker table. He hails from Oklahoma and they reckon he got his luck in cards by selling his soul to the devil. The only* *reason no one's shot him yet is cause they don't want to reunite him with it in hell.*

Goings: *I have been remiss in my duties as a mess of new men have come and gone before I was able to get their stories to paper. Most were sent to hell by each other or Buddy. Hardin shot a few, too. The vampire ripped another fella's arm off, and he bled out. I will list those who had a chance to be put in Sal's ledger and what's believed to have been the cause of their earthly demise.*

—Jack Dougherty, South Dakota, scalped by Indians
—Francis Nugent, Missouri, bad blood
—Tim Clancy, Connecticut, throat cut over money
—Cross-eyed man who couldn't write his name, gut shot
—John Jones, California, got drowned in a river after his panhandle showed some color
—Davey Son-of-a-Bitch Jones, cut with a broken bottle for insulting a man's woman
—Louis Scottsdale, San Antonio, hung for stealing a horse
—Jim Schmidt, Missoula, choked for poaching a man's fishing hole
—Pat O'Malley, New York, drank too much and woke up here, unsure how he died

After speaking to a few folks, I also found out that the sorry sister-screwing geezer who Buddy put out of his misery was a bona fide inventor. He made a pump doohickey that lets people breathe underwater at great depths. Thanks to him, it is now possible to explore regions of the ocean where even the sun's rays can't hardly reach and swim with sea creatures unknown to man. Apparently, he once had a peek at those great depths. Not sure if it was something he saw down there, or just knowing how deep it really was, but it sent him running straight to the plains in fear. Nevertheless, makes you wonder what sort of contraptions he might've rigged up for us here in Damnation. Maybe even a way to get though that wall of dust. Guess we'll never know. Ha!

Chapter 19

New Rules

"You still owe me five bucks!" Red said angrily.

"I don't know what you're on about," Spiffy insisted.

"Don't give me that hogwash. You know damn well what I'm on about. When you was playin' stud with that buck-toothed kid, you didn't have the coin to cover his bet. You showed me a couple kings like they was the best hand in the world and asked for five bucks. I loaned it to ya, and Lucky beat you with triple eights."

"Aw, that didn't count! That was before we knew he was some kinda mind reader. Shit, I wouldn't bet against him now even if I had four aces."

"It don't matter what you know now. That's why they call it gamblin'! You still owe me five bucks, and I'm gonna get it even if I have to take it out of your pocket after I put a few more holes in that fancy suit of yours."

Spiffy didn't bother responding. Ever since Buddy sent Red's gang to hell, everyone knew he was yellow. Every day he drank himself cockeyed just to put off going up against Buddy. His empty threat was swallowed up by the clatter of the saloon.

Four new cowboys had come in that morning, and they were all roistered up and shouting over one another. They'd ate a batch of tainted beef while on a roundup. It turned putrid in their saddlebags, but they were too stingy to slaughter a steer and cut into their profits. They suffered some weeks with blood coming out of both ends as they tried to bring in the herd. When they couldn't mount their horses anymore, the cattle strayed off. Nearest town was over a hundred miles. As they weakened, the coyotes grew bolder, and it was clear they wouldn't be able to fend them off much longer. Decided it was better to go quick and end their misery, so they pointed their guns at one another and pulled the triggers on the count of three. Now that they were dead, they were pleased as punch just to be able to hold anything down. Sal kept their glasses full all day long.

"Ain't them boys drank up their credit by now?" I asked.

"Oh, they're all right," he replied, which was suspicious because Sal didn't think anybody was *all right*.

"I noticed they all got new Remingtons, too."

"Everyone in the room's heeled," Sal defended. "Why should them boys be any different?"

"They wasn't heeled when they come in this morning, and they ain't played any poker yet, so somebody must've given them those pistols. What are you scheming at, Sal?"

"Me?"

"Wouldn't have anything to do with Buddy telling you to feed that geezer for free, would it?"

He just brushed me off. "I don't know what you're on about."

Buddy had been knocking back the bug juice at a hardy pace. He stood in front of the bar, peacefully swaying in his boots. Looked to be feeling about as good as a dead man can feel. He wasn't the truculent sort, unless he was bawling out a logger for disrespecting Ms. Parker or battling a rack of ribs for bites between its narrow bones. One of the rotten beef eaters came by him in a hurry. The fella still had some heft to him, despite the sickness that had done him in. He bumped hard against Buddy's shoulder with the kind of force that should be immediately followed by either an apology or a fistfight. Then he gave Buddy the stink eye, as if he'd been in the wrong.

Buddy wasn't eating drag dust over it though. He just dipped his hat and bowed as if he'd collided with the queen of England, then said, "Pardon me, *ma'am*."

Some men within earshot laughed, which caused the cowboy to redden.

"Don't sass me!" he scolded, and shoved Buddy, who was so drunk he had to squint to see. He stumbled backward but kept on smiling as he caught himself on a stool.

"That how you greet folks where you come from?" Buddy asked cheekily as he regained his footing. "Keep your muck forks off of me."

The man threw a punch. Buddy stepped back to dodge the blow, but wasn't quick enough. It glanced off his cheek, and he winced from the sting. A shove was one thing, but a punch was a whole different matter. Buddy palmed the cowboy's face like a bowling ball and shoved him straight to the floor. The cowboy wasn't quick to rise, but once he got up he started pounding Buddy's stomach, where his wound never fully mended. Buddy drew his gun in a hurry but didn't shoot. Instead, he jammed the barrel down the man's throat, breaking his two front teeth, and tried to reason with him.

"Now see here, mister," Buddy yelled. "I ain't accustomed to shootin' men that ain't pulled on me, but I ain't gonna spend all night trading blows with you. You got two choices. Either go out to the road and draw or walk away, 'cause I had enough. What'll it be?"

Buddy extracted the barrel from between the cowboy's bloodied lips. He spat out some broken teeth and answered, "The road."

Everyone lined the rotted-out boardwalk to watch, except Sneaky Jim, but losing a sip of your drink was a fair price to see a decent gunfight. As Buddy stood in the center of the road waiting, the cowboy conferred with his buddies. Buddy didn't need any advice on aiming and shooting, so he chewed on a piece of straw and gazed drunkenly at the cloud cover.

"I hearda you," the cowboy said as he worked the stiffness out of his holster. "You robbed a stagecoach, then shot up some lawmen. They say you got sent here instead a hell 'cause you was careful 'bout not killin' anyone who didn't draw on you first."

"I hearda you, too," Buddy said.

"Oh yeah?"

"Yer name's shit-for-brains, and you came to Damnation so I can send your ass to hell today."

They took their places back to back in the center of the road. Sal began counting to ten, but the cowboy was not an honorable man. At the count of six, he turned and steadied his barrel across his wrist. The three other cowboys who had eaten tainted beef were in the crowd at Buddy's back. Sure enough, they stepped forward and pulled their guns, too.

I wasn't heeled, but the logger beside me had a sidearm within reach. I probably could've grabbed it and gunned down one or two to even the odds. I'd already gone ten months without shooting anyone though. The possibility of heaven was harder to give up now. Just two more months and I might be saved, or at least know it wasn't possible. After all the turning the other cheek I'd done, I was starting to dream about shooting every loudmouthed bastard that got in my face. Still, odds weren't in my favor. Even if I picked off two of the cowboys, there wasn't much chance of Buddy dodging the other two guns already trained on his back with their triggers half squeezed.

Buddy must've heard the metal barrels leaving leather, because he started counting aloud, drowning out Sal's voice. And when he got to nine, he just kept on saying it over and over, and taking extra-long steps as he did. Must've walked ten paces, just saying, "Nine, nine, nine..." Then he finally turned and drew.

Buddy might've been stink-eyed drunk when he came outside, but it sobered him up real quick to have steel in hand and his survival at stake. As he swiveled forward, he crouched at the same time, like a nimble little ballerina with a cannonball beer gut. The first bullet had real meaning to it. He sent it straight through the chest of the man in the center of the road, like he wanted to make sure he got his point across.

As he fell, the three other men all fired at once. Nobody else in the crowd pulled. Like myself, they must've wrote Buddy off and didn't want to get on the bad side of the winner. Hardin was the only one with enough grit and speed to take them all out anyway. Seeing Buddy facing four men brightened his day. He smiled as the cowboys fired. Likely on account of the extra paces Buddy had taken, all three missed their mark. Hardin frowned. Buddy fired twice more before they had a chance to re-aim.

I'd read a few dime novels about gunslingers and found them all to be wrong about the same thing. It is not the thought of hitting a live target that throws amateurs off. During a gunfight, most first timers do not anticipate how distracted they will be by the sound of their own gun and the echo of their opponent's. They imagine that their hands will be steady, and they will strike their target like the tin cans they have practiced on. They do not anticipate how difficult it will be to concentrate on firing a second shot in the thick of it. And the ones who ain't never shot a gun before are certain to be startled by the loudest noise they ever heard just two feet away from their ears.

Two cowpunchers dropped to the ground at once, both with bullets in their hearts and mouthfuls of dust as their last meals. The fourth man got off a second shot. It shattered a window of the rooming house down the road and some fifteen feet above Buddy's head.

"Ain't ya even *tryin'* to hit me?" Buddy scolded as he stepped forward with his gun at his side. "Let me get this straight. You got four on one, *and* you don't even wait till the count of ten. Hell! I'm flabbergasted." He looked at the man in disgust. "Clearly we can't have any kind of— what'd the vampire call?—*harmonious society* with people like *you* around."

With that, he fired two bullets into the rotten beef-eater's face. Hardin wasn't smiling any longer. He turned and went back into the bar before the Chinaman dragged the bodies to the pigpen.

A couple of newbies fought over the dead men's guns. Sal just gritted his teeth, not being able to claim the weapons since then Buddy'd know he put them up to it.

"So, you decided if you wanna be sheriff or not?" I asked Buddy.

"I suppose I ain't fit for the job," he admitted. "Need somebody who drinks less and won't get drawn into this kinda bullshit." He turned and walked over to the hotel.

"Where's he going?" Sal asked.

"I reckon he's gonna consult the vampire," Red said. "Everyone else in this town sits around drinking all day and fights over nothin'."

Just after supper, Buddy returned to the Foggy Dew with a hammer and a cowhide under his arm. He unrolled it and nailed it to a beam beside the bar so that the fur was facing the wall. On the skin side was written:

Rules

1. Everybody eats.
2. No raping or killing Ms. Parker.
3. No shooting a man that ain't heeled.
4. No back shooting.
5. No killing over dumb shit.
6. The vampire decides whether or not it's dumb shit.
7. If the vampire ain't around, Buddy decides whether or not it's dumb shit, less he's real drunk.
8. If Buddy's real drunk, don't start no dumb shit cause he'll prolly kill y'all anyway.

Nigel wasn't officially declared the sheriff or anything. He didn't want the responsibility of policing men, but it let folks know the pecking order. Hardin glanced up at the rules. His bottom lip curled in disfavor, then he spat some chewing tobacco on the floor and went back to his dice game without a word.

Sal had hoped the notion of free grub would blow over, but it was hard to ignore it written in big letters as the first rule on the wall, and with the backing of the vampire. He wasn't the first to vent his disagreement though. A squeaky voice chirped up from the back of the room, "The wolves are probably gonna come in here and tear us all to pieces any day now, and you're posting *rules!*" We all turned, surprised to find Whiny Pete was doing the talking. The tears on his cheeks showed that the words weren't spoke in anger, but fear. He did give voice to everyone's main concern, and we were curious for a reply.

"Ah, them wolves might come after us in an hour, or it could be ten years..." Buddy said. "Ain't mean we gotta live like a bunch a savages just 'cause we're gonna go to hell eventually."

The room remained quiet as folks considered it in earnest.

"Shit, for a lot of you fellas, this ain't much different from when you was alive," Buddy continued. "Y'all hid out among the willows most days with a bounty on your head and the prospect of a rope necktie not far off. What's the use a goin' on like this? Everybody shootin' each other over nothin'. Ain't no way to live... Or rather, ain't no way to pass the time while you're dead. Can't get no peace! We might as well see if Tom's on the right path with his pacifist ways. Hell, after a year's time, we could all march through the gates of heaven together. Just think... a hundred rotten outlaws up there in the clouds, playin' poker with the saints—and Sneaky Jim stealin' sips from angels whenever they get up to piss. We'd shake things up!"

Red was the first to break the silence with a loud cackle, and the rest quickly joined in till nearly everyone in the room was doubled over in fits of laughter.

"Ah, suit yourself," Buddy said. "Alls I know is I ain't gonna listen to nobody beg for food no more." He stormed out of the saloon. After the laughter died down, folks had to discuss the rules seriously. Couldn't just disregard what the fastest gun and the vampire said. Sal was quietly collecting glasses around the room. He still hadn't replaced Stumpy with a new barback. There were plenty of men willing to do the job, but he seemed happy for the excuse to get away from the bar.

"The way I see it, them rules only hold if someone's around to enforce 'em," Red said.

"Buddy'll enforce 'em," I said.

"Don't be so sure," Spiffy argued. "He's making enemies a man who likes to bend his elbow can't afford to have. Jack only lasted as long as he did 'cause he hardly drank in a town full of drunks."

"He's right," Red said. "Sooner or later, Buddy'll get sloppy, and the guy preparing the grub has a pretty good reason to see him sent to hell. Takes a lot of energy to be on the lookout for hired guns all the time."

"Sal already tried that with them four cowboys and failed," I said. "If he fails again, Buddy's likely to figure it out."

"So what's Sal's next move then?" Red asked. "You reckon he's just gonna lay over and forget about how he was slighted?"

"Not sure what his next move is," I said. "But Sal ain't one to forget a slight."

We reckoned nothing more was going to be said about the matter, at least for the night, so it wasn't worth speculating about. Strong convictions often lost steam between the last whiskey of the night and the first beer of the morning. A short while later though, Sal climbed up on top of a stool. He reckoned he should get out ahead of the issue before folks started thinking he didn't have no more authority in town.

"Gather 'round everyone. I have an announcement to make," he called out. "From now on, there will be no charge for food." Everybody cheered. "One more thing," he added, "drinks will now be four bits instead of two."

Chapter 20

The Whereabouts of Spiffy and Other Mysteries

"I recouped my losses from giving away all that grub," Sal boasted. "And *then some!*" His voice hit a defensive pitch.

"That so?" I said.

"Sure. Fact is, dead men drink much more'n they eat. Shoulda changed things sooner, *a lot* sooner! I was considering it for some time. Long before Buddy came to town."

Red rattled his lips in disbelief.

"Buddy mighta wrote up them rules, but we had words first," Sal added.

"Was that before or after you heeled them four cowpunchers to go after him?" I asked.

"Say what you will, but I ain't had no hand in any schemes against Buddy," he declared and walked off before anyone could press him on the matter.

"Sal seems to have made his peace with the new rules," Spiffy said between bites of free pork chops. He was on his third lunch.

"Don't look good when the clientele decides the prices," Red noted. "Next, some fella might walk in and decide whiskey should be free, too. Then where would Sal be?"

"He's right," Lucky interrupted. The boy didn't say much unless the conversation pertained to cards or strategy, and it was usually worth hearing since he had a knack for calculating odds. "Sal don't act soon, could be taken as a sign of weakness. Gotta raise a weak hand, same as a strong one. Otherwise, folks'll get to thinkin' they can bully you."

Buddy and Ms. Parker came in and sat down at the faro table. They preferred the pace of it to poker, and the odds were a little better—if no one cheated. Ms. Parker proved a better gambler than Buddy. She was more prudent in her wagering, while he threw money around willy-nilly.

She didn't spend any of her winnings on drinks on account of the baby, so she was sitting on a tidy sum.

Hardin took a keen interest in the couple, eyeballing them from across the room at the dice table. There wasn't much cause for him to rub elbows with Buddy, and so long as they didn't have women or gambling to argue over there was no reason for them to lock horns. At least until Sal closed down both the dice and the faro tables that evening. Said they needed mending.

"Mighty convenient," Red winked, "both tables needin' mendin' at the same time."

"General wear and tear," Sal replied curtly. "They're over forty years old!"

"Wouldn't have anything to do with them rules Buddy put up, or how Hardin and his lady drink for free, would it?"

"Too many damn mouths to feed," Sal grumbled. "I ain't scheming nothing, but it sure wouldn't hurt if the town got a little smaller. Don't look at me like that! Alls I'm saying is if they happen to have a disagreement over cards and one shot the other, I wouldn't lose no sleep."

Hardin and Mabel had a late supper that Sal prepared special. Afterward, Sal showed them to a table where Buddy and Ms. Parker were already playing poker. Wasn't easy finding people to play cards with Hardin. Folks feared he'd put holes in them if he lost. Sal knew Ms. Parker didn't have the sense to fold though, and Buddy surely wouldn't let her. It was a tense moment when they first sat down.

"Interestin' rules up on the wall, fella," Hardin said.

"Name's Buddy Baker."

"Baker, huh? I hearda you."

"Really?" Buddy sounded flattered that the famous outlaw knew of him.

"Nah," Hardin laughed, then looked over his cards like he was judging prize ponies on the auction block. Buddy barely glanced at his. Seemed more interested in the shine of the whiskey in his glass.

"Spend any time in the skillet?" Hardin asked, referring to his home state of Texas.

"Had me a little throat trouble in Fort Worth." Buddy pointed to the rope marks on his neck. "Rangers gave me a necktie for it."

After everyone had a chance to look at their cards, Buddy opened with a five-dollar bet, but it scared the others off and they folded one by one.

"Some of my kin caught hemp fever in Texas, too," Hardin said. "Lynch mob broke into the jailhouse, strung up my brother and two cousins. Bastards made the noose hang too low on purpose so they'd die slower. When we cut 'em down, there was tuffs of grass between their toes from trying to clench the earth and keep from strangling."

On the next hand, Hardin bet three dollars. It was still too big to open with and even those with halfway decent cards mucked their hands.

"I heard you did a spell in the crowbar hotel," Buddy said to Hardin.

"Sure did. They got me for killing a deputy in Comanche. Did sixteen years on a twenty-five-year sentence," he said plainly.

"That's quite a stint."

"Got me a law degree while I was in there. Read a mess a them religion books, too. They let me out for good behavior. Then I practiced law for a spell."

"Well, I'll be!" Mabel gushed. "I didn't know we had ourselves a real lawyer here. Imagine that! Handsome *and* smart. Were you lawyerin' for long, honey?"

"Nah, a man in El Paso bet me five bucks I wouldn't shoot some brown belly who was loafing in the sun. By the time the sheriff found him, I dare say that fella had a pretty good tan." Hardin snickered wickedly. "I was playing dice when the sheriff caught up with me. Just got on a roll when I saw him in the mirror behind the bar. Reckoned I could finish my roll before he drew. It kinda precluded my lawyerin' career." He fingered the bullet holes in his skull. "I don't expect I'll let that happen again."

"Have you killed many men?" Ms. Parker asked.

Everyone within earshot hushed up, knowing Hardin had shot men for talking out of line.

"Well, ma'am, I ain't never killed no one that didn't need killin'." He flashed a crooked smile.

The cards were dealt and everybody checked on betting till it came to Ms. Parker. She put in two bucks. Nobody must've had so much as a pair because they all folded.

"Say Buddy, with them rules you hung up, you aimin' to make some sort of civilized society here beyond the grave?" Hardin asked.

"Reckon you could say that," Buddy answered. "Just 'cause we're dead don't mean we can't be civil."

"I suppose a place without rules ain't no good for raisin' youngins neither." Hardin eyed Ms. Parker. The coldness of his stare made her grip her tummy.

The cards were dealt again. Hardin didn't want to scare anyone off, so he only bet a buck. Buddy saw it and raised two bucks. Then Ms. Parker bit her lip and raised it five more.

"It's either feast or famine 'round here!" Mabel said, mucking her cards. "Too rich for my blood."

Buddy and Hardin both saw the bet. There was over twenty-five dollars in the pot. Some of the newer boys gathered around to watch. Folks who'd been around a while took a step back, fearing the bet might be called with gunfire. Sal grabbed his shotgun from the umbrella stand and placed it below the bar.

"What's he doing with the buffalo gun?" Lucky asked.

"Not sure," I said. "If they draw, maybe he's gonna take out the winner."

"Be a smart move. Then he don't have to worry about either of 'em cutting in on his take."

Just then Nigel came through the swinging doors looking bored and restless. There hadn't been a gunfight in days nor any more flashes in the sky to watch. Wasn't anything else to do but drink. He saw Ms. Parker at the poker table, so to be cautious he stayed at the other side of the bar near the door. Sal set his shotgun down on top of the beer cases and poured Nigel a tall glass of gin. He might've been willing shoot Buddy or Hardin, but he wasn't going to do it while Nigel was around, in case he didn't approve.

"The thing about rules," Hardin said abruptly, "is they make a place boring." He laid his cards down, showing three jacks.

"Dang it all!" Buddy thumped down a pair of kings and slid his chips to the center.

Hardin was about to rake in the pot, but Ms. Parker laid her cards on top of his and said, "I think the true measure of a man is how well he can excel *within* the rules." She had three queens.

"Well, I'll be!" Buddy proclaimed.

An awful grimace came over Hardin's face. Losing was hard enough for him to swallow. Losing to a woman tore him up. Ms. Parker quickly gathered up her chips.

"I clocked you while you was shooting them boys the other day," Hardin told Buddy. "You're pretty fast."

"Thanks."

"But if you're gonna race a train, you better not show up on a pony."

Hardin rose and headed to the bar. The men all cleared a path and a fresh beer was waiting for him by the time he arrived. After a respectable but not too noticeable pause, Mabel bid good evening and followed Hardin.

"What the hell did that mean?" Buddy asked. "Ain't no trains in Damnation."

"He means to fight you," Ms. Parker explained.

"Well, why don't he just put it plain instead a going on about trains and ponies."

"He was trying to get your goat. Tell me something," she asked worriedly, "and don't lie to me. Is he fast?"

"Some say he's faster than anyone. Can't really know till you go against a man though."

"But he said he clocked you!" Ms. Parker looked as jittery as a jackrabbit. "Does that mean he *knows* who's quicker?"

"Dunno, ma'am. Ain't never bothered to clock myself. Figured anyone who'd wanna do that is killin' for the wrong reason."

"Please, don't go against him, Buddy. He's a wicked man. Promise me you won't let him goad you into fighting."

"With him speakin' in code about trains and ponies, I don't expect I'll have to, ma'am. But if he comes at me directly, I can't avoid it."

As Ms. Parker sulked, her brown hair fell over her face, masking a pout. Wasn't just protection for the baby she was after. Nigel could do that. Buddy was the closest friend she had in town—though he probably wished they were more than that.

"Don't worry, ma'am." Buddy reached out and tickled her elbow. She smiled and swatted his hand playfully. "Truth is, sometimes the guns come out of their holsters all on their own. Ain't no time for thinking, and if you do, you might get shot on account of it. Guns prolly already decided the matter, so there ain't no use in us frettin' over it."

"Oh, you're a damn fool!" Ms. Parker smiled. She wanted to believe what he said just to keep from worrying. Buddy escorted her back to her room, and by the time he returned to the Foggy Dew, Hardin and Mabel had already left.

"Anyone seen Spiffy?" Red asked.

"Nope," Sal said.

"Bastard still owes me five dollars, and he ain't been in for three days."

"Didja check the rooming house?" I asked.

"First place I checked after I saw he wasn't preening himself in the latrine."

"How about the outskirts of town?" Sal asked.

"What the hell'd he be doing out there for three days?"

"Maybe he messed with them Indians," Buddy suggested. "Coulda picked a fight and got scalped. Anyway, that's where I'd leave a body if I didn't want nobody stumbling across it."

"Maybe the wolves ate him to get even for us killin' their buddies," Whiny Pete said.

"If the wolves were getting even, they would storm this saloon," Nigel said from the other end of the bar. Nobody knew he had come in until he spoke—he just sort of appeared. "That you are talking is proof enough they don't know what happened."

"Prolly ain't nothing to worry about," Buddy advised. "Wouldn't be the first time a man dodged someone he owed five bucks to."

"True enough," Sal agreed, but then he pulled Red aside and told him, "Better go out and check the outskirts anyway. If he don't turn up, could be a lot more of us missing soon."

"Why's that?" Red asked.

"Longer he's away, the more likely he talks."

"So you don't think he's just dodging me?"

"In twenty years, Spiffy ain't never gone a day without a drink. I don't reckon he'd start now just 'cause he owes you five bucks."

Chapter 21

Hardin v. Buddy

Hardin wasn't much of a drinker. He could sip the same beer for over an hour, and never drank more than six or seven over the course of a day, which wasn't a lot in a town full of dead men with no jobs. Since he didn't have drinking pains to recover from, he rose early. You could hear him outside of town shooting at bottles. He'd set up jugs on crates and walk twenty paces, then turn and blast them apart. Did it for hours without taking a break. One morning, I couldn't sleep, so I went to the edge of town to watch. I clocked Hardin from when he stopped walking till the last bottle was broke. He hit all six before the second hand on my pocket watch struck four. Then he set them up again and did it in three seconds.

As I walked back into town, Nigel was sitting on a rocking chair in front of the hotel. He kept odd hours, not having any reason to be awake during chow time.

"Mornin'," I said hesitantly, fearful he might take my arm off if I caught him in a sour mood, but he just nodded. "Couldn't sleep neither?" I hazarded to ask.

"After a lifetime of dodging the sun, it's nice to be able to go outdoors at any hour."

"I guess it might be."

"So how fast is he?" he asked.

"Huh?"

"You were timing Mr. Hardin." A hawk wouldn't have been able to see the shine of my pocket watch from that distance, but he could.

"I reckon he could kill a man in half a second," I told him.

"Is that faster than Mr. Baker?"

"Not sure. Buddy don't shoot sober very often. I never clocked him under a second while he was drunk though. He once shot six men, but he took his time, and they was all lined up. Another time, he squeezed off three rounds in a flash at Jack Finney. One hit the ground and another hit a horse. Got Jack in the face with the third."

"I don't think Mr. Hardin will permit him three shots."

"I guess not. Though Jack didn't intend to either."

"You don't suppose Mr. Hardin could be persuaded to not shoot Mr. Baker?"

"Don't seem like he much likes being told what to do. It'd probably just make him wanna do it even more."

Nigel took a thoughtful puff on his pipe as he gazed up at the twilit skies. Then he got up and walked off without a word. The reporter in me wanted to ask him questions, find out what it was like being the only vampire in town. And what kept him from eating Ms. Parker's baby if he was so damn hungry? The coward in me reckoned it wiser to let him be.

That night, the faro and dice tables were still closed. Sal was hell-bent on bringing things to a head no matter what it cost him. After supper, Hardin and Mabel sat down to play five-card draw. Hardin won a few big pots against some newbie cowpokes, then used his stacks to bully the others. All of the tables were full, but a couple of chairs conspicuously freed up at Hardin's table as soon as Buddy arrived. He drank down a glass of beer as he wiped the sleep from his eyes, then sat down to play. Having the two fastest gunslingers at the same table put some tension in the room, and those nearby scattered for fear of crossfire. Buddy didn't seem to notice it though. He bet on bad hands, then laughed when he lost. He was down to his last ten chips when Ms. Parker sat down beside him.

"Honey, you sure you should be on your feet in your condition?" Mabel inquired.

"Till this baby comes out, I can't be comfortable no matter where I am." Ms. Parker smiled cheerfully. "I might as well have a poker game to distract me instead of staring up at the ceiling."

Hardin wasn't much for pleasantries. He silently picked up his cards and immediately bet a dollar. The two cowpokes folded, but Buddy and Mabel saw the bet. Hardin drew one card. When he got it, his expression didn't change in the slightest. Half the room figured he missed the flush he'd been banking on and was trying his damnedest not to show it. Mabel took two cards, and Buddy asked for four. When he got them, he smiled. No way of knowing what it meant though. After a few beers, Buddy smiled no matter what cards he was given.

"If you're taking four cards, one of them better be an ace," Hardin warned.

"Could be more'n one," Buddy laughed.

Hardin raised four bucks.

Buddy saw it and pushed the remainder of his chips to the center of the table.

"Outta my league," Mabel said and folded. "You boys can fight this one out while I go to the bar for a refill."

Hardin studied Buddy's face for any kind of tell. Wasn't much use trying to read a man like Buddy since he didn't care a whit about his cards. His heft made it even more confusing. Some people touched their ear or lip when they were bluffing, but a fat man in a hot room couldn't keep still even if he was being operated on. Buddy's hands moved over every part of his body as he fidgeted restlessly in his seat.

"Hot as hell with the blowers on!" he remarked while dotting his temple with a handkerchief.

Hardin took it as a sign and raised ten more chips.

"Hey, you trying to buy the pot?" Buddy asked angrily.

"Ain't got the money?"

"You can see right here I already bet all I had."

"Then I guess you gotta fold," Hardin said.

There was a gentlemen's understanding that you didn't bet more than a man had in front of him. If there was a third man in the hand who had more chips, you could always make a side bet with him. Hardin wasn't known for being gentlemanly though. He wanted to win any way he could.

"I'll cover the wager," Ms. Parker said.

"Money's gotta be on the table, ma'am," Hardin said.

Ms. Parker reached into her satchel and dropped forty dollars on the table. Hardin was taken aback, not figuring she had *that* kind of money on her.

"With cards like those," she nudged Buddy, "I should think you'd like to raise, Mr. Baker."

"Good idea." Buddy didn't look at his cards. He just pushed all forty dollars in. "I see your ten and raise you twenty."

"Actually, that's thirty you'd be raising," Ms. Parker corrected. "If that was what you intended."

"Right, thirty. Wow! That's a lot of money." Buddy picked up his cards for another peek.

"*Now* who's trying to buy the pot?" Hardin squawked, wearing a sourpuss. He counted out his stacks twice and was ten bucks shy. "All right, I'll cover it," he said.

"The money has to be on the table, Mr. Hardin," Ms. Parker reminded him.

Hardin started grinding his teeth so loud it sounded like he was chewing pebbles. It ate him up for a woman to give him lip in front of everyone. He looked ready to start making holes in her. And if Mabel wasn't watching, he might have.

"Sal!" he hollered. "Spot me ten chips."

Sal finished pouring a drink and ambled over with a show of reluctance, then placed ten chips in front of Hardin. He couldn't refuse outright, but he wanted to save face in front of everyone.

"Pot's square," the dealer declared.

Hardin didn't even wait for Buddy to show his cards. He flipped over five spades with a wolfish grin. Buddy shook his head in disbelief. "By golly, that's quite a hand!"

It was the happiest we had ever seen Hardin.

Then Ms. Parker nudged Buddy to flip over his cards. He'd was so impressed with Hardin's flush, he'd entirely forgotten what he had. When his cards hit the table, nobody looked more surprised than Buddy. He had a full house, aces over queens.

"That beat a flush?" he asked with a crinkled brow.

"Of course it does!" Ms. Parker laughed.

"You cheatin' bastard!" Hardin yelled and sprang up from the table. His chair kicked over and his fingertips dangled in front of his belly, readying to pluck his pistols from their holsters. Buddy stood as well, staggered some, then cocked his elbow back ready to draw. They both sidestepped to the right, circling around the room with their eyes locked on each other.

Everyone else cleared out. A breeze came through the door pushing the chandelier from side to side with a creak. Otherwise, it was so quiet you could hear a mouse scratch his balls.

"What's takin' so long?" Whiny Pete whispered.

"The real loser ain't just the one who gets shot," I told him. "It's the man who can't stand waiting and pulls just to get it over with. And the real winner is the one who waits long enough to see it and still fires first."

"What if the man who draws first wins?"

"In the end, whoever's north of hell can tell the tale however they like."

I'd never seen two men so eager to draw, yet so resigned to wait. Their eyes were trained on each other's wrist, watching for the first sign of hurried movement.

"Hold it there!" a voice called out from across the room. Nigel positioned himself between the two gunslingers, and asked, "What's the meaning of this?"

"He called me a cheater!" Buddy said.

"What about the rules you put on the wall?" Nigel plucked Buddy's pistol from his holster and turned it over in his hands like he was weighing it.

"If you fire this at him, you'll be 'fighting over bullshit.' Remember that? That's number five on the list. Besides, the wolves could still attack. I dare say we're going to need every last man to protect Ms. Parker."

"All right." Buddy grabbed his pistol back from Nigel and slid it in his holster. "But this ain't over, Hardin. After them werewolves are gone, I'm sending your ass to hell with 'em."

Nigel turned and headed for the door so as not to linger in Ms. Parker's presence. Sal alone looked disappointed that nothing had come of all the hoopla.

Then Hardin called out, "Hell it ain't! I say it's over now!" His hand swept across his belly and plucked his pistol like a feather. The well-oiled holster didn't make a peep as it released the gun. He drew faster than I'd ever seen anyone draw before. Quicker than an eyelid winking at a fleck of dust.

Buddy's hand dropped to his waistline trying to catch-up, but he was caught off guard and already well behind. Hardin's vest rigging also gave him an edge, since he didn't have to extend his arm downward to grab the handle. He could snatch it as easily as he'd scratch his tummy.

Both men's arms rose. Buddy still trailed slightly. As Hardin winked over the level barrel, Buddy was still cocking his wrist. It looked like he wasn't going to be anywhere near fast enough. A shot rang out, followed by a clicking noise. A trail of blue gun smoke floated in the air between them. They were still grimacing with their intent to kill each other. Then Hardin staggered two steps backward. Buddy remained in place. A queer look came over Hardin's face. It wasn't just disbelief—more like shock. A speck of red appeared in the center of his chest, then quickly spread to the size of a silver dollar before seeping down his breast. He dropped to the floor. Even Buddy looked unsure of how he had done it.

"Hardin musta misfired," Red said and went to check his gun. "Nope, still got all six bullets in the cylinder with no hammer marks. He ain't even squeezed the trigger."

Mabel was standing at the bar beside Nigel. She'd been collecting her drink when all the ruckus started. She gasped and let out a cry. Nigel locked eyes with her. She shuddered then quietly backed out of the saloon.

Buddy scooped up all his winnings from the table, then tossed a pile of it on the bar. "Drinks are on Hardin!" he called out, and everyone cheered.

The Crapper

Comings & Goings: *Four cowboys from Wyoming spent the day here last week after they ate some rotten beef. The second* *mistake they made was messing with Buddy, who sent them to hell before suppertime.*

John Wesley Hardin, the notorious gunfighter from Bonham, Texas, and killer of a dozen rangers from said state, was also sent to hell this week with a single gunshot. Hardin claimed to have killed over forty men while he was alive, not including Mexicans and Indians, and he sent a handful of men to hell while among us. For those hankering for more details about his life, there won't be no shortage in the history books to come. I'd just like to note here that the most dangerous gunfighter in America lasted less than three months in Damnation.

Chapter 22

Mabel's Angle

The celebration for Hardin's departure was a hog-killing good time—
even bigger than the festivities for Malachi's leaving. Having a celebrity
around gets real tiresome when you have to walk on eggshells worrying if
he'll shoot you. The night was especially festive since Buddy spent all his
winnings treating everyone to drinks. Old Moe got so drunk he accidently
shot a newbie in the face while trying to reenact Buddy's draw. Everyone
had a good laugh over it—except the newbie. The next day, most folks
didn't rise till late in the afternoon. They stumbled into the Foggy Dew
looking for grub and, the brave ones, a little hair of the dog.

"You find Spiffy yet?" Sal asked Red.

"Nope."

"You look on the outskirts of town?"

"Yup. I even spoke to the chief. The grumpy bastard was haulin' dead
chickens from the road. I asked if he seen a cowboy in church clothes. He
said all cowboys looked the same to him, and the only good cowboy was
a dead one, but they ain't sent none to hell yet—though he was itching to."

"The chief don't lie," I said. "If he says they ain't done it, they ain't done it."

"Well, if the brown bellies ain't got 'em, it musta been the wolves!"
Whiny Pete fretted.

The speculation was interrupted by an argument at the poker table in
the corner. Lucky was playing five-card draw with a bunch of cowboys.
One of them kept hollering real loud. The skinny freckled boy looked
even smaller among the burly sunburnt men. The cowboy shoved all his
chips toward Lucky, then backhanded him and stormed off. Lucky fell
to the floor but got straight up again, dusted himself off, and sat down to
play some more.

He already had two black eyes, a busted nose, and his cheeks were apple green with bruises. He was starting to look worse than Whiny Pete, but he wouldn't give them the satisfaction of complaining. After each beating, he simply asked if they were ready to play another hand. They couldn't do anything but sit back down and play till they ran out of chips. Everyone hawkeyed the boy for signs of cheating, but all they saw was the steady lessening of their chips. The stacks in front of Lucky sprawled across the table like towers of a miniature city. Aside from what Mabel had been putting away, it was a large portion of the wealth in town.

"What happened to the kid?" Buddy asked.

"Cowpunchers beat him up," Sal answered.

"Why?"

"He hasn't lost more'n a hand or two all day."

"Ain't no reason to beat 'em up."

"That's what I thought. Except he's got all the chips, and he ain't spending none. If a fella ain't got no money to buy bullets, then the blacksmith can't lose the money to another fella. Then nobody can buy a drink. I can hardly afford to spot the newbies ten chips when they arrive. When I do, they go straight to Lucky and he doesn't drink, so I don't get them back. The whole system's gone to pot. He's practically begging to be shot."

"I'll have to look into this," Buddy said and went over to the poker table. Just then, Mabel sauntered in with a wink and a smile, then sat down right beside him.

"Certainly didn't take her long to get over Hardin," Sal noted.

"Smart lady," Red said. "Knows she ain't gonna last long without protection."

Buddy folded the first few hands while watching to see if Lucky was palming cards. Then he went in with a pair of jacks. He traded three cards and got another jack. Lucky asked for three cards, then won the hand with three queens.

"The kid's got the right name," I told Sal. "That was some hand to beat."

Buddy folded three more hands while watching the dealer to see if he was in cahoots or maybe had an accidental show that Lucky had caught on to. Buddy finally went in with a pair of nines and drew a pair of deuces. Lucky drew one card and caught a flush.

"His name shoulda been 'Luck*ier*,'" Sal said. "And his last name shoulda been '*Than Shit.*'"

"You cheatin'?" Buddy asked directly.

"No, sir," Lucky replied.

Buddy watched for a few more hands. There wasn't no bottom-dealing or hand-mucking going on, nor any card-marking. It looked like a sound game, except that Lucky hardly ever lost.

"So what'd you do to end up here, kid?" Buddy asked. "Kill someone?"

"Ain't never killed nobody in my life. Ain't even raised a fist, 'cept to defend myself."

"Ah, he's just a boy," Mabel said. "He couldn't hurt a soul. Look at his darling face."

"Musta done something wrong. Or else he'd be in heaven, wouldn't he?"

"I suppose I caused some misfortune," Lucky admitted. "Had a partner once. He got shot up by some cowboys after I cleared them out in cards. Also, I prolly took some wages that woulda fed hungry children."

"Wagerin' ain't no sin," Mabel said, "unless you forced them to bet, and I reckon you didn't need to do that, honey."

"No ma'am, I just let them believe they could win."

"That don't make no damn sense!" Buddy argued. "You couldn't known they was gonna lose."

"No sir, I knowed it," Lucky said plainly. "I always win. Soon as some cowboy sits down in front of me with a stack, I can be sure he's gonna lose it to me. Just like he sees a skinny pipsqueak like me and knows he can whoop 'im in a fight. He may play his cards all right at first, but he'll slip up. When you hate a loudmouthed bully as much as I do, his tells are as easy to spot as the stars on a clear night. So I take his money, and sooner or later he's gonna wanna give me a beating for it."

Buddy folded two more hands before he got some cards he really couldn't resist. He kept them close to his chest so I couldn't see what he had. He only exchanged one card, then went all in. Lucky didn't draw any cards at all. He just called. Buddy grinned laying down a straight to the ten. Then Lucky flopped down a straight to the queen.

"What are the odds of that?" I said to Sal.

"Must be near a thousand to one," Sal replied.

Buddy did what any reasonable man would do in such a situation. He pulled out his gun.

"You cheatin' bastard!" he hollered and pressed the barrel against the boy's lip.

Lucky sat looking at him with his wide cow eyes, like he'd been expecting it all along and there wasn't nothing he could do to stop it. He didn't beg for mercy.

"Hold it there, Buddy," Mabel interrupted. "I thought you said everyone had to follow the rules. How's it gonna look if you break the rules over a five-dollar pot? As far as I can tell, this young man didn't do anything but have a better hand than you."

"I ain't sure how he done it, but he musta cheated. How's he beat three jacks with three queens, then two pair with a flush, and *then* a straight with a higher straight? He didn't even draw no cards! You tellin' me he was dealt a straight to the queen!?"

"You can't shoot a man for what you *think* he might've done, just what you *know* he's done." Mabel didn't raise her voice. She spoke with an even keel and a sweet smile. The bosom beneath her chin didn't hurt her case none either. "Remember rule number five? It says 'no killing over dumb shit.' You wrote it yourself. Besides, the vampire says we're gonna need every last man we have if those werewolves come back." She batted her eyes and placed her hand on Buddy's wrist. "You already got rid of the second best gunfighter in town."

"Damn it all!" Buddy moaned. He couldn't stop himself though. He twirled his pistol around his fingertip till the chamber was in the palm of his hand, then knocked the kid across the jaw with the handle. Lucky took the blow wordlessly. Tears welled up in his eyes and one or two slid down his cheek. He wiped them without saying nothing, then pulled Buddy's chips in with his own. There were still three other players at the table, and he said, "Deal."

"Wonder what her angle is," Sal said.

"What ya mean?" I asked.

"Why's she siding with Lucky? Figured she'd be more concerned with shoring things up with Buddy than arguing on behalf of that runt."

"Hmm, not sure," I said.

Chapter 23

Spiffy's Whereabouts Confirmed

"Last call!" Sal hollered. "You don't have to go home—because there ain't no way back—but you can't stay here."

The handful of men who weren't entirely ruined pushed their glasses forward for a final triumphant round. With nothing to wake up for the next morning, there was little reason to pace yourself, so not many made it to closing time. Quite a few men passed out and soiled themselves by midday. A lot of the rest were airing the paunch by suppertime. Wasn't uncommon for a fella to say he was just taking it easy for the night then wind up shot because he drank too much and picked a quarrel.

As I swallowed the last suds of beer in my mug, a hoarse moan came from the doorway. Spiffy was lying on the floor, propped up on his elbows in a trail of blood marking where he had crawled to the saloon. His arms were crossed and his wrists tucked under his armpits to try to slow the bleeding. Both hands had been chewed to nubs. His church clothes were tattered and soaked with blood from collar to cuff. His feet were gone, too. We lifted him up on a table and tied off his wrists and ankles with rags. He was nearly bled out but could still talk some.

"Wolves done it," he said. "Wanted to know what happened to them others. Chewed on my fingers till I told 'em."

"What'd you say?" Sal asked worriedly.

"That Buddy and the vampire sent 'em to hell. They kept chewing though, so I told 'em the wolves were after Ms. Parker's baby 'cause it was alive and had warm blood in it. They didn't believe me, so they kept chewing. Chewed off my whole hand… then another."

Sal poured some whiskey down Spiffy's throat to dull the pain. He wasn't going to make it. No use in trying to cauterize the wounds and stop the bleeding. He'd already lost too much blood, and there wasn't any way to get more back inside him. Only thing to do was keep him comfortable and hear what he had to say.

"I was tied to a wall for days," he said. "They just kept nibblin' on me. Wouldn't take my word for it. Then they chewed off my feet. I howled like a banshee. Finally, they let me go."

"So they coming after us?" Sal asked.

"They was licking their lips over the prospect of a live baby."

"When they aimin' to come?"

"Tomorrow evening, after the whole pack rises... They're gonna have a hunt."

Spiffy nodded out. Wasn't much use letting him suffer, but nobody wanted to waste a bullet since we'd need all we had. Nigel agreed to quicken his end. "Anyone care to say some final words about the chap?" he asked.

Nobody seemed inclined. Then Sal finally stepped forward. "Spiffy," he said, "sure was a hell of a dresser." He stepped back and gave the nod. Nigel bit into his throat. Spiffy's eyes bulged like a branded steer's. He didn't cry out though. Just grit his teeth, then slipped away. Nigel spit out a mouthful of cold blood, careful not to swallow any, then rinsed his mouth with gin.

"Least he didn't go like no goddamn Fre," Red said.

"What ya mean? He told 'em everything!" Sal said. "Sure as shit, he was hollering like a Fre when they chewed his feet off. We're all done for now!"

"What ya expect him to do?" Whiny Pete said. "They woulda just kept chewing on him till he told them what they wanted to hear. What's a man supposed to do in that situation?" he whimpered. "I know I wouldn't last long if my hands were being ate." Pete was nearly brought to tears thinking on his own straits.

"Well, we'll see who's a Fre tomorrow when the werewolves chew y'all up." Sal poured a round and we drank over Spiffy's body. It wasn't much of a wake, but it was all we could do.

"Can't help but feel a little envious of him," Red said. "Least he's gotten it over with—gettin' chewed up and all."

"Sad to think," Sal added, "there might not be anyone left to drink over us tomorrow night."

"True," I said, "but it's nice to be the one doing the drinking tonight." We all knocked glasses.

"You better rest up," Nigel said and downed the last sip of his gin. "They only let this man go so he could alert us. Werewolves prefer to hunt scared prey. It's in their nature. I imagine they will stretch out the hunt for their own enjoyment."

Buddy and Whiny Pete left with Nigel. Red and I sat for a spell as Sal wiped down the bar.

"I don't reckon there'll be any whiskey served in hell," I said.

"At least it couldn't smell any worse than here. That's for sure!" Red said.

"Ah, that's just Spiffy," Sal said. "He's starting to turn."

"Shit, you can call him stinky now."

"What ya reckon the odds are of us getting through this in one piece?" I asked.

"With a half-starved vampire? Not good," Sal said. "With a fed vampire, it'd be a different story."

"Then we gotta get that vampire fed, goddamn it!" Red said.

"There's only one place in Damnation where you can get warm blood," Sal said.

"You mean Ms. Parker's baby?" I said. "Buddy'd never let it happen."

"Could be us or it," Sal said.

"That baby's gonna get ate anyway. What ya think they're gonna do after they finish eatin' us?"

"Maybe we could get a drop or two of the kid's blood," Sal said. "Not enough to harm it. Just enough to give Nigel the strength to fend off the wolves. We just gotta figure out how to get it out of her."

"She's nearly due, ain't she?" Red asked. "Maybe we could force the birth somehow."

"Buddy ain't gonna like that idea either," I said.

"We got ourselves a real delicate hair-in-the-butter situation here," Sal said. "But if it was suggested properly, real subtle and all, maybe Ms. Parker and Buddy'd both go along with it."

"I'll suggest it," Red said.

"Buddy ain't no fan a yours," I pointed out. "You already tried to shoot him once, and he don't like your schemin' ways none either," I told Sal.

"How about you, Tom? He trusts you."

"That's why I can't bring it up," I said. "But if I second it, that might hold some sway."

"That settles it," Red said. "I'll suggest it, but real subtle-like, and you second it."

Red rifled through Spiffy's pockets till he found some money.

"What the hell you doing?" Sal hollered. "Ain't you got no respect?"

"He still owes me five bucks!"

Chapter 24

The Wolves

Word started getting around at breakfast. Some of the fellas went straight to the rooming house to hide out. Others wanted to wait until after lunch, not knowing how long they might have to hold up. Most decided they were better off making a stand together in the saloon where the vampire was. "Gonna be a long one," Sal remarked.

"Could be the last one," Red added. "Might as well be long."

Just before suppertime, a series of long eerie howls summoned the wolves to gather in front of the Foggy Dew. There were just a few at first, then the rest joined in like a chorus of hungry carolers. Sal quickly slid the storm door over the flimsy swinging café doors. The miners looked scared as schoolchildren. Most of them had died of black lung but had done their share of mistreating women and children. In the rooming house, they were known to be fitful sleepers, always worrying there would be some reckoning for their earthly misdeeds. Seeing all the wolves, they quickly regretted their decision to stay put.

"We're surrounded!" one declared. "I say we tear up the floorboards and tunnel our way out."

Sal grew oddly possessive of his floor. "You ain't doing nothin' of the sort! You're just gonna have to fight, and that's all there is to it."

"Ain't gonna need the floor if we all get ate up," another one argued.

While they were bickering, a sodbuster tried sneaking out the back window and got dragged around to the front of the saloon. His yelling drew all eyes to the window. Four wolves clamped down on his limbs and all pulled at once, ripping him to pieces. The largest wolf ended up with the head and torso still attached to a leg. The dead man looked around at the pieces of himself strewn across the road. He screamed and shook like he wanted to collect them, but had no hands to hold anything with. Two wolves fought over an arm with the fingers still twitching.

"Push that piano up against the door!" Sal ordered. "And break up those tables to cover the windows!"

"I say we open fire before they come in and get us," a soldier suggested. "Gotta stay on the offense."

"Why should we be taking strategy advice from you?" Red argued. "You got scalped by a measly Indian, and he'd didn't even have a gun!"

"Don't go underestimating Indians," he said in earnest. "I'd rather face a werewolf than an Indian with a purpose any day of the week. You get one Indian with a cause, and pretty soon there'll be a hundred by his side."

"Do we have to listen to this hogwash?"

"But we got Buddy," Whiny Pete said. "If they come in here, he can shoot a mess of 'em. Tom and Sal can take out a couple, and the vampire'll take care of the rest."

"I am too weak to face the entire pack," Nigel said.

"Don't go counting on Tom neither," Red said. "He's got his pacifist sights set on heaven. He's still trying to make it a year without shooting no one."

"That include not shooting wolves or just people?" Lucky asked.

"Suppose it'd include all God's creatures," I said.

As the howling went on, more folks started coming undone. They hadn't realized the vampire was so worn out. Then the wolves started pulling men out of the rooming house, mangling their legs and leaving them to bleed out in the road.

"They're gonna get us for sure!" Whiny Pete cried out, "Just like they'd done to Santa Anna at the Alamo."

Nigel just chuckled and lifted his glass. "Those who are doomed to repeat the past sometimes read about it beforehand."

"If you had some warm blood, you could take on the pack, couldn't ya?" Red asked him.

"Where we gonna get warm blood in Damnation?" Lucky asked. "I thought everyone's blood is cold as ice."

"You can heat mine up," a farmer volunteered.

"Only blood pumped from a living heart will do," Nigel said. "You are just a sack of brackish water to me. It would be no better than you trying to quench your thirst with sea water."

Red saw his opportunity. "Don't Ms. Parker got fresh blood in that child growing in her belly?" he said a little too eagerly. "I say we cut it out now and give it to the vampire to protect us!"

"Real subtle, you shit heel," Sal muttered.

"Ain't nobody doing nothing of the sort," Buddy hollered.

"Now hold on a minute," Sal said. "Nobody's gonna harm Ms. Parker. But say she was to deliver naturally. There'd be some of that afterbirth leftover, right? That's gotta have warm blood."

"When you due, ma'am?" I asked.

"Not for another few weeks, at least," she replied.

"We could all be torn to pieces by then!" Whiny Pete wept.

The cowboys took a practical view of the matter. Most of them had delivered valuable calves at the risk of their less valuable mothers' lives. They didn't have no qualms about tearing the baby out of Ms. Parker if it would improve their odds. The crowd grew unruly. Some wanted to toss her to the wolves and be done with it, but they'd have to go through Buddy and Nigel first.

A farmer spoke up. "My wife had all of our children early. She didn't take no bed rest neither. Kept working right up to the day she delivered."

"That gives me an idea," Sal said. "Maybe if Ms. Parker keeps active, she'll deliver early. Worryin' 'bout them wolves might help trigger it, too. Buddy, you get her up and walk her around the room. Let her get a peek out the window while you're at it."

"It might not be good for the baby!" Buddy protested.

"Well, it might not be good for the baby if it ends up as supper," Red said.

"No, he's right," Ms. Parker said. "I'd rather the baby come early than we all get eaten."

"Now, you boys get some Winchesters up in those windows and fire if a mutt gets within ten yards the building. We'll hold them off as long as we can."

The windows on the second floor were boarded up with slots to fit a rifle barrel. The men took turns sitting in the rafters, keeping the wolves in check with the occasional warning shot.

"They might enjoy a hunt, but they ain't too keen on getting lead poisoning for it," a cowboy called out merrily as he blasted the ground before their skittish paws.

Buddy had Ms. Parker up half the night doing laps around the saloon carrying a sack of grain. Everyone else camped out on the floor. Hardly an hour passed without some howling. A burly logger wept in the corner, blubbering about how he didn't want to end up dog food.

Just after dawn, Ms. Parker's water finally broke. The baby wasn't ready to come out though, and the wolves were getting more restless. There was a sudden crash and glass shattered across the floor. Then a wolf came sailing through the small window above the front door that we'd neglected to board up. Nigel kicked it square in the teeth, then tossed it out the way it came.

"Board that up now!" Sal ordered. "Where the hell's Buddy?"

Lucky went upstairs to look for him. A minute later, he called down from the catwalk, "He's gone!"

"What?"

"Took French leave!"

"Buddy wouldn't a skinned out," I said. "He got more guts than you can hang on a fence."

"Well, he ain't here. I searched everywhere. Whiny Pete's gone, too."

"I'd have expected it from the kid, but not Buddy. Shit, that's a good share of our firepower!"

"Buddy wouldn't desert us," Ms. Parker said. "He just wouldn't!" She was panting like a horse run ragged. The baby pains were coming on more regularly now. The wolves were also getting more daring. The lookouts in the windows had to fire warning shots every few minutes to keep them at bay.

"At this rate, we're gonna run out of bullets before we kill any of 'em," Red said.

"Might be their plan," Sal said.

The sound of breaking glass came from the backroom, and two cowboys ran back to check on it. A gunshot sounded, and one of them didn't return. "Gotta seal up the door to the backroom," the other one said. "They've overrun it. I stuck a board under the knob, but it won't hold for long."

"Dang it all! Get Ms. Parker up to the second floor," Sal said. "And get some boards to secure that backroom."

While Mabel was helping her up the stairs, two wolves broke into the barroom. There wasn't any time to take aim on them. One raced after Ms. Parker, nipping at her heels. Red jumped out from behind the bar, leaving himself exposed. It was the first selfless thing I'd ever seen him do. He squeezed off a shot, striking the wolf in the mid-section. It tumbled down the steps with a whimper. The other wolf leapt for him and bit into his shoulder before he could get back to cover. He cried out as the long teeth sunk into his flesh and struck bone. Sal pressed a pistol against the wolf's face and shot its jaw off. Red managed to crawl back behind the bar and wrap his wound.

"Board up that back door now!" Sal yelled.

"Where's that skinny freckle-faced kid?" Red asked.

"Right here," Lucky said, crouching behind a barrel.

"Shit, boy!" Red smiled. "Looks like today's your day. You may just see hell after all!"

Chapter 25

The Horse Thief

The charges came in bursts throughout the day. The wolves smashed against the door and tried to squirm between the boards that covered the windows. When their noses slipped through the cracks, they nipped at the men, taking chunks out of their arms. The ancient beams in the walls began to buckle from the constant ramming. Luckily, the wolves got tuckered out before they gave way. They needed rest just like any other dogs that'd been chasing their tails too long in the sun.

"It's your turn to take lookout, Tom." Red handed me a Winchester and a sack of bullets.

"Don't put him up there," Lucky said. "He's still trying to get into heaven by not shooting anyone."

"Ah, who cares about that now?" Red said. "Probably all be torn to pieces by tomorrow. Why would God take you just 'cause you managed to not shoot no one for a few hundred days? Hell, there ain't even no sunup or sundown to count the days by. It could all be one long day for all we know! And why would God give a piss what you did with it?"

"Now hold on a second there," Sal interrupted. "How long's it been you ain't shot no one, Tom?"

"Well, I had about three months on me when Ms. Parker arrived. That was nine months ago, so it's nearly a year," I said. "Maybe a few weeks shy."

"You better hide out behind the bar," Sal said. "If them wolves overrun us, it'd be worth it to know if there's a way out of Damnation. Could be a while before anyone lasts that long."

Everyone was watching, and I didn't want to shirk my duty for some pipedream. Morale was low enough. "Ah hell, there's always next year." I grabbed the gun and bullets.

The perch in the rafters was a tight space, and I had to squeeze in with my back against the joist and the rifle in my lap. Between the boards over the window, there was a clear view straight down the road to the dust cloud that surrounded the town. Across the road, the fellas in the rooming house were held up without a lick to eat. It had been a full day since they had any grub. One man tried to sneak to the general store for rations, but the wolves caught him and tore his throat out mid-scream. Then they lay back down behind some barrels and planks of broken-up boardwalk so we couldn't pick them off.

The town was completely still. Ms. Parker's panting had slowed. Even the wind had died down. My back began to cramp up. Then there was some ruckus behind the wolves' barricades. The shouting of orders and the banging of tools could be heard. After about an hour, six large wolves appeared on the road, marching two by two at a slow, labored pace. They kicked up a big cloud of dust, so thick I couldn't make out what was keeping them from moving faster, let alone get a clear shot. Without breaking rank, they trotted straight toward the saloon, picking up some speed as they approached. When they got within a hundred yards, I could make out a long, thick beam between them that was lashed to their haunches. Looked like a rafter that'd been taken from one of the buildings.

"They got a battering ram!" I yelled, and fired a shot into the dust. The farm boy in the other window fired as well. They passed below the pitch of the roof where we couldn't hit them. I climbed down from the perch just as they mounted the porch with a creak of the floorboards. A loud crash shook the whole building and sent a century's worth of dust raining down from the ceiling. I hobbled down the steps to see the piano was nearly dislodged, and there was a crack in the door.

"It won't hold," Sal yelled.

"What can we do?" I hollered back.

"Pray." he shrugged.

The wolves had to back up down the road a ways to get another running start. They needed at least fifty yards to pick up speed. One more hit would surely split the door in two. Then they'd be able to slide the pieces aside and climb over the piano, easy as pie.

"Get back up there and try to pick off the lead wolf," Sal ordered.

I hustled back up the steps, but it was a lot quicker coming down than going up—the bum leg being easier to slide down than lift up. Finally, I hopped back on the joist and raised the rifle. Only now, I had trouble seeing. Everything looked dim. I reckoned all the running around had made me light-headed. Then I realized that the sky had actually grown darker. The streaks of violet and yellow had faded to a plain dreary gray. My eyes were slow to adjust to the vanishing light. The wolves were looking up in confusion as well. It wasn't quite pitch black. A faint glow still shone beyond the brooding clouds, but its shape couldn't be made out. Looked like a candle behind some dirty curtains.

Before anyone could gather their wits, giant drops of rain—as big as fists—began falling from the sky. They struck the ground with a loud patter. After half a minute, the rain was coming down in sheets so thick you could hardly see the other side of the road. The dry cracked earth muddied and every footprint filled with a puddle.

"That's a real gully washer!" called out the farm boy at the other window.

"Keep your eyes peeled," I ordered. "They might use it as cover."

Sure enough, a long howl bellowed from beyond the veil of water, and a moment later the wolves came charging down the road toward the door. Their pace was slowed by the freshly drenched ground, and there was no more dust being kicked up to hide them.

"Shoot the lead wolves and the rest'll trip over 'em," I said. "I'll get the one on the left. You get the one on the right."

We each fired in turn, but both shots struck the mud. We fired again, but the rain made the bullets descend too quickly, and every shot was off by five feet or more.

Fortunately, the mud didn't give them much traction, and the soggy beam swung from side to side, throwing the wolves off balance. As they mounted the porch, I climbed down to look through the window above the door. There was a hell of a clatter, but the door didn't budge. The beam had slipped from the harness and crushed one of the wolves. The rest scrambled to their feet and ran for cover as the boys opened fire.

"I thought it didn't rain here," Lucky said.

"So did I." Sal shrugged.

"I ain't never seen a drop myself," Old Moe added. "And I been here longer than anyone."

"Must be a sign from God," Red decided. "First, a lightning bolt fries a wolf. Then this. Can't be no coincidence."

"Why the hell's God need to use signs?" Sal asked. "Don't he speak American?"

Twenty minutes passed before the rain suddenly let up all at once. The sky brightened with its normal violet and yellow streaks, and the town was silent except for the gusts of wind cutting between the buildings. The wolves must've been tuckered out from their attack, because there wasn't a peep from behind their barricade.

"What we gonna do when they get that battering ram going again?" a lumberjack asked. "That measly timber door ain't gonna hold."

"I don't know, you damn tree humper," Sal said angrily. "Give me a minute to think on it."

I climbed back up on the perch beside the joist with the rifle in my lap. It wasn't five minutes before my back began to cramp up again. There was nothing to do but sit and wait. For the living, pain was a warning of damage done to the body that might eventually lead to death, but dead men couldn't get any deader so it was just pain for pain's sake. Eventually, I just accepted it and began to drift into a light slumber.

I hadn't dreamt much since I died. They were more like fantasies, and if I thought on them real hard, I'd get to believing they were real for a minute or two. I was back in the Dakota Territory, and my wife was beside me. We had just picked out a patch of land in a field where we were going to build our home. I made love to her something fierce. It faded to the newspaper office, and Mr. Hearst was laying down the law, saying how I should write up the massacres in the Black Hills. Only this time I didn't have no fear. I could see how it would all go down, with me getting gut-shot and ending up in Damnation.

This time I was angry. I was angry for my whole life, for every second I let some misbegotten fool lead me astray. I could see that they didn't know no better than me. They were just more forceful with their will. I was standing there getting angrier and angrier at Mr. Hearst, and this time I didn't back down to him. His man trained a gun on me, and I gripped the barrel. As the blast went off, it burned my hand. Then I began to float upward toward the sun, because there was nothing holding me to the earth anymore. Before I reached the clouds though, the dream started to break apart. I tried real hard to believe it was true, just so that I could keep rising up to heaven or whatever was above.

A neighing in the distance woke me. When I opened my eyes and saw that I was still in gloomy old Damnation, the awful emptiness returned. A piebald stallion with a black face and a white stripe down his nose came bolting out of the dust. His coat was shiny with blood and sweat. Looked to be an Appaloosa. A bridle wrapped his jaw and there was a bit in his mouth, but no rider atop and the reins fell slack.

"Lookie there!" I shouted down to the others. "A horse just came out of the dust!"

"Now that's gotta be a sign," Red said.

The horse trotted up the center of town and stopped in front of the saloon beside the hitching post. He lapped up some dusty water from the trough, then stood still as a statue. His eyes were dead black, and his hindquarters riddled with bullets. Looked like a military horse, shod as he was and wearing a fancy saddle. The werewolves didn't show much interest in the cold horse meat, still having a hankering for a warm-blooded meal. A few minutes later, a man hobbled out of the dust and limped down the road. Some of the wolves lifted their heads to peer over the barricade, then quietly rested their jaws back on the ground. An urgent knock sounded on the door.

"Who the hell you suppose he is?" I asked.

"Maybe he's here to help," Lucky said.

"Could be Jesus," one of the Christians suggested.

"Maybe it's the Antichrist," Red said.

"Ah, shit! Open the door up before them wolves tear 'im up," Sal said. "Maybe he can shoot straighter'n you cross-eyed halfwits."

A few of the miners pushed the piano aside and unbolted the storm door while the boys upstairs provided cover from the windows. The man squeezed past the broken boards and collapsed on a stool in exhaustion.

"There a doc in town?" he asked, fanning his face with his Stetson. A blood-soaked rag was tied around his leg. "The law's on my tail!"

Everyone in the room broke into laughter at once.

"What's so dang funny?" he said. "Soldiers shot up my backside for stealin' a horse in Abilene. Didn't know it belonged to a general. Woulda been shot to pieces if that storm hadn't come on. I fell off my horse a ways back. Lucky I made it to this thirst parlor before they could catch up. Where we at anyway? This Buffalo Gap? I know I ain't made it as far as Sweet Water, though I was hauling tail. I tell ya that!"

Sal placed a bottle of whiskey and a glass in front of him. "The law ain't gonna catch you here. And that wound ain't worth worrying over no more."

"What's with all them big-ass dogs on the road? Some kind of kennel?" The horse thief poured a glass and had a long gulp. Then he took off his bandage, surprised to find blood wasn't flowing from the wound. It had thickened up like day-old gravy. He stood and took a few cautious steps, finding no need to favor it.

"Golly! Seems good as new." He looked at his back in the mirror. "Think I got some buckshot in me, but I don't feel no pain from it. It's the damnedest thing! Why is that?"

"'Cause you're dead, friend," a farmer said.

"What ya mean *dead*?"

"I mean you done died from them soldiers shooting you in the back. And your horse is dead, too. How many horses you seen walking around with bullet holes in their legs?"

"You're just joshing, right? The army put you up to this? Staged it to stall outlaws or somethin'?"

"Ever seen a thirst parlor filled with shot-up men like this before?"

The horse thief looked long and hard around the room. He grew a shade paler and started to sweat. Then he took another drink of whiskey.

"Maybe this is some kind of infirmary," he said, trying to convince himself.

"Does this look like something you heal from, boy?" The farmer pointed at a gouge in his skull made by a hay thresher. "You can see my dang brains!"

The horse thief nervously poured more whiskey in his glass.

"We don't have time for this," Nigel called down from the top of the stairs.

"Who's that?"

"He's a vampire," I said. "Kinda looks out for us sometimes."

"A what?"

"Those werewolves will be rested enough for another attack soon," Nigel warned. "I strongly advise you all to be on your guard."

Sal grabbed the bottle off the bar and hammered the cork into the rim with a whack of his palm. "Your credit's done, newbie."

"Can you shoot?" Red asked him.

"Sure can," he replied.

Red tossed him a repeating rifle. "Get in that corner."

"What's he mean about werewolves attacking?"

"Means you picked a bad day to steal a horse," Red said.

Chapter 26

Argus

The door wouldn't hold for long. That much was clear. Another line of defense was necessary, so we piled the chairs up on the bar as a barricade, and ducked behind them with our gun barrels sticking out. The sodbusters turned tables on their sides in the corners and pointed their rifles outward. Everyone had their sights trained on the front door, ready to cut down the first wolf that entered. Then two wolves suddenly burst through the back door. The horse thief picked one off, then cocked the lever ejecting the spent shell, and reloaded a fresh one into the chamber. He caught the second wolf in the side before anyone else had time to take aim.

"What the hell was that?" he asked afterward.

"I tol' ya, werewolves!" Red said. "And there's gonna be a lot more of 'em."

"Good shot, newbie!" Sal said. "Now go secure that back door."

Without any hesitation, the horse thief grabbed some boards and a hammer, and went to the back room where the whacking of nails was soon heard.

"Now that's a fella with some gumption!" Sal remarked.

A moment later, the hammering was interrupted by loud screams. His hollering was drowned out by the cracking of bones. Sal stuck his scattergun through the doorway and blasted away till the wolves fled. A couple of loggers helped him board up the door to the back room.

"Imagine that! He done died twice in the same hour," Red declared. "It's a shame. Seemed like a nice fella."

"Well, if Ms. Parker's baby don't come soon, you might see him again," Sal said.

"Ah, he wasn't that nice."

Howling came through the walls from all sides of the saloon. The whole pack was up and getting frisky. They'd already made us plenty scared and worked up an appetite in the process. They probably had more casualties on their side than they counted on. All that was left was to finish the hunt.

"You really think we'll go to hell if they eat us?" Lucky asked.

"Could be," I said.

"Think they have cards in hell?" he asked.

"I suppose not."

"Good, 'cause I'm sick of beating folks anyways. I'd rather be just like everybody else for a change. Even if I gotta burn in lakes of fire, like the Bible says. Least we'll all burn the same."

We had neglected to shove the piano back after the horse thief came in, and a lean brown wolf squeezed through the crack. Sal caught it in the belly with a pistol shot. We provided cover as two men tried to push the piano flush against the door. The rotted-out timber walls began to buckle from the weight of the wolves' charges. A few mutts slipped through the holes.

"You think there'll be big ol' cowboys ridin' me down there, too?" Lucky asked.

"Nah, in hell them cowboys'll be getting scalped by Indians, I suppose."

"Good 'cause I ain't taking no more shit from cowboys or anyone else!" Lucky climbed on top of the bar and fired a pistol in each hand. Two wolves fell. Then two more. Lucky was on a roll. There wasn't no more fear left in the boy.

The front door broke apart, and more wolves poured through than we had hope of fighting off. They pulled down the riflemen perched on the catwalk. A wolf sunk its teeth into Lucky's leg, then another caught him in the shoulder. He went down with a fight. When his guns clicked empty, he jabbed the barrels in their eyes.

"Guess he wasn't no Fre after all," Red said as he ducked to reload.

One of the wolves that got Lucky scrambled toward me. I leveled my rifle. Heaven would have to wait. The blast caught the beast in the mouth, shattering its jawbone. As soon as it fell, I regretted it. The saloon was already overrun. If I was going to get eaten anyway, it would've been nice to go with no blood on my hands just to see what'd happen—even if I was a few weeks shy of a year.

There was no time to reload our weapons. When they realized we were out of bullets, a dozen wolves surrounded us and stood snarling. A large white wolf marched to the center. Its withers were three hands higher than the others. He let out a triumphant howl.

"That's Argus, the pack leader," Sal whispered.

"We're goners for sure," Red said.

I dropped to my knees and clasped my hands together. I wasn't the religious sort, but it seemed like a good time to start. The last time I prayed was when I got gut-shot by that kid for writing lies in the newspaper. Time before that was when my wife got consumption. It didn't do any good in either case.

A racket of gunfire erupted outside the saloon. Bullets rained in through the doorway, and four wolves dropped to the ground. The rest scrambled for cover, but they didn't know where the shots were coming from. Two more wolves were shot. I looked over to see a large round figure crowding the doorway.

"Take that, you mangy dogs!" Buddy was wielding two pistols and a jolly grin. He unloaded them into the pack like he was picking off tin cans. Then he reached for the scattergun hanging by a rope on his shoulder. Before he could raise the barrel, Argus jumped on him and pinned him to the ground. Some sodbusters tried to help but got ripped to bits for their trouble.

The door to the upstairs room blew open, sending splinters of wood through the air. Nigel jumped down to the center of the room, hissing with his fangs out. He kicked Argus off Buddy, then impaled another wolf with the barrel of a rifle. He grabbed a third wolf by the neck and twisted its head till its spine broke.

Argus stood on his hindquarters, and the fur fell away as he took the shape of a man. He was tall, with a long white beard, but he wasn't frail. Stood half a head above the tallest man and just as wide as Red, but with muscle instead of beer fat. Looked like he could take on five men in a fistfight.

"Surrender, vampire," he ordered. "You've put on a good show, but you no longer possess the strength to defeat all of us."

"I do after I've consumed warm blood." Nigel pulled out a gooey mess from his coat pocket and held it in the air. "The afterbirth of a human child born in this underworld." He bit into it and his eyes glowed like hot coals. His chin reddened as blood drizzled over his mouth. He grabbed the nearest wolf, lifted it over his head, then threw it across the room with ease.

"So it's true," Argus said.

"The remainder of your pack is no match for a well-fed vampire," Nigel said. "Leave now or I will slaughter you all."

Argus dropped to all fours, assuming the shape of a wolf again, and howled to the others. He snarled at Nigel as if to say it wasn't over, then fled out the door. The rest of the wolves followed. After the last one was gone, Nigel collapsed to one knee and you could see the effort it had taken for him to stand, let alone toss that last wolf.

"I knew it weren't no afterbirth," Sal said. "It's yesterday's sloppy joe with ketchup, ain't it?"

"So you was just bluffin'?" Red said.

Just then, a small wolf shuffled beneath a pile of wood. As soon as he got to his feet, he took a bite out of Nigel's neck, then dashed for the back door.

"Get him before he alerts the others!" Nigel moaned.

Nobody had any bullets left, so two men tried to dive on top of the little beast as he darted by. Their heads crashed together as they missed. He was almost clear of the room when a pistol shot rang out behind me. The wolf rolled over, and the fur around the bullet hole was still smoking. At the doorway stood Whiny Pete.

"You didn't skin out on us after all," Sal said.

"Well, I tried to," Pete said shamefully. "I saw Buddy creeping out the latrine window this mornin' so I followed. Figured if he wasn't gonna stick around, we didn't stand no chance. Then I watched him come back when all hell broke loose. Musta been his plan all along. When the wolves left, I reckoned y'all whooped 'em, so I came back. Sorry I skinned out. I just ain't ready to go to hell yet."

"Ah, I don't care if you did skin out on us," Sal said. "Long as you came back to kill that wolf. He was the most important one. If he'd told the others Nigel tricked 'em, it woulda been the end of us."

The gash on Nigel's neck wasn't too deep, but it leaked a fair amount. We helped him to a stool. Luckily, it had only been a pup that bit him and his teeth weren't very long.

"I guess Ms. Parker didn't deliver in time," Buddy said.

Nigel tied a rag around his neck while Sal placed a bottle of gin in front of him. He poured a tall glass and emptied half of it in a gulp.

Ms. Parker soon started up again with her panting and yelling. It went on for nearly hour with Mabel tending to her. Finally, the cries of a baby came from the storage room, and everyone except Nigel rushed upstairs to see it. Ms. Parker had the child wrapped in a sheet and was smiling sweetly. It didn't have devil's horns or angel's wings. It was just a regular boy. Seemed to have a bit of a glow around him though, perhaps on account of being the only living thing in Damnation.

"What ya gonna call him?" I asked.

"Martin," she said, "after his father."

Chapter 27

Mabel's Bargain

I wasn't much of a baby person, my wife having died before we could have any of our own. I soon grew bored of making goo-go onoises at the tot and went back down to join Nigel at the bar. Mabel followed me, and I poured us tall glasses of whiskey, while Nigel opened another bottle of gin.

"Ain't you gonna go up and see the kid?" Mabel asked him.

"I think it would be best if I kept my distance for now," he replied. "I haven't been in the same room with a warm-blooded creature in a century. I might not be able to control my appetite."

Nearly every inch of the floor was covered with wolf carcasses or chewed-up men. Hell-sent corpses didn't keep long, and the scent of decay weighed heavily in the air. If you didn't haul them to the pigpen quick enough, even the pigs wouldn't touch them. I kept my glass of whiskey below my nose to filter out the smell.

"I know it wasn't Buddy who killed Hardin," Mabel announced out of the blue.

"Why you say that?" I asked.

"When they drew, there was a clicking noise immediately after the gunshot. Only Hardin hadn't misfired. They checked his gun. All the bullets were in it, and there were no hammer marks. That means Buddy's gun must've clicked empty."

"I always did wonder about that," I said, "but how do you know Buddy didn't shoot Hardin?"

"Buddy always reloaded his gun right after he used it. It was the one thing he was careful about, so his gun must have been fully loaded. Nigel had grabbed his gun when he tried to talk them out of fighting. He knew Hardin wouldn't be put off. Nigel must've slipped a bullet out of the first chamber before he gave it back. That way Buddy'd click empty and still think he shot Hardin."

"Then who shot Hardin?" I asked.

"Nigel did," she said. "He fired over Buddy's shoulder. I was standing right beside him. He moved real fast. Could hardly tell he shot at all, except that a smoke trail came from behind Buddy. Then I saw Nigel slip a gun back in his pocket."

Nigel didn't say anything.

"I was wondering why you did it," she pressed him. "With Hardin's speed, he'd a been more help against the wolves than Buddy."

Nigel packed a tobacco pipe in no particular hurry as blood seeped from the gash in his neck. Finally, he answered, "Hardin wasn't exactly the fatherly type. Buddy was a better choice to raise the child and keep it safe in my absence."

Mabel couldn't argue with that. Even if she had shared her bed with the man, she knew Hardin was too cold for fathering anything but fear.

"But why'd you make Buddy think he done it?" I asked. "You coulda just killed Hardin outright and let it be known it was you."

"Buddy needed the confidence," Nigel said. "If he knew I fought his battle for him, how would he fare against the wolves, or *me*? Someday I might not be able to control my hunger, and someone has to be able to protect the child."

A long, drawn-out moan came from under a pile of bodies. It sounded like a bleating goat. Nigel staggered behind the bar and filled a saucer with water. Then he put it below a mangled cowpuncher's face so that he could lap it up.

"Why do you have such an interest in Ms. Parker anyway?" Mabel asked.

"She reminds me of someone," he said.

"Your wife?" I asked.

Nigel nodded. "I guess we do look for redemption in this little town of ours. If I couldn't keep my wife safe, perhaps I can protect a lady who reminds me of her."

Nigel topped off all of our glasses. The saloon walls were sprinkled with bullet holes and the windows were shattered. There were hardly enough men left to help the Chinaman drag all the bodies to the pigpen.

"Buddy doesn't have to know you shot Hardin," Mabel said. "But I need something from you. The way it is now, a woman doesn't stand a chance around here unless she attaches herself to a man, and I don't aim to be hitched to the likes of any of you. But if I open my own place, I can make the rules. Lucky was going to be my investor, and he already gave me his share before the wolves got him. Together, we have half the coins in town. I'll need protection if I'm gonna go out on my own. Sal's sure to kick up a fuss, and there's bound to be others. I reckon a vampire'd be a pretty good bouncer."

Nigel didn't seem keen on taking sides. He preferred to remain impartial to human quarrels.

Ms. Parker called down for Nigel to see the baby. He ignored her, but she just called louder.

"So, we got a deal?" Mabel asked.

Nigel didn't shake on it or nothing. All he said was, "I think I know a way in which I can protect your interests."

Since Ms. Parker wouldn't stop hollering, Nigel reluctantly crept up the stairs, but he remained at the doorway, as far from the child as possible.

"Oh, come in here," she demanded. "If his blood does make you hungry, I wanna know about it now."

"She's right," Buddy said. "Best to test the waters while we're on alert. Don't worry." Buddy plucked his pistol from his holster. "I'll shoot you if you start salvatin'."

Mabel placed the child in Nigel's arms. Sal trained the scattergun on his head and cocked the hammer.

"So, you got the hunger?" Buddy asked.

"Oddly, no."

"You ain't trying to trick us so you can eat 'em later, are you?"

"No, I have no hunger for him at all." Nigel was puzzled. "He's cute and all, but I don't have the same reaction that I used to have toward living humans."

"Maybe your hunger for us died when you did," Ms. Parker suggested.

"No, the hunger is always there," he said. "I just don't have any hunger for this creature."

The Crapper

Goings: *In all, thirty-eight men left Damnation, including six cowboys named Jonny and some horse thief who rode up in the middle of the action and took a couple of wolves with him. Twenty-five wolves were counted among the casualties. I think Old Moe phrased it best when he said, "We done good for not having no fangs or claws or leaping abilities—just a few old* *rifles and some rusty bullets. We live to drink another day, for whatever that's worth."*

Comings: *Martin Parker: 6 lbs., 8 oz.*

Chapter 28

Jarvis

For a spell, the Foggy Dew wasn't so crowded. No need to shout or wait for a drink—unless Sal was sore at you. One thing that livened things up was a piano player came to town, and he was good enough not to get shot right away, so in the evenings a waltz or one of them newer ditties filled the air of the saloon. Otherwise, it was hard going to round up enough hands for a game of cards. No one complained though since at least there was plenty of elbow room at the bar. But the stools slowly filled with new dead men, mostly soldiers that had gone up against the Indians, and they had their stories to tell.

One day, a kid named Jarvis showed up with buckshot wounds dotting one side of his face, which wasn't easy to look at. He wasn't a soldier, just the son of a preacher from Cincinnati. His pa had been real strict and beat the daylights out of him for every little thing, so one day he ran off and fell in with a gang of train robbers.

"What the hell's a train?" Sal asked.

"Just how long you been here!?" Buddy asked. "Don't you know they done laid down metal rails for transport? Got carriages powered by steam that cross the whole country. You can go clear out to California in a couple of weeks."

"Why the hell'd anyone wanna go out there? Injuns'll get you."

"Injuns ain't gonna be a problem much longer," said a soldier with a couple of broken-off arrows in his chest. "We got them on the run!"

Jarvis had caught the spray of buckshot while trying to rob a Wells Fargo payload. He didn't know a Pinkerton was hiding behind the compartment door guarding the safe. When we explained to Jarvis where he was, he took it pretty well. Ever since he could remember, his pa told him he was going to burn in hell. Seeing as how he didn't wind up there, he was a bit skeptical and took everything we told him with a grain of salt.

"So how you know you go to hell if you get shot?" he asked.

"Don't know," I told him honestly. "Guess it was Sal who told me. Hey, Sal, how you know we all go to hell when we get shot?"

"Ah, I don't know," Sal shrugged with some irritation. He poured a beer from the tap and blew the suds over the rim. "Where else would you go?"

"Could go to some other town like this one," Jarvis suggested. "Maybe every time you get kilt, you end up in a new town. Could go on like that forever. Maybe you only remember that last place you been, even if you been to hundreds before that."

"Ah, what'd be the use of that?" Sal sneered.

"Shit, you mean to tell me you made all that up about us being in hell's sifter?" I said bitterly to Sal. "I been telling it like it was God's honest truth!"

"I didn't make nothing up!" Sal defended. "Some gold panner told it to me when I first came to town. Said he was here because he fiddled with his little girl. Said he done good stuff too though, so God was probably givin' him a second chance. He reckoned God was sifting through the dead souls like a panner would, checking to see if any of 'em's got a heart a gold worth keeping."

"And what happened to that panner?" I asked.

"I shot the bastard," Sal said proudly. "A man shouldn't go fiddlin' his daughter. And if he does, there's gotta be a hell to send him to. So that's where I sent him!"

The room grew quiet as everyone considered the origin of Sal's hell. It was unsettling to think everything we believed might just be the tall tales of a bartender.

"Guess it doesn't really change things much when you think about it," Old Moe said. "We still wanna avoid gettin' shot, and if we do we still hope to wind up someplace better."

The fellas shrugged and drank.

"So what did *you* do to end up here?" a soldier asked Sal.

"Ah, I don't remember."

Some of the men nodded, as if this gave credence to Jarvis's theory about past lives we couldn't remember.

"Seems we can't be any more sure of things here than when we was alive," a sheep puncher declared.

Jarvis sat quietly as the men bickered over the possibilities. One of the miners called the sheep puncher a pagan. Then the sheep puncher reached for his knife. He didn't know what the word meant, but he didn't like the sound of it.

"Hey, fellas!" Jarvis called out. "Lemme ask you another question. How you know it's always dusk here?" The sheep puncher and the miner stopped their fighting and stared blankly at Jarvis.

"Huh? Look outside!" Sal laughed. "It's dusk. Always has been. Ain't no disputing that!"

The kid turned his head to the window.

"Dunno..." He shrugged. "Could be dawn for all I know."

"Shit!" Sal said. "I'll be doggone! The kid may be right. Everybody reset your pocket watches."

Laughter broke out around the room. The miners showed their blackened teeth as they cackled and pounded on the bar. After a minute, it quieted down as the fellas gave it some serious consideration. Finally, Red gave voice to everyone's deepest concern: "Not sure whether I should have breakfast next or supper."

"I don't care if it's suppertime or breakfast time," one of the loggers added. "I'm having bacon either way. Them wolves sure fatten up a pig mighty tastily."

Everyone agreed, and Sal sliced up some sowbelly. The smell of it sizzling in a frying pan filled the air. To pass the time as it cooked, we told the same tired old jokes we'd told a hundred times before. Finally, Sal placed a heap of charred pork strips in front of each man. Food was still free, but Sal didn't mind because bacon was salty, which made you thirsty.

"Ah, nothing finer than a beer and a plate of well-done overland trout," Red said looking a little misty-eyed after he finished eating. We sat patting our bellies and sipping beer in agreement.

"There's one thing I don't get," Whiny Pete said. "If Ms. Parker didn't kill her baby when she drowned herself, why'd she end up here? There ain't nobody in Damnation that deserves to be picking grapes in God's vineyard."

"Quit beating around the bush," Red hollered. "Put it plain!"

"She musta done something wrong. Otherwise, she'd be in heaven, right?"

"Hmm, guess so," I said. "Reckon she got a story she ain't ready to tell us yet. Maybe she will when the time's right."

"Maybe it'll account for why little Martin didn't drown like a normal baby woulda," Sal added. "And why Nigel didn't feel no hunger for the little tot."

On hearing the child's name, Nigel got up suddenly and stormed out the door.

"What's botherin' him?" Pete asked.

"Damn moody vampire," Sal said. "Who knows."

An after-lunch lull set in. Everyone was too tired to drink or play cards, so they stared out the window into the dusk, which might very well have been dawn, and thought about their old lives. Some men had been dead so long they could hardly recall what their mammas and their sweethearts looked like. Things didn't pick up again till later in the evening when folks got their second wind and gave up thinking about the past.

The floorboards creaked loudly, and we looked up to see a large man in the doorway. He had long yellow hair, even longer than Nigel's. You might've taken him for a lady if he wasn't so tall and broad. He was nearly the height of Stumpy, but not so skinny. He wore a long dark duster even though it was hotter than blazes, but he wasn't even sweating. Looked as cool as a gator that just crawled out of the marsh. He certainly didn't have the scare in him.

"Think he's a wolf?" Whiny Pete asked worriedly. It was a fair question. The last men to come in without the scare in them were the two werewolves looking for Ms. Parker. The time before that, it was John Wesley Hardin, and he was worse than a wolf in some ways.

"Could be a gunslinger," I whispered. "Mighta been expectin' it."

Sal approached cautiously and placed a glass of whiskey in front of the man. He just glared back without touching it.

"What's your name, friend?" Sal asked.

"Luther," he said coldly.

"Better get Nigel," I told Whiny Pete.

"Why?"

"Just get him."

"But what'll I tell him."

"Tell him a tall fella named Luther just came to town. It's the same name as the vampire that kilt him, so that oughta get his attention."

THE DEAD INDIAN WARS

Keep reading for a preview of the next title from Clark Casey

Coming soon from LYRICAL UNDERGROUND

"Out of the crooked timber of humanity no straight thing was ever made."
—Immanuel Kant

Chapter 1

Luther

"Hey, blondie!" one of the soldier boys called out. The stripes of a colonel decorated his sleeve and, judging by the pain-in-the-ass tone of his voice, he reckoned that still meant something. All afternoon he'd been teasing the other newbies, and now he figured the big fella in the duster was due for some good-natured ribbing. Even a large newbie was easy pickings. Usually. The colonial strolled up with his shit-eating grin and said, "What's with the—"

Before he could finish his question, the fair-haired giant palmed his face like a grapefruit. His long fingers stretched from ear to ear and nose to scalp. In a single motion, he drew the colonel in and cradled his neck. Yellow fangs, much longer than Nigel's, dropped below his lip. His gumline was high, like a mare that'd seen more winters than nature intended. He pierced the soldier's flabby sunburned neck and sucked hard. His eyes immediately widened in horror. He spit out the cold blood, then collapsed to one knee in a coughing fit. Some of it had slipped down his throat and was cutting up his insides like shards of glass.

"*Scheisse!*" he yelled, then tore open his shirt and began beating on his chest in desperation. Men dove under tables, fearing he might explode.

"I see you have endeavored to sample the local fare, old chap," a voice teased from the doorway.

"Nigel!" he gasped for air. "So that would mean I'm... Is the dark one here?" he asked nervously.

"No, he is absent. I believe we are just short of his domain—though you may still reach it."

Nigel suddenly dashed forward, closing twenty paces as if they were one, then hammered his fist into Luther's chest with a thud that sent him to the floor. The big fella wasn't down for long. His eyes glowed angrily and he popped to his feet, then charged. He lifted Nigel on his shoulder like a bull between the horns, and the two of them struck the bullet-ridden wall. They broke clear through to the other side and tumbled into the road. As soon as they stood, they began trading blows.

Luther had the advantage with his reach, but Nigel wasn't weakened from drinking cold blood. He crouched low and worked away at Luther's midsection. Finally, Luther got fed up and smashed his knee against Nigel's face, then gripped him by the slack in his shirt and heaved him through the air. His body landed some ten feet away on the boardwalk. Luther quickly grabbed Nigel's legs and dragged him back to the center of the road to finish him off. Nigel managed to take a piece of wooden plank with him, and when Luther flipped him over, he met with the two by eight. A twisted nail poking out from the board had pierced his forehead, and blood poured over his face.

They both lunged for each other's throats at once. Nigel's short powerful forearms were locked inside of Luther's, both squeezing with all their might as they hissed breathlessly. Neither would release their grip to try to save their windpipe from being crushed. It was clear that whoever could hold on the longest would be the winner.

There was no way of knowing how the outcome would affect the town, if the new fella would be better or worse than Nigel. We'd gone from bastards like Jeremiah Watson running things to worse bastards like Jack Finney. Buddy was about the nicest top gun we'd ever had. Nigel usually let folks be, but this new vampire might be more of the meddling sort. On the other hand, it looked possible that they might both suffocate each other at once.

Just then, the clouds shifted. From the corner of the sky, the blanket of gray slipped back to reveal a sliver of the brightest light I had ever seen. Everyone had to shield their eyes. The years of dusk had made us too sensitive for anything brighter than candlelight. I squinted up, but it hurt too much to examine directly. A single beam shined down on the two vampires. Their clenched hands immediately began to smolder. Then a flicker of blue flames shot across the length of their interlocked arms. They had to release their grasps to pat it out, but it kept spreading over their bodies. The skin on Luther's cheek melted like lard in a frying pan. He threw his duster over his head for shade. Nigel had already put his arms over his head with his back to the sky. Their closest escape from the light was the saloon. They both bolted for the hole in the wall and dove through it at the same time, breaking off bits of wood to make it even larger. A moment later, the clouds shifted and the sky darkened.

The blisters on Nigel's face looked like they'd heal, but Luther hadn't fared as well. Smoke was still rising from his blackened skin. It made his blond hair look even lighter. Much of his jawbone and teeth could be seen where the skin had melted away.

"That was for killing me," Nigel said after dusting off his singed lapel, then extended his hand. Luther stared at him silently for a moment.

"I suppose I had it coming," he admitted and took Nigel's hand.

"Two gins," Nigel called out. Sal hustled from the back where he'd been hiding and put the bottle and two glasses on the bar.

"Odd, isn't it?" Nigel remarked. "To feel such pain. Those blows would have been like mosquito bites when I was alive and well fed."

Luther rubbed his battered ribs. "Also, you put up a better fight than last time. *Prost!*" He lifted his drink, and they knocked glasses.

The two vampires sat chatting cordially in the room they'd just destroyed. Everyone gave them a wide berth, but I situated myself just within earshot and scribbled some notes with my head down so as not to attract their attention. Luther had a funny way of talking, but not in the same way as Nigel. Wasn't as proper-like.

"Hear that?" Luther asked.

"What?"

"Absolutely nothing."

Nigel smiled knowingly.

"These men have no thoughts for me to hear," Luther said.

"Yes, I find it a welcome silence."

"It is rather nice," Luther agreed, "especially for an old vampire like me."

"If not for the hunger and boredom," Nigel said, "it might make this place bearable."

"So none of them have warm blood then?" Luther asked anxiously.

"Tell me," Nigel changed the subject, "Who finally defeated the Scourge of Saxony?"

"The council turned against me," he replied bitterly, pushing his yellow hair out of his charred face. "We disagreed on ideology. They wanted to permit mixing with the humans."

"Still a hardliner, huh?"

"Speaking of that, is your woman here? The one you killed your brother for."

"No, I suppose she went someplace else."

"So you're not going to hold it against me then, what I did to you?" Luther asked.

"Ah, you were just doing your job," Nigel replied a little too breezily.

Luther studied his face. He didn't have much practice in reading a bluff since he was accustomed to hearing thoughts. "Besides," Nigel added, "it can get rather boring here when there aren't any gunfights to watch. The Americans are no great conversationalists. They lack our European sensibilities."

"*Ja*," Luther agreed.

"So why did the council finally decide to allow relations with humans?" Nigel prodded delicately, like he was hunting for something.

"They believe it is inevitable, the next stage in evolution."

"And you don't agree?" Nigel was surprised. "I suppose you wish to keep our bloodline pure, not muddied by those human traits you abhor."

"I don't abhor humans. In fact, I'm looking out for their best interest. I want to spare them from our offspring."

"You fear the mixed-breeds' appetites would cause our kind to be discovered."

"No," Luther scoffed. "I fear the hunger of the mixed-breeds could bring about our starvation. They consume too much! If one of them can dispose of an entire town in a matter of hours, what would a dozen do, or a hundred? Let alone thousands! The only way to keep up with their demand would be to farm the humans, keep them caged and continually reproducing. They'd be nothing more than sacks of blood. I wish only for them to remain free as nature intended, and happily ignorant of us!"

"But only one in a thousand mixed-breeds become vampires."

"It is still too risky. Ah, but now we are both beyond the world where such things matter. So you say the dark one is not here?"

"Not openly, but I've sensed his presence," Nigel said hesitantly. "I was never a believer when I was alive, and the last hundred years have given me little reason to think otherwise, but there have been signs recently." Nigel became very serious. "Like that blast of light that separated us."

"The dark one using light!" Luther scoffed.

"I never would've thought it possible, but things are different here. Even the human priests kill in Damnation."

"Is that the name of this place?" Luther bowed his head solemnly and made the sign of the cross in reverse order.

"Oh, don't get so high and unholy!" Nigel teased. "The name was given in jest. Just after I arrived, some cowboy asked me where he was and I told him Damnation. He got shot the following day, but the name stuck. They have no idea it is the name of our Eden."

Whiny Pete barged in the saloon just then. He nervously eyed the hole in the wall, wondering if he should scatter. Nigel looked at him expectantly.

He nodded eagerly, perhaps a little less subtly than Nigel would have liked. Luther took it all in wordlessly.

"What's that all about?" Sal whispered to Pete.

"The vampire asked me to move Ms. Parker and Martin to the general store."

"You think that other vampire can smell the warm blood in Martin?" Sal asked.

"If Nigel can smell it, he probably can, too," I said.

"Think he'll wanna drain the child?" Pete asked.

"Why else would Nigel have you move 'em?" Sal barked. "Better get the word out that nobody should mention the kid in blondie's presence."

"Ain't gonna be easy with all the loudmouths around here," I said.

"Then we gotta put the fear of hell in 'em."

After it was scrubbed down real good, Luther moved into Ms. Parker's old room, and Buddy was left in the room between the two vampires. Everyone reckoned the new vampire was going to cause a big hoopla, but nothing much happened right away. Since he wasn't accustomed to going without warm blood, it made him real tired. For the first few weeks, he slept pretty much around the clock. But there were other things to worry about aside from the new vampire.

Chapter 2

The Unknown Soldier and the Apache Woman

"Am I dead?" a new soldier asked as he sat down at the bar. Wedged between his shoulder blades was a tomahawk with greased goose feathers dangling from the grip. The hollow stem of a pipe was attached to the end. Presumably, the owner didn't find occasion to bury the hatchet in the earth and smoke in peace with the fella. The edge of the blade was peeking out from the front of the soldier's sternum, where chunks of heart muscle had been pushed out. They clung to his shirt like dinner scraps. His arms were red from trying his damnedest to push the blade back out the way it came.

"Yup," I told him. "You're as dead as a doornail, but twice as useless."

"Figured I was done for when they ambushed us." Judging by the silver strands in his beard and the metals on his tits, he'd been soldiering awhile. "This hell?" he asked matter-of-factly.

"Nah."

"Then why's there so many dang Indians outside?"

On account of the wars, more and more of them were coming to Damnation every day. They marched out from the dust with the feathers of their headdresses swaying in the wind. Some came whooping and hollering atop dead-eyed ponies, still rallying the bucks with war cries. Others were shot in the back, likely on the run from larger forces. They built teepees outside of town with scrap wood from old covered wagons. The barren flatlands between the buildings and the dust cloud quickly filled with their camps, and eventually we were surrounded. The tribes might not have gotten along so well when they were alive, but in Damnation the Navajo, Cherokee, and Sioux all banded together. Their ideas about the spirit world were somewhat vague, so when they wound up in a place with tumbleweeds, horses, and a few white men, they figured it was close enough.

"I suppose them Indians wasn't good enough for heaven," I told the soldier. "Nor bad enough for hell—like yourself—so they were sent here. Some miner called it 'hell's sifter.' Thought that God was giving us all another look-see to check if any of us might be worth saving from the fire. Another man thought that if you could manage to keep from shooting anyone for a whole year, the gates of heaven'd open up for you. Nobody's managed it so far. The truth is, I can't say for sure where we are. Alls we really know is you can stay here and play poker as long as you like. But if you get shot, you don't get to see your cards."

An Indian brave on horseback came riding by, shrieking and howling at the window, then threw a rock. It shattered the pane of glass. Wasn't meant to be an attack or anything. He just wanted to let us know he was out there and didn't care much for us. The soldier took it as an omen though.

"Should've known what we done'd come back to haunt us," he said uneasily. "Government gave 'em land, but it weren't near big enough and the soil no good for growing nothing. Meat rations were slim and often spoilt. Lost ten men in my battalion when they finally revolted. Guess I was the eleventh."

A breeze blew the doors open, bringing with it a mess of dust and rattling the rusty fixtures. Nigel burst in like a twister and stopped in front of a toothless man huddled in the corner. A shiny tin star was fastened to his lapel. As sheriff, Nigel found he could make good on his promise to look after Mabel while still remaining impartial. His wounds from the fight with Luther had healed up good as new, though every passing day without warm blood made him weaker. He was still a far shot stronger and faster than any man or wolf in town. Just not the other vampire. Luther had healed, too, except for his blackened skin and the cheek that had melted away. Nigel might have missed his only chance to take out the big blond in a weakened state.

"This is a child's toy, sir. Not a derelict's." Nigel yanked a wood-carved rattle out of the toothless fella's hands, then tore out of the saloon as quick as he'd come.

"Who was that?" the soldier asked.

"The sheriff," I told him.

"How's he move so quick?"

"He's a vampire."

"You got vampires here?"

"Just two and some werewolves," I added. "But most of them got wiped out when they came after Ms. Parker's baby."

"So there's babies?"

"Just Martin. Only living thing in Damnation."

"*Shh*, keep it down," Sal scolded. "Luther might come in and hear ya."

"The other vampire don't know about him," I explained to the soldier. "We're afraid he might eat the little bugger. So if you see a tall blond fella missing half his face, pipe down about the kid."

Ever since Martin was born, the wolves had been afraid to attack because they reckoned Nigel had a steady supply of warm blood to keep him strong. He never had a drop of the kid's blood though. Some folks reckoned he was just waiting till the child got bigger, fattening him up like a hog. There were also concerns about a vampire being sheriff, so Buddy was made deputy. He took the position with the best of intentions, but when Ms. Parker began spending more time with Nigel, his mood soured. Buddy didn't bother interfering in quarrels unless one of the rules was broken, and he was a little loose on their interpretation. One hungry man pointed out that rule number one said everybody eats. Buddy lifted his face from his glass, squinted angrily, and said, "It don't say what though." Then he shoved a gun barrel in the man's mouth.

"Got any whores 'round here?" the soldier asked.

"Whores go to heaven," I told him.

"So there is a heaven then?"

"Wherever they end up must be heaven," Red added. "At least you can get a reg'lar poke there."

"Wouldn't be heaven for the lady suffocatin' beneath you!" Mabel laughed.

"I can't stand that damn racket!" Sal complained as he peered out the window to the half-finished building across the road. "The hammering's driving me crazy."

Mabel had hired a bunch of dead carpenters to build her saloon just opposite the Foggy Dew. She used Lucky's money to pay them. On account of their thirst, they worked fast, framed up the walls with a balcony and a pitched roof in a couple of weeks. The top floor was already finished. It was going to be larger and grander than Sal's dingy saloon. They had some brand-new wood for the exterior that came in on a lumber wagon. There weren't any new nails though, so they had to yank old ones out of the rotted buildings. The rusty round heads stood out from the shiny new cedar, giving it an odd look, like the new was being held together by the old. She was going to call the place the Rusty Nail.

"Why we need another saloon anyway?" Sal grumbled.

"Town's growing," Mabel smiled with no apologies. "'Sides, a girl's gotta keep herself busy somehow."

"Don't think about underpricing me," he warned. "If folks start crossing the road for cheaper whiskey, I ain't gonna bother feeding 'em for free."

"Who says I won't serve food?" Mabel said. "Just 'cause you got a frying pan don't mean you have claim to every dead pig that wanders out of the dust."

"The whole system's going to pot!" Sal huffed, then he counted out ten chips for the soldier. "We'll all be in hell before the year's through. Mark my words!"

The tomahawk sticking out from the soldier's back parted the crowd as he stood. He took his money straight to the poker table, where he lost a few hands. The gray in his hair had long overtaken the brown. He was likely the grandpa of some little tot he'd rather be holding than a straight flush somewhere shy of hell. When he got down to his last chip, he bought a bullet and borrowed a gun. He stuck the barrel in his mouth and squeezed the trigger. As the bullet broke apart the back of his skull, the piano player paused till the body hit the floor. Then he took up the song again right where he left off.

"Imagine that," Old Moe remarked. "He literally wore his heart on his sleeve!"

"Just another soft army boy who didn't care much for whiskey or poker," Sal said. "Get the Chinamen to haul that sad sack away."

As the day wore on, more dead soldiers arrived with stunned looks in their eyes and loads of fear-shit in their drawers. There'd been a battle in Florida, and for every soldier that came out of the dust four Seminole followed. Their whooping and hollering made the army boys nervous. Some of the same Indians they'd killed were outside with their war paints on, making bows and arrows out of scrap wood.

"I seen that prairie coon before," a soldier barked angrily. "He followed me here, damn it! How many times I gotta kill that sumabitch?"

"Settle down now, boys," Sal tried to soothe them. "You may a been winning the battle, but you're losing the war here. We're outnumbered! Best you can do is keep your head down and hope they don't dig up the tomahawk and start a war."

"What them red bellies want anyway?" an old sodbuster asked.

"So far they just wanna dance around the fire whoopin' and hollerin' same as always, but if you stir up trouble they might wanna kick us out of their spirit world."

"They gonna chase us outta here like we chased them out of Oklahoma?"

"I expect they'd like to," I said.

The rooming house was packed as tight as a barn during a twister, with hardly a foot of floor not covered by some wretched body. Smelt worse than a slaughter house with all the open wounds festering. I stayed at the saloon as late as I could to avoid it. One evening as the crowd was dwindling down, a squaw in a buckskin dress staggered through the door. She was skinnier than a desert steer, but feisty. Her shawl was torn and muddied from some sort of scuffle. Her hair was tied up in braids, revealing a round pretty face. Rough as she was, her skin was as smooth as any powdered society lady. She didn't have a single blemish, except the bullet hole in her temple. The flesh around it was singed, probably from a hot barrel pressed against her head while someone had their way with her. It would've explained the crazed look in her eyes. Her own kind probably chased her away for causing a ruckus. They didn't stand for their women getting out of line. She sidled up to the bar and a few of the fellas offered to buy her a drink.

"This is gonna be trouble," Sal warned.

"Think the Injuns will come looking for her?" Whiny Pete asked worriedly.

Sal shrugged. "Who knows, but if she's trading her wares for drinks, there's bound to be a fight over her."

The soldiers didn't much care for her kind, and most hadn't been dead long enough to change their minds. To the rest of the fellas, a woman was a woman no matter what color she was or how many bullet holes she had in her. The squaw accepted a drink from Red. Then one of the loggers put his hand on her thigh.

"Git your own damn woman, you tree humper!" Red hollered. "I done called her first."

Normally, a fella wouldn't take insult, but a woman was watching, even if she couldn't understand what it meant. Some dead pride surged within the chubby logger, and he lunged at Red. Their bellies knocked together as they swatted one another like a couple of walruses. Red got the upper hand and shoved the logger to the ground. As he went down, his foot kicked the poker table, sending stacks of chips to the floor, and everyone started shouting.

"Ain't you gonna do something about this?" Sal asked Buddy. "You're the deputy after all."

Buddy sipped his beer. "They ain't broke no rules."

"Rule number five says no killing over dumb shit."

"There's only one dang woman in the saloon and thirty men," Buddy told him. "I'd say that's a darn good reason for fighting."

"All right, you fellas take it outside." Sal grabbed his scattergun from the umbrella stand. "I ain't having you break apart what's left of my bar over some dirt-worshipping woman."

Red and the logger headed out to the road, while the squaw stayed at the bar drinking. Nobody was interested enough in the outcome of the fight to vacate a stool.

"Ain't you gonna watch?" I asked her.

"No matter who win," she snarled. "Somebody get shot. Somebody buy me whiskey. All white man same. All filthy dog." She spat on the floor.

A gunshot sounded outside, and a moment later Red trotted back into the saloon rubbing his hands in satisfaction. "Now that that's all settled," he announced, "what do you say to a poke, little lady?"

"How the hell'd you shoot that logger so fast?" Sal asked. "You're so drunk, you couldn't shoot a barn if you was standing in it. Wasn't even out there long enough to count off ten paces. Musta shot him in the back," he decided.

"You calling me a back shooter?" Red was feeling bold after shooting the logger, and Sal's scattergun was on the other side of the bar.

"Settle down!" Buddy called out. "Rule number five says no fighting over dumb shit. Now Sal, if you cared so damn much about whether or not it was a fair fight, you shoulda went out and watched it for yourself. It's over now, and both of you better quit your yapping 'cause it's giving me a headache."

The squaw's eyes wobbled in her half-closed sockets, looking off in different directions at once like a blind man who couldn't focus on anything in particular. When she noticed all the pale faces around her, she sneered with real hatred. Red was no friend of mine, but it was only fair to warn him. I pulled him aside and told him to watch himself.

"Ah, you'll get a poke if you wait your turn, pencil pusher."

"You ain't listening. She ain't right in the head," I said. "Got it in for the white man."

He brushed me off. "They all got it in for the white man. Makes 'em feisty under the covers." Red laughed and pinched the lady's backside. She squirmed away, saying she wanted another drink, so he ordered whiskey. She kept gulping it down like there was a bottomless pit inside her. Probably already put away more than a man twice her size. Might've been trying to blot out whatever horrors had been done to her.

The piano player was playing a quick little ditty, and she hopped from foot to foot like a caged rabbit rearing to be free. Red took her for a whirl around the floor. She shook her hips savagely and kicked her dark legs in the air. Soon enough, they caught Buddy's eye. He wandered over like a cow to hay and cut in on Red. She didn't seem to care much who her partner was.

"Better get the sheriff," I told Whiny Pete.

"Hold it there," Sal interrupted. "When Red and his boys came after Buddy, he shoulda shot him then. I say he'd be in the right to do so now."

"You've certainly changed your tune. Wasn't so long ago you were trying to have Buddy kilt."

"I did nothing of the sort, Tom. I've always backed the deputy. 'Sides, Red ain't paid his tab in weeks."

"We can't go back to killing each other over grudges," I argued. "Especially with all these dead soldiers in town. Ain't like managing a bunch of cow punchers and churn-twisters. They actually know how to shoot—some of 'em anyways. If they start settling old scores, there's bound to be a war with the Indians."

Red stood stupidly eating drag dust as Buddy sallied about with the squaw on his arm. "What's the big idea, Buddy?" he finally blurted out. Buddy ignored him, which made Red angrier. There was nothing else for him to do but draw. He lifted his gun just as Buddy turned his back. Even stinking drunk, Buddy had a sense for these things. He must've seen the glint of the metal out of the corner of his eye, because he spun the woman around an extra turn and pulled as well.

"Buddy!" Nigel yelled from the doorway. Both men froze with their fingers on the triggers. "As deputy, you are supposed to maintain order here, not steal other men's women and provoke them into fighting you."

"But he drew first. 'Sides, who's to say I stole her. He don't have no claim on her just 'cause he bought her a few drinks. You woulda seen so for yourself if you wasn't playing house with Ms. Parker."

It was clear that Buddy reckoned all the time Nigel was spending with Ms. Parker was akin to him stealing *his* girl. Nigel weighed his words before responding. It wouldn't have been prudent to go against his own deputy. Besides, Nigel wasn't heeled, and if anybody was fast enough to shoot a vampire it was Buddy. Each day without warm blood made Nigel slower, and Buddy had gotten quicker. He'd taken to shooting bottles on the outskirts of town like Hardin used to.

"We've got more pressing problems," Nigel said. "There's a hundred Indians outside and only thirty soldiers in here. If a gunfight breaks out, *somebody* could get caught in the crossfire." He winked slowly. Buddy looked at him blankly, so Nigel whispered, "*Little Martin.*"

Buddy shrugged and let the squaw go. After Nigel left, Red didn't waste any time in leading her upstairs. She swayed drunkenly, nearly falling over the banister, so he threw her over his shoulder and carried her up to the storage room. A few minutes later, her screeches could be heard above the barroom.

"Red's really givin' it to her!" Whiny Pete snickered. A moment later, Red started screaming even louder than the woman. "Or maybe *she's* givin' it to *him*!" Jarvis said, and everybody laughed. Then a gunshot sounded.

Meet the Author

Clark Casey is the author of three novellas: The Jesus Fish and Slaughter Bird, Pale Male and the Infertile Girl, and The Perfect Defective. He was born in New York and currently resides in Northern California.